THE THIRD GIRL

Molly Sutton Mysteries 1

NELL GODDIN

Beignet Books

ISBN: 978-1-949841-01-5

For my wise aunt, Claudia Teass

CONTENTS

❧ 1 ❧

2005

She was being ridiculous, no question about it. Yes, it had been years since she had studied French, and she hadn't exactly been a top student. But having moved to Castillac just three days before, surely she could muddle along well enough to buy a pastry to have with her afternoon coffee. The shops were there to sell their wares, not judge her accent, right? And with that thought, Molly Sutton perched a straw hat (brand new, *véritable* Panama the sign had promised) on her wild curls and marched down her short driveway and into the village, determined to get her first éclair.

Three days had not been long enough to learn her way around the rabbit warren of narrow streets, but Molly had a good sense of direction, and she was having one of those moments of elation expats sometimes experience when they are not in the grip of their adopted country's bureaucracy, or finding out they have just eaten something like lark pie. The golden limestone of the buildings was warm and lovely. It was the end of summer but there was no chill in the air, and she kept up a brisk pace, peering into windows and backyards, drinking it all in. She had no idea where to find a *pâtisserie*, but steered toward the center of the village.

Interesting how everyone seems to hang all their underwear on the line—doesn't it dry hard as cardboard, she wondered. She stopped at the stone garden wall of one house, stepping on a rock so she could see over. Clothes were strung out on the line, dancing rather gaily in the breeze. She was tempted to reach in and touch a pair of those expensive-looking panties to see just how soft they were, but maybe trespassing to touch the neighbor's underthings might not make the best first impression.

She could see that the underwear was La Perla. Soft, well-cut, *très cher* and probably worth every penny, she mused. I think if I had underwear that nice, I wouldn't hang it out in the baking sun. It deserves hand washing at the least and should be, I don't know, dried by the beating of hummingbird wings or something.

Molly stood at the wall, looking at the three bikinis and a cami, neatly clipped with wooden clothes pins. The alley was so quiet. No sound but the steady hum of cicadas. She looked to see if anyone was around and slowly leaned against the wall and reached her fingers toward a pair of bikinis with a pink ribbon running around the top.

Someone shouted something she didn't understand. Molly jerked her hand back and looked around to see who had spoken. The man next door had come into his backyard and was talking to his neighbor over the fence between their houses.

Quickly she ducked her head and trotted around the next turn. A street of shops was just ahead. A bustle of people out doing errands, having a midmorning *petit café*, and gossiping with neighbors. Molly wandered along looking at the unfamiliar shapes of the rooftops, at the signage in windows; listening to French but not catching a single word; smelling roasting chicken that smelled so good it brought tears to her eyes.

Everything was not what she was used to, and she loved everything if only for that.

The street curved around to the right, and then straight ahead was a large fountain. Several students from the art school were perched on the rim with drawing pads and serious expressions as they sketched. Molly walked up and sat on the rim, people-watching until she remembered the éclair and went off to look for a pâtisserie in earnest. She had loads of work to do; the cottage on her property was nowhere near ready for guests, and she had her first booking coming in a matter of days. She should have been shopping for sheets and pillows, and giving the place a good scrubbing instead of wandering around hunting for sweets. But she was feeling indulgent: after the couple of years she had just been through, she was in France seeking pleasure and calm. And she was going to wallow in it, savoring every delicious moment.

Ahh. Yes.

She found herself in front of a small shop painted on the outside in red enamel, with gold lettering over the doorway in a flourishing script: *Pâtisserie Bujold*. The smell of butter and vanilla practically grabbed her by the shirt and pulled her inside.

"*Bonjour*, madame," said a small man behind the counter.

"*Bonjour*, monsieur," said Molly, her eyes wide. Under the glass, row after row of pastries so beautiful they looked like jewels. Delectable, mouthwatering jewels, arranged by a true artist, color-coordinated and symmetrical as a *parterre*. Should she go for the *mille-feuille*, with its bajillion layers of crisp pastry sandwiched with custard and swirly icing on top? She leaned forward, nearly pressing her nose against the glass. The strawberry tarts looked amazing, but berries were out of season and probably didn't taste as good as they looked. The cream puff with whipped cream spilling out of it was calling to her. But she had so dreamed of an éclair...

"Madame?"

Molly snapped out of a sort of trance. She took a deep breath and gathered her courage. "The pastries, she pretty," she said, wincing at her horrible French.

The man smiled and stepped out from around the counter. His eyes went straight to her chest and lingered there. Molly sighed.

Then, so quickly as to verge on rude, she made her choice, paid, and left with a small waxed bag and a silly grin on her face.

She was in Castillac, her new home, about to eat her first real French éclair in almost twenty years.

I'm finally here. Finally in France, for good.

❧

"Yes, mademoiselle, how may I help?" asked Thérèse Perrault, who had only joined the tiny Castillac police force a few months ago.

"It's, well, I'm at Degas," the young woman said, meaning the prestigious art school in the village.

Perrault waited. She was already so weary of dealing with nothing but traffic violations and lost dogs, she hardly dared hope this call would turn into something more intriguing.

"My roommate is—she's missing. I haven't seen her since yesterday, I'm getting worried."

"May I ask your name?"

"Maribeth Donnelly."

"American?"

"Yes."

"And your roommate's name?"

"Her name is Amy Bennett. She's British. And she's the most responsible student in the whole school. That's why I'm so worried. She just wouldn't run off without saying anything to anyone."

Perrault was scribbling notes, trying to get the student's phrasing exactly. "I understand. Have you notified anyone at the school?"

"I—I mentioned it to one of the teachers this morning, *Professeur* Gallimard. She didn't show up to his class."

"Exactly how long has she been missing?"

"I had dinner with her last night. Then I went out with my boyfriend, and she went back to the studio to work on a drawing that's due. She never came back to the dorm, and I haven't seen her all day," the young woman said, her voice catching.

"It's not even twenty-four hours," said Perrault, her tone not dismissive but sympathetic. "And I'm afraid the *gendarmerie* only actively searches for missing minors—can you tell me how old Amy is?"

"She's nineteen. I'm sorry," said Maribeth. "I don't know what the missing-persons procedures here are or anything. I'm just—I don't want to sound like a flake, officer—but I...I have a bad feeling."

Officer Perrault told her that almost always these situations resolve themselves happily. She asked if Amy had a boyfriend, if she had a car, if she had access to money—and she carefully wrote down Maribeth's answers in her notebook.

Before calling her boss, Chief Dufort, on his cell, Thérèse Perrault took a moment to think through everything Maribeth Donnelly had told her, and to fix the young woman's voice in her head. It was only an impression, and she did not have enough experience to be able to know yet whether her impressions tended to be correct—but Perrault trusted Maribeth Donnelly, and did not think she was a flake, or unstable, or anything but a concerned friend who had something legitimate to worry about. Then, in quick succession, she grinned and looked chastened, as she felt thrilled that something had finally happened in the village of Castillac now that she was on the force, and then felt guilty for being so excited about someone's else's potential tragedy.

Like everyone else in the village, Perrault knew about the two other women who had disappeared without a trace, but those cases had been several years ago. The first one, Valérie Boutillier, had actually been part of the reason Perrault had pursued a career in law enforcement. Thérèse had been eighteen when Valérie disappeared, and while she had not known her personally, in the usual way of Castillac, she had friends who had known her, and family members who knew Valérie's family one way or another. Perrault had followed the investigation closely and tried to puzzle out what had happened. She still thought of it from time to time, and wondered whether new evidence would someday turn up that would allow the young woman's abductor to be identified.

No body had ever been found, nor even any evidence of wrongdoing. But Thérèse had no doubt someone had killed Valérie Boutillier—no doubt at all.

Valérie had not been the only one. And now there was another.

2

It had taken a full year for Molly to find her new home, *La Baraque*. On the day her divorce was final, she was handed a check for her half of the proceeds from the sale of their house. The check was big enough for her to buy a house all her own, and she had had no doubt whatsoever that she wanted that house to be in France. She had been extravagantly happy there as a twenty-year-old student, but for one reason or another, had been unable to return since. In that weird, post-divorce phase, when her life was collapsing around her and she felt alternately morose and exhilarated, she spent hours every day looking at websites and reading about different regions of France, learning about *notaires* and contracts and cooling-off periods, and reveling in the stunning photographs of old stone houses and manors and even *châteaux* that were for sale. The endless pages detailed the most glorious habitations ever made, and depending on location, they were sometimes cheaper than a ranch house in the suburb where she lived. It was about the best house porn ever.

After a good friend had been held up at gunpoint and a cousin had nearly been raped in her own living room, Molly had accepted that life, where she lived—a place that until then she had not thought of as a hotbed of mayhem—had become dangerous. Part of the appeal of the French house porn was imagining living in a place where crime was lower, and people weren't getting shot every three minutes. She could retire the canister of mace she carried in her purse, and just relax. Of course, France wasn't crime-free—no place was these days—but still she felt she would feel safer there. Chill out, garden, eat some magnificent French food, and put her bad marriage and dangerous outer Boston neighborhood far behind her.

A fresh start in a place she adored. What could go wrong?

It had never occurred to Molly to see if she could find actual crime statistics for the places she was considering moving to. It was grotesquely naïve, she realized later, but she had simply assumed that a village with a pretty historic church, a Saturday market where old people sat in folding chairs selling mushrooms, where fêtes were organized several times a year in which the whole village sat down to eat together—she had assumed all of that charm and community spirit translated to almost complete safety. And how, she had wondered later, when it was too late, how can you correct a faulty assumption if you don't even realize you're making it?

She had spent months considering the vast array of house choices and locations. Her check would cover a house a shade better than modest (for which she was extremely grateful), but one big house would take it all. In her new life as a thirty-eight-year-old divorcée, Molly needed an income, and so she looked for places that had at least one separate building that she could rent out. If that went well, and she could find a place with enough old barns and stables to convert, she could expand and run her own empire of vacationers, with a whole flock of *gîtes* (France's closest equivalent to a B&B) just waiting to be filled by joyous travelers.

Well, empire might be overdoing it just a little. But she had hoped before too long to at least be able to cover her bills. The trick was finding a house that wasn't already renovated (too expensive), restored (way too expensive), or in such a ruinous state that it would take more money than she had to put it in working order.

While the glossy websites had incredible pictures, she suspected she might find something more affordable if she looked deeper into the less-shiny corners of the internet, and in fact, one day she saw an interesting listing on a stray expat blog. The blog itself was sort of sketchy, and she wondered whether the writer even lived in France: the grammar was iffy, the design poor, and the posts about French life had a strangely wooden quality about them, as though they were fifth hand or possibly fictional. The photographs of La Baraque were blurry, but she could make out the golden limestone southwest France, and especially the Dordogne, is famous for. She could see outbuildings galore, even though some, like the ancient pigeon house, appeared to be crumbling. She could imagine herself there, in the garden, drinking kirs and eating pastries.

Molly fell in love, hard.

Six months later she was bumping down the driveway of La Baraque in a taxi, having sold almost everything from her old life except a small crate of her most treasured gardening tools and kitchen equipment. The sale had gone through without a hitch, and although what was left of her family and most of her friends thought she was insane, she shipped the crate over and booked a one-way ticket to Bordeaux without looking back.

Castillac was a large village with a weekly market and a lively square. It had the orange-tiled rooftops, narrow streets, and ancient stone buildings she loved so, but no particular attraction like a *château* or cathedral, so while a few tourists were drawn to its quiet charm, the streets were not deluged with visitors, which Molly thought might get tiresome if you lived there full-time.

Southwest France was known for its caves, its duck and mushrooms, its truffles; the weather was temperate, real estate prices low, and the pâtisseries plentiful. The perfect place to recover from a marriage turned bad.

Months before moving, she'd set up a website and began to get bookings almost right away. Once in Castillac, Molly had two and a half days to get things ready for her first guests, which was not remotely long enough, time management not being one of Molly's particular talents. Those two and half days had gone by in a flurry of sweeping and painting and scrubbing, when she received a text saying the guests were forty-five minutes away.

Molly managed to get the cottage looking spiffy in time, but barely. The old stones were beautiful, but they seemed to exude dust so quickly that everything was covered again before she had even put away the vacuum cleaner. The windows were small and she rubbed them violently with newspaper and a vinegar solution so that they let in all the light they could. When she was done, she tried to stand back and look at the place critically.

Well, she thought, I hope nobody sues me after smacking his head on that beam. But it is charming, in its way. I think. Maybe.

She staggered out with a mop and pail, sweaty and grubby and looking forward to having a shower and a drink before doing any greeting.

She was just pouring the white wine into some crème de cassis and admiring how the dense purple color swirled up when she heard a car honking.

Not much of a praying woman, nevertheless she looked heavenward and said to herself: Please don't be loud people. Or pushy. Or too chatty or quiet. Or scary. And, um, please don't let this entire idea have been a huge mistake.

"Bonjour!" Molly said as the couple climbed out of a grimy-looking taxi. The taxi driver pulled himself out of the car and nodded and smiled. "I am Vincent," he said, grinning. "I know English, Molly Sutton!"

Molly was taken aback by this stranger knowing her name, but she managed to say "*Enchantée*," and then "Welcome, Mr. and Mrs. Lawler!" She was glad they were American, so at least on the first time she didn't have to struggle to communicate. Plus they'd be as jet-lagged as she still was.

Mr. Lawler strode up and shook Molly's hand vigorously. "So happy to be here," he said. "And please, call us Mark and Lainie."

Mark shook hands with the taxi driver and paid him. "Now give us the grand tour!" he said to Molly.

Molly smiled and chattered away as she showed them around La Baraque and got them settled. But underneath her bright expression, she was wondering what the deal was with Lainie Lawler, who never said a single word the entire time, and whose face was apparently so Botoxed she appeared to be frozen in a state of childish astonishment.

Not for me to judge, thought Molly. Repeat 60,000 times. And really, this *is* a good way to have an income. A little chat, some handshaking—easy peasy. I just need to get enough bookings that I can hire a cleaning woman and leave the dust-busting to her.

A DAY. That could be everything. Or nothing.

Chief Benjamin Dufort of the three-person Castillac gendarme force walked around his desk and picked up the phone, then put it down again. He looked at Perrault and pressed his lips together, his thoughts inscrutable. "Maron!" he called to the officer in the adjoining room.

Gilles Maron appeared in the doorway, an easy expression on his face although he did not like the way Dufort barked at him. He was in his late twenties, an experienced officer, having moved to Castillac from his first posting in the *banlieue* of Paris. Dufort had been pleased at his arrival and happy with his performance so far.

"Bonjour, Maron. Perrault took a call at 3:00. Student at the art school, said her roommate was missing. Perrault judged the caller to be level-headed and not just drumming up drama the way students that age sometimes do." Dufort paused, rubbing a hand over his brush cut. "Unfortunately, as you know, we no longer search for missing persons unless they are children."

"Stupid bureaucracy," Perrault muttered under her breath.

"I happen to agree with you," said Dufort. "I had a case a few years ago, a woman came in to report her husband was missing. Do you remember, Perrault? It was in the papers and on local television. Turned out the poor man had been put on a new medication and the stuff was giving him delusions. Three days later we found him in a cave, up off the road that goes up by the Sallière vineyard.

"People think if their doctor gives it to them, it's perfectly safe, whatever it is. They don't question anything." Dufort shook his head. "At any rate, that's another subject. We found the man and got him home unharmed." He pressed his palms together, then clapped his hands.

"*Bon*, I don't see why we can't keep our eyes open in regard to this art student. Just don't neglect your other duties."

He did not mention the two older cases of missing persons, the first of which had occurred just after he was posted to Castillac. He had investigated both and solved neither. Doubtless Perrault and Maron knew all about them, as unfortunately, the cases were now part of the lore of Castillac. When he was by himself again, Dufort reached into his drawer and pulled out a small blue glass bottle and a shot glass. He uncorked the bottle, which contained a tincture of herbs prepared for him by a woman in the village, and poured himself a careful ounce. He grimaced as he tossed it back. He did not like this news of the girl. Somehow, he could sense something was wrong, even though he had not been the one to take the call and had no idea where the bad feeling was coming from.

But it was there, no question about that. It was there. Same as the other times.

3

Early the next morning, Molly walked into the village to get croissants for the Lawlers' breakfast. She could feel a nip in the air and wore a sweater for the first time, and shoved a cap over her red hair, which was crazier than usual. About halfway to the village, on the other side of a road, was a small cemetery. Molly hurried past its mossy wall with only a glance at the mausoleums on the other side. She took a peek at the neighbors' gardens to see what kind of fall vegetables they had put in, and admired the cauliflower and ruffled kale. The French way of gardening was so neat, so orderly, so un-Molly. She passed one garden and stopped for a moment to appreciate its late-summer lushness, cucumber vines overrunning a trellis, zinnias in a profusion of orange and red, and the slight yellowing of leaves hinting at the end of the season.

She had big plans for her own garden, but had been too busy with the house to do anything yet; the real work was going to have to wait until spring. A neglected *potager* was right off the kitchen with an ancient rosemary bush in the corner, and a perennial bed along the stone wall in front of the house had a few sturdy things—black-eyed Susans and coneflowers, mostly. In fact, maybe she could find an hour to spend in that bed this afternoon, just to get some of those nasty-looking vines out. It would be bliss to kneel in the grass and get her hands dirty.

She had been up and had coffee, but never minded having another, so she took a seat at the Café de la Place in the center of the village and ordered a *café crème* from the very good-looking waiter whom she heard the hostess call Pascal. And well, why not just get the breakfast special—a tall glass of freshly squeezed orange juice and a croissant to go with the *café crème?* Why not, indeed.

Pascal set down the oversized cup of coffee. It had a deep layer of milk froth, and Molly beamed at it and then at Pascal, who smiled back and disappeared into the kitchen. She sprinkled a little sugar over the froth and drank deeply, in a state of ecstasy, moving from coffee to juice to croissant. Some Brits at a nearby table started talking loudly enough for her to eavesdrop, making her breakfast even more delightful.

"I really think we ought to consider taking Lily home right now."

"Come on, Alice, you're overreacting. Lily is doing well and this is her dream, remember? Her work has been quite impressive here, don't you agree? Degas is doing an excellent job."

"Don't tell me not to mind it. That girl's been missing nearly two days."

"Oh, I really wouldn't worry, my dear. Girls run off for a million reasons, don't they. Probably nothing. A boy, I'll wager."

"I heard she is a very serious student. Not flighty. And if she had gone off with a boy, she'd have contacted her mates! You know they text each other every minute. Someone would have heard from her."

A family with two young children sat at the table next to her, and Molly had to stop herself from shushing them so she could hear the rest of what the couple were saying. But they had moved on to an aunt's lingering illness, and Molly stopped listening.

For a moment she wondered about the missing girl, and which parent was right—nefarious abduction, or romantic getaway?

She didn't want the Lawlers up and about, hungry and unattended, so she washed down the last of her breakfast special, gathered her bag of croissants, and headed back down the cobblestone street to La Baraque. She was flooded with memories from twenty years ago, when she had been a young student in France. There had been that weekend with Louis, the one with green eyes and the sly sideways look, who could make her laugh like no one else...

THE OFFICERS usually met unofficially in Dufort's office about an hour after arriving at work. Dufort had come in early after a run even more punishing than usual, wanting to clear his desk so he could focus on the missing art student.

"Bonjour Perrault, Maron. I've just spoken to the school and listened to a list of platitudes, help any way we can, blah blah blah. I'm afraid the president over there is more concerned with the school's reputation than with what has happened to the girl."

"You do think something has happened? Other than she went off on some lark?" asked Maron.

"You know the percentages," said Dufort quietly. "She's too old for this to be a custody matter or something of that sort. Either she's taken off by herself without a word, or there's been an accident or abduction. Perrault, I want you to make some calls—airports, hospitals, car rental agencies, etc. Maron, you go around town, talk to people, look around, see what you can find out. We've got a description from the roommate. If it comes to that, I will call the parents, and we can get a photo from them. But I don't want to call them just yet. They can't help beyond the photo, and we're not even supposed to be investigating this." He paused. "First we need to find out something about her movements that night. Make sure you check the bars," he said to Maron, even though from the description the roommate had given, it did not sound as though Amy Bennett would have been in any of them.

Dufort headed to L'Institut Degas. He walked through the village, greeting old friends and acquaintances, taking his time, keeping his eyes open. Sometimes information came from unexpected sources, and he wanted to make himself available to it. On one side of the main square were three places that stayed open late: a wine bar that served "small plates"; *La Métairie*, an expensive place that hadn't yet earned a Michelin star, but was trying hard for it; and a bistro called Chez Papa that was run by a much-loved inhabitant of Castillac, which is where Dufort turned in.

"Alphonse!" he shouted over the din of pop music. Alphonse was mopping with his back to the door. "Bonjour, Alphonse!"

Alphonse startled and turned around. "Bonjour, Ben! I would offer you some lunch but the hour is all wrong, and I can see besides that something is the matter. Tell me!"

"You tell *me*," said Dufort, with a faint smile. "What about last night? Anything unusual?"

Alphonse leaned on his mop. "A Dutch family was here with twelve children, if you can believe that. You don't see big families like that anymore, do you?"

"Not so much. Many students? From Degas?"

Alphonse looked up at the ceiling and thought for a moment. "Oh, I don't know," he said finally. "I hate to admit it, but my memory isn't what it used to be. The nights, they start to run together." He shrugged.

"I understand. I wish I could sit and have a glass with you, but I've got some work that can't wait." And with a wave, Dufort was back on the street, alert, looking around for anything out of place, anything calling out to him, no matter how subtly.

Dufort had grown up in Castillac, and his mother and Alphonse were old friends. He could remember how Alphonse would come to dinner on Sundays, and make his parents laugh themselves sick with his imitations of other villagers. He brought homemade gooseberry jam that was Dufort's all-time favorite. Most people in the village were known to Dufort his whole life, except of course for the tourists who passed through and the occasional new person such as the American woman who had apparently bought La Baraque and moved in recently.

It had taken some doing, getting himself posted to his hometown. Officers in the gendarmerie were routinely moved from place to place precisely so that they did not get too close to the communities they served. At first, he had been told it was impossible, but Dufort had a way of convincing people to do what they did not necessarily want to do, and in the end, he got sent to Castillac. Perhaps he suffered from nostalgia, or was just a man who belonged in one place, but he had been happy there for the last six years.

When young Perrault had gone off for her training, she begged him to figure out a way for her to come back too. He had called in some favors and pulled some strings, and Perrault was allowed to come, but only for six months. They both expected to be posted to another village by the first of the year; their time in Castillac among the people and places they had grown up with was coming to an end.

L'Institut Degas was a short ways out of the village, just a little over a kilometer, and Dufort covered the distance quickly. He was not a large man but he was fit and athletic, and he arrived at the main building where the administration offices were without breaking a sweat. He did not call ahead, and he did not expect to get much help.

4

The Lawlers only stayed for two nights, and then Molly was back in the cottage for another round of dusting, scrubbing, and mopping. At least they weren't slobs. And oh look, a tip for the maid!

Molly snatched up the five-euro bill and shoved it in the pocket of her jeans. More bookings were coming in every day, but she needed to sit down and write a budget before running out to hire a cleaner. She went back to the house, got her phone and some earbuds, and listened to Otis Redding while she worked, singing along with "These Arms of Mine," her voice cracking in a satisfying way. She hoped the neighbors couldn't hear.

When she turned to leave, an orange cat was standing in the doorway looking at her.

"Hello, little puss!" Molly was happy for the company. "I'll get you a little saucer of cream if you come with me." The cat not only followed, but wound itself between Molly's legs, nearly causing her to trip and split her head open on the slate walk. She put her cleaning stuff away in a closet, and got together a saucer with a bit of cream and set it down. The orange cat looked at her, then walked slowly over to the saucer as if it didn't really care one way or another, and took a lick. Then the tail went straight up but with a little kink at the end, and the cat polished off the cream in under a minute.

"Thought so." Molly smiled and reached out her hand. The orange cat bit her on the finger and ran into the bushes. "Fiend!" she called after it.

The house was still unfamiliar and exciting, and she spent some time not accomplishing anything but wandering through its rooms, most of which had low ceilings with ancient beams. The original structure had been added on to several times so that the building was something of a hodgepodge, stuck together at odd angles. The staircase turned almost in a spiral, its treads worn, and Molly wondered at how many families had lived here, how many feet had trudged up to bed stepping just where she stepped.

She thought of walking around in the meadow behind the *potager*, but decided she had better get some more work done, so she spent the next hour at her desk, confirming bookings and emailing friends at home, sounding a little sunnier than she actually felt.

Back in Massachusetts, after the divorce, she usually ate lunch at the sink, or even just crammed in any old thing while standing in front of the refrigerator with the door open. But in her new French life, she was trying to change her habits and pay more attention to the small ceremonies of the day. She took a butter lettuce out and washed a number of leaves, broke up some goat cheese she had gotten at the market that morning along with the lettuce, sliced some carrots, opened a can of sardines and crumbled those in along with a few little potatoes from last night's dinner. For a dressing, she chopped up plenty of garlic and whisked it together with lemon juice, an egg yolk, more mustard than seemed right, and lots of salt and pepper and olive oil.

She stepped out the kitchen door to the garden, searching for herbs, but there was nothing besides rosemary. How can a French garden have no tarragon? What sort of infidels used to live here, anyway? she thought, stomping back inside.

After tossing the salad and pouring herself a glass of rosé, she went out to a terrace off the living room, pulled a rusty chair up to a rusty table, and had a long, luxurious, lonely lunch.

Jet lag had finished having its way with her, so she didn't feel like a nap after eating. Instead she put her dishes in the old porcelain sink and went out to the garden. Just inside the garage was the crate she had sent from home, minus the kitchen equipment which was unpacked and put away. She selected a tool whose name escaped her. It had a sort of fork on one end and a pick on the other—great for weeding out the nastiest garden invaders. Molly knelt in the grass and got to work on a patch on the side of the house, more Otis Redding coming out through the window, the sun on her back. That sort of weeding can be a kind of meditation, and as the pile of ripped-out vines and grass grew, her thoughts quieted down until she wasn't having any at all, nothing but the sound of Otis and the smell of plants and the feel of dirt on her hands.

"Bonjour madame!"

Startled, Molly sprang to her feet and turned around. Standing at the stone wall that separated her property from the neighbor's was, well, the neighbor. A small, bird-like woman dressed in a housecoat, her white hair flying out from a bun.

"Bonjour madame," Molly answered, her hands becoming clammy at the prospect of a conversation in French. It had been too long since college, when she'd studied it last.

"I would like to say hello and welcome you to Castillac," the neighbor said.

Okay, I actually understood that, Molly thought, feeling a little surge of optimism. "Thank you very much," said Molly. "She pretty."

The neighbor nodded vigorously and then spoke so quickly,

and with a stutter, that Molly was hopelessly lost. "*S'il vous plaît,*" she said, "Speak slow?"

The two women worked hard for the next ten minutes, both of their brows beginning to glisten from the effort of communicating the simplest things, and by the time they said *à tout à l'heure* they at least had each other's names, although Molly forgot the neighbor's more or less instantly. What did stick in her mind was the mention for the second time that day of the girl, the art student, who was missing. The neighbor had looked solemn, and said it might be a good idea to lock her doors, living alone and all.

Molly was quite happy to be living alone, thank you very much, and she was not going to get frightened just because some young girl ran off with somebody else's boyfriend. She stayed firm in her belief that her new country was much safer than her former one. Spitefully—although whom she was spiting was a little unclear—she left the French doors to the terrace not only unlocked but cracked open that night. The orange cat came in for a look around, but no other uninvited visitors crossed the threshold that night, unless you counted the spider and a couple of flies.

L'INSTITUT DEGAS HAD either a sterling or an unsavory reputation, depending on whom you talked to. The school had been founded in the 1950s by an artist who had tried to ride the wave of Abstract Expressionism but found himself beached with not enough income to get by, and so turned to teaching. He was a much more gifted teacher than artist, and soon had more students than he had time for himself, so he brought on other teachers, and L'Institut Degas was born.

Over the years, other talented teachers had come to the school, and some of their students had gone on to illustrious, and sometimes very lucrative careers. This track record meant that applications were almost always steady, which meant the school could be choosy about the students it admitted, and the tuition fees stayed hefty.

However, some of the teachers—including perhaps a few on the present faculty—had turned out to be capable enough as artists, and their classroom work was creditable, and yet, still, one might say that they were not precisely the best choices to mold young minds. That at least was what Jack Draper, head of the current administration, hinted to Dufort, when he was asked about the faculty and their relation to the students.

"It's *France*, after all," said Draper. "Some of the students—Americans in particular—they expect to have flirtations, maybe an affair or two. It's part of the experience of studying abroad. You know how it is."

Having an American remind him that they were in France might have pushed a less seasoned officer right over the edge of annoyance, but Dufort merely gave a faint smile. It had not come naturally, but he had learned over the years to keep his feelings and reactions from showing in his expression. And so, without having to work at it, the urge to tell Draper he was a jackass passed without a trace.

"Are you saying, *Monsieur le Directeur*, that you believe Amy Bennett was romantically involved in some way with a faculty member? That there was a relationship beyond that of teacher and student?"

"Well, of course it's *possible*. Here at Degas we do not follow those old rigid classroom models, where the teacher is all-powerful and the students are meek and never dare to express themselves. We are open. We make room for creativity—yes, for *passion*—to bloom."

With some effort, Dufort kept his eyes from rolling.

"I am happy to hear that creativity is blooming here at L'Institut," said Dufort. "Would you be so kind as to print out a list of Bennett's classes, with the schedule and teachers' names and cell numbers? I would be interested in talking with some of them, only for background, you understand.

"The most likely thing is that the girl has run off, for any of the reasons that young women find to do that. But at the same time, I wish to be thorough. You said that Bennett was a serious student, a conscientious one. That doesn't quite fit with a flighty girl running off for romance, do you think?" Dufort's expression was open and questioning, perhaps a bit slow-witted.

"Of course I will provide you with anything you ask for, anything at all," said Draper. "As for flighty—who knows what lurks in these girls' minds? Sometimes it is the most serious ones who have the biggest screw loose, am I right?"

"Are you suggesting Mademoiselle Bennett has a screw loose?"

"Not at all, not in the least. I'm only saying that girls that age —*young women*—they can be unpredictable. The students here are not studying to be bankers, Officer Dufort. They are creative spirits of a rather high order. And that means, yes, that we might see more, how to put it, *instability* of behavior and emotions than one would encounter at a school for, say, tax accounting. You understand?"

Dufort nodded. He understood that *Monsieur le Directeur* was saying that if Amy Bennett was missing, it was her own fault, not the school's, and moreover, that her flightiness was just part of how very special she was. Dufort appreciated art as much as any Frenchman, and he also had a sensitive bullshit detector, which at the moment was letting off a piercing shriek.

5

The Wolfsons were due in two days, so after drinking her morning coffee and checking her email, Molly went over to the cottage to make sure it was ready, feeling pleased that she was staying organized and ahead of schedule.

Oh. Forgot to make the beds. Needs vacuuming again. Please tell me that's not the faucet leaking. Or worse.

It *was* the faucet. Molly wasn't completely useless as a handyman, and she managed to get the water to the cottage turned off and the faucet taken apart. It just needed a new washer. Hoping to avoid getting in the car and driving out to the big box stores, she glanced in a mirror to make sure she was presentable and hurried into the village to see what she could find. Perhaps there was some sort of general store, preferably in the vicinity of Pâtisserie Bujold.

The elementary-school-age kids had Wednesday afternoons off, and the streets were thronged. They pushed each other, ran in circles, sang, held hands. Molly wondered if she would ever be able to look at a group of kids and not feel a stab in her chest. The bad marriage—that she could get over, and was most of the way there. But being nearly forty, without the children she had wanted so deeply...she wasn't sure if there was any getting over that.

A world of regret and sorrow bubbled up in such moments. But Molly had learned to carry on anyway, and at the moment, that meant finding a washer and preparing for the Wolfsons, no matter how hard she was being jerked around by her emotions.

She found a hardware store, and by deft use of her pointer finger, got what she needed to repair the faucet. While there she stocked up on some tools (a wrench, some decent pliers, a drill) she was clearly going to need to keep La Baraque from falling to pieces, and wondered how much local handymen charged, since she assumed before too long she would encounter emergency repairs that went beyond what she had learned from watching her mother fix stuff, or what she figured out from watching YouTube.

Pâtisserie Bujold was only about four blocks from the hardware store, practically right on the way, so she swung down that street, her mouth already watering. No art students out by the fountain today even though the weather was perfect, but more throngs of schoolchildren and their happy chatter.

She decided not to take her pastry home, but to enjoy it there at the shop, with a petit café. There were only two tiny tables outside, and she sat at one, waiting for her coffee with her face turned up to the sun, freckles and skin cancer be damned, the bag of new tools at her feet. Her sadness had faded, and the *pain au chocolat* was brilliantly sweet and salty, the outer layers shattering in an explosion of buttery flavor, and the inside moist and dark and delicious.

Life was good, if sometimes annoying and never perfect, and she sat back and watched people going about their errands and stopping to have long conversations with their friends and neighbors. It felt so much less busy here, somehow, even though she had plenty to do. Or maybe it was simply that she felt less rushed, less like everything had to be done yesterday.

She would get the drippy faucet fixed before the Wolfsons

arrived. And eventually, no matter how long it took, she would get the *potager* in the back of the house producing again, and the borders in the front free of vines and bursting with sweet-smelling color. Her gîte business would continue to grow. She would read good books and eat more *pain au chocolat*, and the loneliness she felt from not having children or a partner would simply be part of the fabric of her life, and not its defining tone.

Molly ventured into Pâtisserie Bujold again before heading home, with the idea that she would be so happy to wake up the next morning knowing there was a pastry waiting for her, even if it was a little bit stale.

CHIEF DUFORT CLOSED the door to his office and passed his hands over his face. Stress was part of his job; it was inevitable and expected, even in a village where the crime rate was low. He had handily withstood a number of extremely stressful situations: a sea of blood from car accidents, several attempted suicides, a chase or three in which he was pushed to his physical limit. Yet making a call to inform parents that their child was missing filled him with dread.

He was going to be firm in his reassurances, and of course do his very best to believe his own words. But he and the parents knew the percentages—everyone who reads the paper or watches television knows them. All three would feel the dark abyss opening in front of them, even if they didn't speak of it. Dufort had been born in Castillac and never lived anywhere else, but in a moment like this, he wished he lived and worked in a big city where he imagined getting lost in the crowd, even as a cop, somehow always too busy to be the *flic* who had to make the call.

He sat at his desk for some long moments looking at the sheet of paper with the Bennetts' phone numbers. Always the possibility loomed that a parent was involved in a case like this. Mental illness, personality disorders, family dysfunction—they could all lead to a parent doing something unimaginable, and he would have to listen for any indications of that when he spoke to the family.

Another woman, vanished. The third time. Will it be like the others, with no evidence, no trace, no resolution?

A little part of his brain, the weaselly part everyone has, wondered if perhaps it might be better to call later, first thing in the morning being not so convenient after all. Why ruin their day right at the start? Why not give them several more hours of blissful ignorance? Dufort chased the weasel away and took a deep breath, then slowly tapped the numbers into his cell.

Jack Draper should be making this call. Dufort had no official responsibility for Amy Bennett, but he knew the call needed to be made and he did not trust Draper to do it.

"Hello, I'm looking for Sally or Marshall Bennett," he said, in passable English.

"This is Marshall Bennett."

"I am Benjamin Dufort, chief gendarme of Castillac," he said. He knew the word "gendarme" would send a chill through Bennett, and he paused a moment even though he knew Mr. Bennett would not have time to recover from it.

There was not enough time in the world to recover from it.

"I call because your daughter Amy is reported missing from L'Institut Degas, and I am hoping you have some information about her location."

"What?" said Marshall Bennett, his voice sounding far away.

"Amy's roommate called my office to say that Amy was not seen. We have looked, but not found. Mr. Bennett, I am sorry for my English."

"I'm going to get Sally. Please hold on."

Dufort sighed. He took another deep breath and let it out slowly, but felt just as tense. He had the strong sensation of wanting time to stop and then roll backward, zipping back to the place where Amy was still with her roommate, at which point time could reverse again, this time everyone being careful not to let Amy out of their sight until the moment of her disappearance was safely past and the awful mistake was corrected.

He could only imagine how deeply the parents would wish for this, if the feeling was so strong for him when he had never even met the girl.

"Hello?" said Sally Bennett.

"Hello madame, I am Benjamin Dufort of the gendarmerie of Castillac. I spoke to your husband about your daughter. I wonder if you have heard from her in recent days?"

"I don't understand. Amy is in school, at the L'Institut Degas. She is a painter."

"The school tells me she is a good student, Madame Bennett. I am calling you because she is not seen, her roommate does not know where she is. I wonder if you have these informations?" He closed his eyes and smoothed his palm over his face.

Silence on the line. Dufort heard a strangled sort of grunt, then Mr. Bennett came back on the line.

"We have not heard from Amy since last week," he said. There was a long pause. "She works very hard. She is not in touch every minute the way some girls her age are. Are you saying...what exactly are you saying, Chief? Is that what I call you, Chief?"

"*Oui*, that is good. What I say is that your daughter is reported missing. This is not an official phone call because in France, the gendarmes do not investigate missing adults. But, Monsieur Bennett, the roommate of Amy called my office, and I do not want girls missing from my village, if you understand me. I want to know where she is, and I'm sure you do too."

"I appreciate your concern."

There was another long pause. Dufort tried to imagine what it was like, receiving a call such as this one. He knew that there was never any preparation, never a way to know how you would react until the thing actually happened to you. He suspected the

Bennetts were in shock, and there was no guessing how long that phase would last.

At least he had not felt anything untoward in either Bennett's voice. It was of course way too early to know for certain, but his intuition said that they were truly shocked by the news, and not perpetrators in any way.

"I would thank you if you would call me if you hear from her," said Dufort gently. "I will give you my cell number and my email, please to use anytime at your convenience." He really should get some tutoring for his English. It was excruciating to struggle so hard to make himself understood.

"Thank you for calling," said Mr. Bennett. "I'm sure she's off somewhere working on something and forgot to let her roommate know. Something like that, at any rate. We will let you know when we hear from her."

After giving them his contact information and several exchanges of *politesse* and gratitude, Dufort ended the call and put his phone down on the desk. Even though he had no children, it was not hard to imagine the horror the Bennetts were in for if their daughter did not turn up soon.

He was thirty-five years old with no girlfriend at the moment, but had always assumed he would have a family someday. He wondered whether he might have resisted settling down because having a family, having children, meant never being able to avoid the possibility of something very bad happening, something so bad it would take everything in you to get past, if you even could. A loss of the very worst kind.

He was mature enough not to think in certainties, and not to be superstitious. But he could not forget the bad feeling he had from the moment he first heard Amy Bennett's name. He knew the percentages, and he believed the calm of her parents was unfortunately going to be quite short-lived.

6

By that evening, just at dusk, Molly had more or less finished unpacking, and she wandered around the house at loose ends even though there were a million things she felt she should be doing. She went out to the garden and inhaled. A summer scent of mown grass with a hint of roses was still in the air, but the garden itself was so overgrown that it was overwhelming to contemplate how much work needed to be done. The orange cat sidled up and rubbed against her leg. Distracted by the garden, she reached down to stroke it and once again the cat bit her and ran under the hedge.

"Nasty beast!" she called after it, and then fled through the gate and into the village for a drink and some company, hoping to find at least one person who could speak English. It was Friday night, and she hoped villagers would be out enjoying the nice weather and in a welcoming mood, tolerant of her subjunctive tense (which was utter rubbish).

Chez Papa looked promising. It was right on the main square with a large number of tables outdoors, and a small crowd seemed to be enjoying themselves, having apéritifs, drinking beer, and eating peanuts and potato chips from bowls on the bar. Three small dogs were underfoot. The place looked lively but not too intimidating. Molly made her way inside to the bar, and when the bartender gave her his attention, she pointed at the drink that belonged to the woman next to her and said, "*Comme ça!*" The bartender gave a short nod and took down a bottle.

Molly felt happily victorious for getting out a phrase and being understood.

"Let me guess—American, Massachusetts?" said an older man in probably the best-looking suit Molly had ever seen.

"Um, yeah?" she said, mystified.

"Lawrence Weebly," he said, holding out a hand, then taking hers and kissing it. "I have a little hobby of guessing people's accents. But I admit, yours was not much of a challenge."

Molly laughed. "I'm Molly Sutton. But you only heard me speak two words of French! It's not like I asked where I should pahk the cah or anything," she said.

"That would be fish in a barrel. So thank you for providing the evening's amusement by giving me only the two words, and not in English."

"But seriously, how did you do that?"

Lawrence just smiled and sipped his bright red drink. "Now tell me, you are the new owner of La Baraque? How are you finding Castillac so far?"

Molly flinched. "It's a little unsettling having everyone know who I am before I even meet them," she said, managing a weak smile.

"That's life in a village," said Lawrence. "For better or worse. Even in the age of the internet, most of us find our neighbors make up a decent portion of our entertainment. We gossip, we pry, we want to stay informed of the latest. Another!" he said to the bartender, pointing at his empty glass.

"Well," said Molly. "I may fit right in then." She turned and surveyed the other customers with curiosity. "I've been called nosy. Once or twice," she added in a lower voice.

"Here in Castillac we just consider that to be interest in humankind," he said, taking a long swig of his fresh drink.

Molly nodded and smiled. She liked Lawrence Weebly. And it was really wonderful to speak English, face to face, after days of struggling to make herself understood or having only herself for company. Now that she had someone interesting to talk to, she could feel just how lonely she had gotten.

The bartender had placed her drink on the bar in front of her, and she'd been too distracted to try it. She took a sip and nearly choked. The bartender grinned. "Cognac and Sprite," he said in English, shrugging. "It is what you ordered."

"But—" said Molly, pointing at the woman's drink. "*That's* what she's having?"

"It is a fad," said the bartender with a sigh. "Unfortunate, as most fads are."

"Spoken like a true Frenchman, Nico," said Lawrence. "And I couldn't agree more."

"You speak English like a professor," said Molly to the bartender.

"I studied in America for three years," Nico said, shrugging. "Your French will come along, now that you're here. You'll see."

"Your lips to God's ears," said Molly. Then she turned to Lawrence. "What are *you* drinking?" asked Molly, looking at his red cocktail.

"Lawrence always, but always, drinks Negronis," said a large man with an even larger belly who leaned over Molly's shoulder to join the conversation, but in French.

"*Bonsoir*, Lapin," said Lawrence.

"I don't think I've ever had a Negroni," said Molly, pleased that she could make out the man's French.

"Expensive way to get a buzz on, if you ask me," said Lapin.

And indeed, it looked as though Lapin liked to get a buzz on quite frequently, if his red-rimmed eyed and bloated face were any indication. "Hey, you're *la bombe* who bought the big place down the rue des Chênes?"

"*La bombe?*" said Molly.

"His idea of a compliment," said Lawrence. "Molly Sutton, meet Laurent Broussard, called Lapin for reasons unknown to me."

Molly nodded to Lapin, and tried to move on her stool to keep him from leaning on her shoulder.

"*Enchanté*," said Lapin, smiling, and he moved around to get in front of Molly, at which point the focus of his bloodshot eyes drifted south and stayed on her chest.

Molly tried to cross her arms but really there was no position that would camouflage her body enough to hide the fact that her bosom was quite large and extremely perky.

Lawrence watched Molly, then thoughtfully ate a handful of peanuts. "Hey Lapin, I saw a woman in the back, a tourist, just your type." He motioned with his head toward a small back room which was furnished with comfortable chairs for customers to drink and socialize, or play some cards or chess if they felt like it.

Lapin's eyes did not budge from Molly's chest. She rolled her eyes and took a sip of drink, then scowled at it. Lawrence slid off his barstool and put his arm in Lapin's and slowly pulled him toward the back, giving Molly a wink as he did so.

"Back in a minute," he mouthed before stepping out of sight.

Molly tried to overhear the conversation going on behind her, but the couple was speaking French too rapidly, and she was only getting bits and pieces that she couldn't knit together into any sense. She narrowed her eyes at her drink and then took a long slurp of it, hating it but wanting to be done, making herself drink it instead of ordering something else as a kind of penance. Penance for what, was not clear.

She saw Lawrence winding his way back through the crowd. Already he felt like a friend, and she felt unreasonably happy to see him.

"All right," he said, settling himself back on his stool and interrupting himself long enough to sip his Negroni. "What's the story?"

"Which story?"

"The girls. Not real, are they?"

Molly guffawed. "Hell no, they're not real!"

"Then why have them? You don't enjoy the attention. So what's the point?"

"My ex."

"I see." He sipped his drink and reached for some chips. "I don't think you need to say anything more. That spells it out rather neatly."

"The real question," said Molly, "is why people work so hard to try to save bad marriages. In retrospect, we'd have saved a lot of time—and *these*—if we'd quit five years earlier." She looked down at her buxom self and laughed again, and Lawrence Weebly laughed with her.

The two of them sat at the bar for another few hours, drinking Negronis and talking about former loves, broken relationships, and Castillac, until finally Lawrence stood and took her arm.

"All right, this has been a lovely evening of overdoing it, now let's get you home safely to sleep it off."

Molly stood up unsteadily. It took some time and concentration to get her feet under her. After finishing the dreadful cognac and Sprite, she had tried a Negroni, and liked it so much she had another, and now was, well, shit-faced. "I feel like singing," she said, giggling.

"I'm sure you do. Come on outside, I'm sure Vincent is hanging around out here, you can take his taxi home."

"I don't need a taxchi," said Molly.

"Taxchis are quite nice when one is blotto," said Lawrence. He waved at Vincent who was leaning against the hood of his tiny taxi, chatting to someone. "Here we are." He opened the door and poured Molly inside. "She lives at La Baraque," he said to Vincent. "Just put the ride on my tab."

"*Bonne nuit, mon petit chou*," he said through the open window. "Nice meeting you. Next time, one Negroni only."

Molly flopped her head back and laughed, even though some part of her noted that nothing was especially funny.

"Vincent," she said, and laughed again.

He reached over the seat and patted her knee. "No worry, I'll get you home safe," he said. He took a look in the rearview mirror and grinned at her, and pulled away from the curb and down the rue des Chênes, on the way to La Baraque.

BENJAMIN DUFORT STOOD up when his officers came into his office, both of them carrying takeout coffee. "Bonjour Perrault, Maron. Thank you for coming in on a Saturday. At some point I will find a way to make up your day off."

"Chief, that's not our concern right now," said Perrault. Maron nodded.

"Well, I thank you. All right, let's get to it. As you know, Amy Bennett was last seen on Wednesday afternoon. That was nearly three days ago. I'm going to fill you in on what I've learned, which is next to nothing, and then I'd like to hear from you." Dufort reached his arms up over his head and stretched from side to side, then twisted one way and then the other. His officers were patient, used to the way Dufort stretched while he paused to think.

"I spoke to Jack Draper, head of Degas. I'll leave my personal judgment aside for the moment, and say only that he was not much help. On the surface, he made all the right remarks about how the school will do anything to help find Amy, but just under the surface, he hinted that she was possibly unstable, might be having an affair with a teacher—in short, that if anything has happened to her, it's her own damn fault.

"Let me say this: it's a common reaction, blaming the victim. It happens in the press, in the village, even in the court. Perhaps it's simply a human reaction and there's nothing anyone can do to put a stop to it. It can be subtle, but it is always poisonous, and we in the gendarmerie need to be vigilant against it. Whatever bad decisions a victim makes leading up to a crime being committed, he or she did *not* make the choice to be victim to assault, or abduction, or rape, or anything else. And *that* is where the fault lies—with the person making that choice. Stupidity is not equivalent to criminality, or anywhere close."

He looked up to see Thérèse's eyes open wide and Maron looking a little grim. "I'm sorry, I did not mean for that to take quite the tone of lecturing that it ended with. I am not accusing the two of you of this bias any more than I accuse myself. You understand?"

Perrault and Maron nodded.

"That's it for Draper, for the moment. I plan to go back to Degas today and see if I can have a word with Monsieur Gallimard, one of her teachers. Also, I called the Bennetts. They did not express worry in words, but of course a phone call such as that stirs up quite a lot of anxiety. I expect to hear from them soon, if they have no luck contacting their daughter. Now, let me hear from you. Perrault?"

Thérèse sat up straight and scraped her teeth over her bottom lip. "I made the calls, Chief. Bergerac airport, Bordeaux airport, all the car rental agencies within seventy kilometers, same with hospitals. I got zero. Nobody has seen her, talked to her, nothing.

So, I thought I would see if I could turn up any information in the village. I went around to the restaurants and bars—" she put up her hand to deflect the criticism she felt coming—"I know, it was premature without a photo or even a description. It was just casual conversation."

"Let's not get too far ahead of ourselves," said Dufort. "Of course, when any young woman goes missing, the first thought is abduction and subsequent sex crime. We would be looking for anyone who might have crossed paths with Amy after the time she was last seen.

"But I don't want the previous unsolved cases to make us jump to any conclusions. There could be other motives leading to Amy's disappearance."

"Like what?" asked Thérèse, and then wanted to kick herself for asking a dumb question.

"Jealousy, for one," said Dufort. "By all accounts, she was the top dog at Degas. An ambitious but less-talented classmate could want her out of the way."

"There's always love triangles," said Maron quietly.

"Yes, something in that line, as well," agreed Dufort. "Draper wanted to steer me in that direction at any rate." He paused, noting that he resisted going where Draper was pointing, only because it was Draper doing the pointing.

"I know I keep harping on it, but remember we're essentially doing this investigation off the books and not as gendarmes. We need to cut things a bit close to make sure I don't get sanctioned, you understand?"

The officers nodded and took sips of their coffee in unison. Perrault grinned, happy to have something besides traffic violations to work on, and Maron, inscrutable as always, kept his feelings buried deep and out of sight.

"Just between us, I am calling this a murder investigation. Perrault, I know it's your first. What we need to try to do is put ourselves in the mind of a person who would want to take this girl and hurt her. Of course we need to look for evidence and see if we can painstakingly account for her movements. We need to interview anyone we think might shed light on the case. But all that work will come to nothing if we do not use our imaginations to good effect."

"Yes, Chief," said Perrault, beaming.

7

1983

The little boy stood on his tiptoes to look inside the window. The glass was fogged up with condensation because Aline, the cleaning lady, was washing some curtains in the big metal sink and using gallons of boiling water. Billows of steam rose up from the sink, obscuring her face. But it was not Aline's face that Laurent was looking at. He was watching her body, specifically her breasts, which were generous and on the verge of spilling out of her work-dress as she bent to her washing.

He was five. His mother was long dead, and he yearned to have Aline's attention for more than a few minutes. Longed for her to stop working and stroke his hair and comfort him, to take him on her lap and allow him to rest his head on her bosom. To tell him she would take him away from Monsieur Broussard, his father, who was so cruel to them both.

As he watched, he felt some relief. Even though it was cold outside, seeing the steam tricked him into feeling warmer. He rubbed a little corner of the window and could see more clearly Aline's rosy skin, could almost smell her earthy fragrance.

But then he heard heavy footsteps, and the boy startled, and scampered around the side of the house. He couldn't let his father see him hanging around Aline, or he would get rid of her, like he'd gotten rid of all the others. And after getting rid of her, he would beat Laurent, snarling at him, and the boy would have to stay home from school until the bruises subsided.

Little Laurent slipped into the big garage stuffed with old furniture and knickknacks, and hid inside an armoire, shivering against the cold.

8

2005

The Saturday market in Castillac was typical of markets all over France, with farmers setting up stalls for their flowers, vegetables, meats, seafood, and cheese, alongside purveyors of mostly cheap clothing, used books, homemade jams, spices, and other odds and ends. At a few folding tables, collectors of mushrooms, nuts, and various wild greens sat with small bundles for sale, and occasionally salespeople of things as disparate as air conditioners, mattresses, and cookware set up shop as well. The market went from early in the morning until noon, when everything was packed up and the scene deserted because everyone in the entire village was having lunch.

It was the first Saturday market since Molly had moved to Castillac, and she was not going to miss it no matter how dreadful her hangover. Damn those Negronis! She smiled about the night before as she dug around in the kitchen trying to concoct a remedy for her slamming headache. Surely she was too old to be getting drunk with strangers, but it had sure been fun, and she only hoped that Lawrence Weebly would turn out to be as entertaining and friendly during the sober light of day as he had been last night.

Glass of tomato juice, loaded up with hot sauce? Seemed like it might help, or at least distract her mouth from the dire cottony feeling that was making her so nauseated. She chugged it, popped a few aspirin, and went out to the terrace to sit at the rusty table and think things over, and drink one last cup of coffee before heading into the village.

But the sun was shining right in that very spot, and her head throbbed and her eyes burned. She gave up and went inside, grabbed a hat and sunglasses, and set off down the rue des Chênes, market basket in hand, thinking that she would look just like a Frenchwoman, what with walking to the market with a basket, except that she suspected most Frenchwomen weren't showing up with hangovers as prodigious as this one. Most of them seemed so controlled in their pleasures, or, "controlled" wasn't it, maybe...moderate. So perhaps one small éclair on Sunday, instead of stuffing them in at every opportunity. *Ahem.* And perhaps one Negroni, not two plus that horrid Cognac and Sprite.

Well, she thought, I may live in France, but I'll always be an American. Long live immoderation! And then she winced, as having even a thought with an exclamation point made her head hurt.

The street was crowded with market-day traffic, and cars were parked almost all the way to La Baraque. Molly held one hand on her stomach and thought about cheese and éclairs, about fresh sausages and mushrooms, and all the other gems she was sure to find. She gently rubbed back and forth, trying to soothe her unhappy belly.

Stalls were set up in the center of the Place and all around its perimeter, as well as going down some side streets. Molly walked around, gaping, letting all the chatter sweep over her, not trying to understand conversations but just looking and walking slowly so as not to upset her head any further. She was grateful that no one was putting on a hard sell, and she could walk along and check things out without having to fend off overeager vendors.

Perhaps a vegetable plate for dinner, she thought, something healthful and not taxing to the system. She spied a middle-aged woman manning a vegetable stand and went over.

"Bonjour madame," said Molly.

"Bonjour madame!" said the woman, beaming at her. She was rather round, wearing a grubby apron, and her eyes twinkled with good humor.

"I think for dinner I have some vegetables only this night," said Molly, bravely.

"Only vegetables? I love them, I grow them, as you see. But madame, they are best cooked in meat broth, or in a nice butter sauce alongside a steak. Have you had potatoes cooked in duck fat?"

"No, madame." Molly grinned, because she could understand what the woman said. Though she still struggled to speak, at least understanding was coming back—an amazing feeling, like having closets inside her brain opened up and finding treasure inside.

"Well, Molly, you cannot come to live in the Dordogne and not have potatoes cooked in duck fat at least once. Of course, once you try it, you will want it every week! Or every night!" The woman gestured to a basket of gnarled potatoes flecked with dirt.

Molly felt her face flushing. It was just weird how everyone seemed to know her name, that she was the woman who had just moved to Castillac, before she had a chance to tell them.

"I need...I wonder," she began, and then gained steam as her determination grew, "Everyone knows my name and how I am come to Castillac to live. How is this?"

The woman laughed. "We talk," she said, shrugging. And then

she leaned over a basket of peppers and took Molly by the shoulders and kissed her on each cheek. "I am Manette," she said, "*Bienvenue* to Castillac! I am only sorry you have come right when we are in the grip of a crime wave."

"Crime wave?"

"Well, my next-door neighbor had his wheelbarrow stolen right out of his front yard. Who ever heard of something like that in Castillac? And also Robert tells me that someone went into his garden and took all of his artichokes, right at the peak of ripening. This sort of thing is unheard of here! And on top of all that, there is that girl missing from the art school."

"I heard about that," said Molly. "Are you worried there is...bad?"

The woman rubbed her hands on her apron. "Who can say," she said. "People say oh, young girls run off all the time and it turns out they've stolen their best friend's boyfriend or something like that. But me, I think this is nothing but stories from the movies. Wishful thinking, you see? In real life, I think when girls disappear, it's not a joke with a happy ending. It's usually because someone *made* them disappear, and they don't come back."

Molly's eyes widened. It was one of those *bang!* moments when she realized her thinking had been totally wrong, and the woman was exactly right—when she heard about the missing girl, she had supplied any number of reasons to explain her absence, and it was absolutely true that the reasons came from movies and novels more than real life.

"I see," she said. "And...I think you are right."

The two women stood looking into each other's eyes for a long moment, sharing sympathy for the missing girl, and also a flash of fear for themselves and the other women in the village, for if the art student had been taken by someone, and if she was still missing and maybe not coming back, and no one had been caught, then weren't all the rest of them in some danger as well?

Then Manette brightened, gestured to the peppers and said,

"They are at their peak right now, Molly. Just the right amount of rain, so the flavor is exquisite, if I do say so."

"I'll take three," said Molly, thinking with relief of dinner instead of violence. "And can you show me a person for sausages?"

Manette smiled. "That will make a nice supper," she said. "Go to Raoul over on the far side of the Place. Politically he is crazy as a loon, but he has great talent for raising pigs and making sausage. They are treated like princes, those pigs, which is funny because Raoul is so far to the left he makes Mitterrand look like a royalist."

Molly bought her sausages and headed home without making a detour to Pâtisserie Bujold. Her head was pounding and she felt like she needed to lie down. Manette's words were disturbing. Had she really left the high crime of her native country only to find herself in the middle of a village crime wave, complete with abduction and murder? She really believed she had not.

But she knew even as she was putting some effort into hoping, that hope, in circumstances like this, did not count for much.

BENJAMIN DUFORT LEFT the backstreet where the office of the herbalist he frequented was tucked away, a new blue glass bottle of a stress-relieving tincture in his pocket. He made his way through the market, chatting with old friends and neighbors, always with an ear out for the thing out of place, the chance bit of information that would help him with his new case. So far, not a single bit had crossed his path, or at least, he had not recognized it as such. It was always possible that he had come across it but did not grasp what it was, no matter how attentive he was trying to be.

He was headed to L'Institut Degas again, hoping to catch one of Amy's teachers for an informal interview. A chat, nothing more, just for background—that's what he would say to Professor Gallimard, who was not on the list of suspects, which unfortunately at this juncture, was entirely blank. By all accounts he was a serious man who was entirely wrapped up in his art and his teaching, and Dufort had not heard a single word to suggest there was anything untoward in his relationship with Amy Bennett. A serious, dedicated student and a serious, talented teacher—that can make quite a profitable pairing, thought Dufort, and he hoped that Gallimard was going to have something helpful to say, though he did not try to guess what it might be.

In the meantime, Dufort enjoyed the beautiful Saturday morning. The weather was absolute perfection, clear and sunny but not hot, with occasional cumulus clouds puffing by with a light breeze. He smelled a strong scent of lavender and saw that he was passing a vendor from Provence who had sacks of the flowers open, with small signs stuck in each sack giving the price. Farther along he saw Rémy, an organic farmer, who had a mountain of beautiful tomatoes for sale. They kissed cheeks, one peck to each side, friends since childhood.

"*Mon Dieu*, Rémy! How many varieties are you growing now?"

"Bonjour Benjamin! I've lost count. They are all heirloom, *bien sûr*, you should see my seed-saving files! It's complicated keeping track of it all and takes up a lot of time, but when I come to market with a haul like this, it's worth it. Come on, even a crusty old bachelor like yourself needs some tomatoes on your kitchen counter—look, try one." Rémy took a serrated knife and sliced through a round yellow tomato with green stripes, then held out a slice.

Dufort shook his head but took the slice and ate it. Quickly he nodded and said, "All right, I won't argue! Give me a few kilos, something I can finish up in a few days' time."

Rémy smiled and started putting tomatoes on his scale. Dufort turned and surveyed the market, watching.

"So what's the story with the missing girl?" asked Rémy.

"Nothing's secret here, is it?"

"Of course not. Everyone's talking about it, got their pet theories, you know how it is."

Dufort absently reached for another slice of the yellow tomato and ate it. "I have nothing to tell you. Not holding anything back for official reasons—I'm saying I have nothing. No idea where she is, whether she's been abducted or went somewhere on her own by choice. *Nothing.*"

Rémy put his hands on his hips and looked at his old friend. He wished Benjamin had something in his life besides work, but somehow now, in his mid-thirties, that is what Benjamin had. Work, and working out. Rémy shook his head.

"And I have to ask..." Rémy lowered his voice and leaned close to his friend, "...do you think there is any connection...with the others?"

Dufort's face looked stony. "I don't know," he said simply. The men made eye contact then, all their emotion in the looks they gave each other.

"So, good to see you as always," said Dufort, feeling his anxiety ramp up. "I should be off, got much to do as you might guess."

Rémy nodded. "Here," he said, holding out the bag of tomatoes. "But be gentle with them, they don't like being knocked about."

Dufort dug in his pocket for some money but Rémy waved him off. "Just take them," he said. "And invite me over for an *apéro* someday, huh?" He grinned and looked behind Dufort at a woman waiting her turn.

Dufort moved out of the way and walked out of the Place, down the road that led to L'Institut. He was thinking about questions he could ask Gallimard, wondering what unexpected route he could take with the conversation that might produce something helpful, and on the outskirts of his thoughts was Valérie Boutillier and the tiny handful of details he had gathered on her case. She too had no apparent reason for disappearing—in fact, she had been celebrating her acceptance to a prestigious university program the night before she went missing.

As he walked, he took a tomato out of the paper bag and bit into it absently, but the flavor was so intense he stopped in his tracks, giving it his full attention, making sure not to drip juice all over his shirt, amused at how horrified his mother would be to see him eating by the side of the road like a barbarian.

9

Sunday mornings in Castillac were quiet. The Romanesque church on the Place had a trickle of visitors because it was something of an architectural oddity, but the congregation attending weekly services shrank nearly every year as the elderly members passed away. What the village did on Sunday mornings was spend time with family, prepare the big Sunday meal, go to Pâtisserie Bujold or its competitors for pastries, and laze around in slippers reading the paper or perhaps a new detective novel. The more ambitious might putter in the garden.

It was a day for family, for relaxation, and food.

For Gilles Maron, Sundays were a boring nuisance. He was from the north of France, near Lille, and he was glad to have that much distance between him and his family because they were a poisonous pack of hyenas, and it was much better that way. He appreciated food, of course, but had found that ambitious cooking for one person was more depressing than satisfying, and he had developed a hatred for leftovers after living alone for eight years.

After breakfast, Maron strolled over to Degas, figuring that students far from home did not have Sunday plans either, or at least if they did, the plans would not involve family obligations that would be difficult to extricate themselves from. He wanted to talk to Maribeth Donnelly, the roommate who had called in to report Amy missing.

There was only one dormitory, and he found that easily enough, but saw no directory or anything that would tell him which room was hers. The main door was locked. Maron wandered around campus for some minutes, wondering how tight a rein Dufort expected him to be on. Could he investigate on his own, without direct instructions? Would his boss be pleased if he came in with some evidence, or annoyed that he had acted on his own?

Maron had been in Castillac for over a year, but they hadn't had a real case yet, nothing but a few domestics and a stolen wheelbarrow, if you didn't count drunk driving and parking violations. Parking violations! He certainly had expected to be much farther along in his career by now, not writing stupid parking tickets. Of course he had heard about the other disappearances, but they were way before his time.

When he came back to the front of the dorm, he saw a young man ahead of him on the path. When the student swiped his ID to unlock the door, Maron was right behind him, and slipped inside the door so quietly the student heard nothing. He trotted up the stairs and out of sight. There were two hallways going off the foyer on the ground floor, and Maron opened the door to the left and walked as silently as possible, looking for some way to identify Amy and Maribeth's room, and hopefully find Maribeth there. Some of the students had stuck whiteboards on the outside of their doors—odd in this era of texting, thought Maron, but most had drawings on them instead of messages, which made sense since it was an art school dorm, after all.

He heard some young women talking, and went toward the sound, cocking his ear. When he got to their room he held his breath and listened, and when their voices were still a little too indistinct, he furtively pressed his ear up against the door.

"I don't know, I just...don't think so."

"I'm telling you, he's interested! Why do you think he comes to our room all the time?"

"He just wants my class notes."

"Your notes *are* really good." Pause. "Listen, I know he flirts with me, but I'm telling you, he's only doing it to try to rile you up. It's about you, not me!"

"Oh, shut up!" The women laughed.

Maron lifted his head from the door and kept going down the hallway. He considered knocking, showing his badge, and asking where Maribeth's room was, but he wanted to find a less direct way, something less noticeable. At the far end of the hall was a set of stairs, and Maron went up two at a time, and then started down the hallway on the second floor, straining to hear voices, footsteps, clues.

Just as he crept past a door, a student came out and nearly knocked into him.

"*Pardon*," said Maron. "Could you tell me the room of Maribeth Donnelly?" He had his hand on his badge but hoped he wouldn't have to use it.

"Third floor. 314, I think," said the young man, and hurried down the hallway and clattered down the stairs.

Maron smiled and followed him to the stairs and went up to the third floor. The hallway was quiet. He heard no talking, no movement. Security was obviously inadequate—he had gotten into the building with barely any effort. The students kept their doors shut, but Maron was willing to bet, mostly unlocked. At least on Sunday morning, there was no activity in the halls, no groups of students socializing that would be a deterrent to anyone who didn't belong there.

If a person wanted to, he could treat these hallways as hunting grounds. Students were easy marks—young and distractible, often gullible, still confident in their immortality. And beautiful, too. Often very beautiful indeed.

He found 314 and put his ear to the door first. He thought he heard something, not talking but movement, possibly the sound of a book dropping to a table. He knocked firmly.

A young woman opened the door a crack. "Yes?" she said.

"Bonjour mademoiselle, I am Gilles Maron of the gendarmerie. I am sorry to bother you. Are you by any chance Maribeth Donnelly?"

She opened the door. "Yes, I am," she said. Maron noticed that her French accent was quite good. She was wearing sweat pants—so American!—and a hoodie, and flip-flops. Closing the door behind her, she stepped into the hallway. "Are you here about Amy?"

"Yes," said Maron, wishing she had invited him into the room. "You haven't heard from her by any chance?"

Maribeth shook her head.

"Then I wonder if you might have a photograph of her you could give me. If we're going to search, we need to know what she looks like."

He smiled, but Maribeth did not smile back. She thought there was something cold about this gendarme, and wished that the pleasant woman she had spoken to when she called had been the one to pay her a visit.

"Sorry, I'm afraid not. I have tons of snaps on my phone, but no hard copies of anything."

"Snaps on your phone will work," said Maron. "Of course I am not suggesting I take your phone from you," he added, seeing her expression of horror. "Perhaps you could come to the station with me, and we can make some prints there?" He knew this was unnecessary, but thought he could get her talking on the walk back into the village.

"Yes. I'll do anything to help," said Maribeth, seeming suddenly to remember that her roommate was missing, and feel the force of her anxiety about it. Over the last days, Maribeth had found that if she didn't put the whole thing aside at times, she went absolutely insane. And then once she remembered and realized she had been going about her business and blocking it out, she was wracked with guilt.

"Could I email them to you? I can do it right away?"

"Of course."

Maron dug in his pocket for his card, and handed it over. "My address is right there. Thank you very much for your help, Mademoiselle Donnelly. While I am here, may I ask—what is your opinion of the situation? Do you think your friend might have gone off for some reason—a boyfriend, or perhaps something to do with her art?—and simply forgotten to let anyone know?"

Maribeth jammed her fists into the kangaroo pocket of her hoodie. "Zero chance of that. Amy's not a flake. I mean, at *all*. She's a fantastic painter, super talented, but she doesn't go in for all that bull about artists being wild and crazy and practically mentally ill. Amy's like, you know, serious about stuff."

"And...I'm sorry to bring this up, but no inkling that she may have committed suicide? Anything like that?"

"God no. She'd just won the Marfan Prize, she was on top of the world!"

"Marfan?"

"It's a prize given every year to a very promising art student. People who've won it tend to go on to successful careers. Plus, she was going to get some cash."

"Any idea how much?"

"Nope, sorry. Don't think it was huge. Just that anything is huge to students, you know?"

Maron nodded and tried to smile amiably. "And her things—is her handbag still here? Wallet and so forth?"

"She always carried a backpack with her, a pretty large one. Art supplies and junk food," said Maribeth with a thin laugh. "That's not in the room, or her phone either."

Maron hesitated to continue the interview since he was conducting it without Dufort's knowledge. He could call for permission, but for reasons he didn't identify, he wanted to keep this meeting to himself. "All right, that is helpful, mademoiselle. And the photographs will be as well. Thank you and have a pleasant Sunday."

Maribeth nodded to Maron and then watched him go down the hallway and through the doors at the end. He was a handsome enough man, tall and fit, with a face almost chiseled enough for a model. Yet she did not find him attractive. Quite the opposite in fact.

❧

MARON WAS NOT the only junior officer working on Sunday, or at least trying to. Thérèse Perrault had spent the morning with her family: parents, both sets of grandparents, her older sister with her husband and two children, and an uncle who was "strange" and had been coming for lunch every Sunday as far back as Thérèse could remember. For her, Sunday lunch was a pleasant part of her week. She looked forward to whatever delicious things her mother and grandmother produced from the kitchen, she enjoyed joking around with her father, and she even tolerated her older sister.

The only less appealing part of it was that the older she got, the more hints got dropped about how her career as a gendarme was getting in the way of having her own family. She was tired of deflecting the comments. It wasn't that Thérèse had any objection to husbands and children, she just wasn't interested yet. She was only twenty-four, after all— not exactly a wizened old crone.

And this Sunday she was jumpy and a little impatient, wanting lunch to be over with so she could go to the station, do a bit of research and think in peace, and then later on, when the Place got lively, she planned to go mingle and see what she could find out.

Someone had to have seen something or heard something, if Amy Bennett hadn't gone off on her own. Thérèse just needed to talk to the right person. Or persons.

Amy *could* have just gone off on her own, that's still possible until proven otherwise, Thérèse reminded herself. She stood by the old cast iron stove in her mother's kitchen where she used to play all winter when she was little, and peeked in a copper saucepan at sliced carrots bubbling away in a butter sauce.

"Love these, *Maman*," she said brightly.

"You're not fooling me," her mother said. "You want to get back to the office, don't you? You'd skip lunch right now if we let you." She wiped her hands on her apron and picked up a chef's knife and started cutting radishes into paper-thin coins.

"First of all, it's a station, Maman, not an office. And plus, yes, finally I have something to do that's important, and it's not like my kind of work can just be put off until I get around to it. It's time-sensitive. You understand."

"I do understand," said her mother, turning and looking into her daughter's face. "And I am glad for this girl that she has you looking for her."

The two women didn't speak for a while after that, both of them thinking about Valérie, Elizabeth Martin, and now Amy, and grappling with their desire to be optimistic, as well as their fear. The kitchen was warm and smelled of butter and roasting duck. "Wash the lettuce, will you?" said her mother.

"*Oui,* Maman," said Thérèse, wondering where her grandmother was since she was so fussy about lettuce she usually did the washing herself.

After arranging the washed and dried leaves in the salad bowl, she stepped through the kitchen door to the outside, where her niece and nephew were playing a game that involved a home base made of a broken plate, various super powers, and brandished sticks.

"Don't hurt me!" laughed Thérèse as she went by. The children charged at her and threatened to poke her, shouting a gibberish of incantations. "I surrender!" she said, holding up her hands.

The children shrieked and ran around the side of the house, crashing into their father, Frédéric, which brought on louder shrieking and more waving of sticks and shouting of spells.

Frédéric walked over to where Thérèse was pretending to look at the garden, but was actually thinking over the scant details of the Bennett case.

"Bonjour, how are you, Thérèse?" They kissed cheeks.

"Not bad, Fred. I'm just—I'm anxious to get back to work. We finally have something to do. I mean something real."

Fred nodded. "You're happy in your work?"

She beamed. "Very much. I mean, I don't want to sound glad that someone is possibly in trouble or hurt, I know that sounds awful. But I admit, a missing persons investigation is a whole lot more interesting than giving tickets for speeding, you know? It feels like what I'm doing counts for something."

"I understand," said Fred. He turned to watch his children zoom by and disappear around the other side of the house. "Is it all right for me to ask what you are doing to find her? I mean, I've been trying to imagine what needs to be done, and it seems overwhelming. Even if, say, someone murdered the girl here in Castillac—there are empty buildings galore, and then there's all that countryside. Impossible to look everywhere, no?"

"It is daunting," answered Thérèse. "That's why we put so much effort into looking for information, for clues, so a search can be targeted, instead of just randomly attempting to cover a wide area. We're all conditioned from watching cop shows, but of course television makes it look easy since everything has to be wrapped up in an hour. In real life, as I'm sure you'd guess, the work is much more time-consuming and painstaking."

"I'm a little surprised you have taken to it so," he said. "In school, I remember...."

"I know, I was a terrible student," said Thérèse laughing. "And those office jobs I got after graduating—I was just as bad. I guess I'm one of those people who just has to find the exact right thing."

Then they stood listening to the children yell, and waiting for Maman to call them in to eat, both of them wondering about Amy Bennett and where in the world she might be.

10

It was nearly dusk on Sunday evening, and at long last Molly could proclaim freedom from the wretched hangover that had kept her in sunglasses and popping aspirin all weekend. She was feeling so much better that she thought she would venture out for a walk. Sadly, Pâtisserie Bujold would be closed, so perhaps she would go in the other direction, out of town, to see how things looked out that way, and feel gratitude for not dying a death of two Negronis.

Rue des Chênes was quiet, and before long, the houses were quite far apart and she was in the countryside. She strolled along, wishing she had a dog for company, and checked out the houses and then farms along the way, trying to be sneaky about her staring, but it seemed everyone was inside, gathering themselves for the week to come. She remembered how unpleasant Sunday evenings had been when she was working in an office—how hard it had been not to feel consumed with regret at the weekend's being over, and the prospect of the week ahead, not even begun, seeming to stretch to infinity.

Molly had not been happy in her work as a fundraiser. She had gotten the job because she was chatty and sociable and generally good with people, but as it turned out, that did not include being good at asking people for money. She much preferred sharing gossip and laughing at their jokes. When the moment arrived for her to ask for a check—and she recognized the moment all right, her sense of timing was just fine—she would start to mumble and change the subject. Running a gîte business was turning out to be infinitely more suited to her, though she acknowledged she could hardly make an informed judgment yet, after barely a week.

The road was curving and a forest had sprung up on either side with no houses in sight, but instead banks of ferns with a tinge of autumn yellow, darkening as the sun dropped with no sunset color in the sky. It was so quiet she could hear nothing but choruses of birds. I should really get a CD of birdcalls so I can learn which birds I'm hearing, she thought, knowing full well she would do no such thing.

She heard footsteps, someone running. Suddenly her heart seized up and she thought of the missing girl. Fear coursed through her body and her veins felt like ice. She stopped walking, frozen, unable to decide whether to turn and run or jump into the ferns and hide.

She flapped her hands out at her sides and tried to pull herself together. If anything had happened to the girl, and no one even knew that it had, then whoever went after a college girl was unlikely to be coming after her, practically forty years old whose husband had unceremoniously left her after going off with a barista at Starbucks. And then she closed her eyes tight and opened them again, realizing how utterly nonsensical that thought was.

The footsteps got louder. They came from in front of her, just around the next bend. Molly arranged her face to seem more in command of her emotional state than she felt, and strode forward pretending to be confident. Around the curve, a man appeared, jogging easily. He was powerfully built, of medium height with broad shoulders and muscular arms and legs. His hair was not cut in the current fashion, but in a brush cut, very short. He was sweaty, and Molly noticed, in spite of her qualms, that he was rather handsome.

Yet as he got closer—he sped up, she was sure he was moving faster now—she felt another stab of fear, simply because there was not much daylight left, and she was a woman out on the road alone.

Alone except for a strange man who could run fast and who was heading straight for her.

When he reached her, he stopped. "Bonjour!" he said, making a slight bow. "You are Madame Sutton, of La Baraque? I am Benjamin Dufort, of the gendarmerie. I am pleased to make your acquaintance." He nodded and smiled.

The tension in Molly's legs relaxed so quickly she nearly fell over.

"Enchantée," she said, her voice sounding a little funny. She figured she didn't need to mention that he had just transformed from being an axe-murdering rapist to a cop in a split second.

He *was* a cop, right? This wasn't just a line to make her drop her guard?

Hold on a minute. I'm in Castillac, she reminded herself, not some sketchy neighborhood back home where the murder rate is through the roof. I shouldn't be expecting to see sex offender cop imposters around every bend in the road.

She realized the man had been talking to her while her brain tried to get the situation sorted.

"*Pardonnez-moi*," she said. "My French is not good and I lose concentration easy." She tried to have a friendly expression on her face and hoped it would make up for her deficits in language. He *was* very handsome. There was something deep about this man, she could feel it.

Although she should have learned by now not to trust her feelings when it came to handsome men, she told herself in something of a shriek inside her head.

"A pleasure to meet you. Welcome to Castillac. I'm going to continue my run," Dufort said. And with a smile and a sort of salute, he took off.

Molly stood for a long moment and watched him go. She smiled to herself, shook her head, and started back home, deciding that maybe she had recovered enough that she could risk drinking a kir while she was making dinner.

❧

"IN LONDON, we wouldn't have this problem," said Dufort, slamming his hand down on his desk.

Perrault's eyes widened.

"They have CCTV everywhere, I mean *everywhere*. You don't sneeze without its being recorded. Sure, people protest about the loss of privacy. I say—yes, let's take away the privacy of the cretins who commit violent crimes. Let's get their asses on videotape so we can lock them away where they can't hurt anyone else."

Maron looked impassive, his lips pressed together.

"I'm right with you, sir," said Perrault. "At the least it might give somebody pause, make them think they might get caught before they act."

"I don't think the people who commit this kind of crime worry about getting caught," said Dufort. "The person who takes these actions, he thinks he's above everyone else, the normal rules don't apply. He can use other people however he likes, because they're not even real to him, you see what I'm saying? Other people are nothing more than props—necessary perhaps, for his drama—but props all the same. Replaceable. Disposable.

"Right now, he is consumed with thinking about the next time, and enjoying memories of the other times. He is not bothering about getting caught, even a little."

"So, definitely a man? And...do you think the disappearances are connected, even being so far apart?"

Dufort took a long breath in and out, and looked up at the ceiling. "I don't know anything," he said carefully. "I'm talking about likelihood, and I'm talking intuition. Could be female, but you know the stats, it's highly unlikely, nearly impossible. Should we keep a door open in our minds in case this turns out to be very unusual? Of course. And the intuition part...yes, I'll tell you and Maron, no one else, that I'm working under the assumption that whoever took Amy also took Valérie and Elizabeth. Unproven, of course. Nothing linking the cases except for our village."

"Then it is someone who lives here, one of our neighbors."

"I believe so. Yes."

A long pause while they all considered this. "Maron? You have any thoughts?" Maron was young, it was true, but Dufort thought he had a decent head on his shoulders. There was something bitter and disconnected about the young man, and Dufort made extra effort to show that he wanted to hear his opinions.

"The video. How many do we have?" asked Maron.

"Three. Well, two plus some that are of limited use, as I'll explain. That's it. Chez Papa put a camera in after the break-in last year that turned out to be some tourist's kids, teenagers looking for alcohol. The *Presse* has one because Michel verges on paranoid about everything. And *Crédit Agricole* and the other banks have cameras on their street-side ATMs, but I'm afraid the angle of vision is quite limited since they're aimed directly down on users of the ATMs. At best, you can see the bottom third of people going past on the sidewalk, no more. I don't expect them to be very helpful."

"How soon are they getting the videos here?" asked Perrault.

"They're sending them digitally right away," said Dufort, making it clear with his annoyed expression that "right away" was not nearly soon enough. "I will be open with you," he said after a pause. "I have a bad feeling about this situation. Something turned overnight, I don't know how to explain it, but—I had the bad feeling before, but when I woke this morning, it was closer to a certainty." He pressed both palms on his desk and dropped his head. Maron and Perrault heard him inhaling deeply through his nose.

Perrault nodded her agreement. Maron narrowed his eyes as though the talk of feelings did not sit well with him.

Dufort lifted his head and said, "We are going to treat this as an active investigation. No more pussyfooting around because of a law that should never have been changed. That young woman needs us. Her family needs us. So we are going to find Amy Bennett, and find out what happened to her." He clicked his mouse and a large photo opened on the screen.

Amy Bennett was smiling, eyes into the camera. It was an interior shot, a close-up. Several paintings on the wall behind her were out of focus. Amy had chestnut hair, shoulder-length and wavy. Freckles across her nose. Green eyes, wide apart. Dufort studied her face for any distinguishing characteristics, and at first he saw none. She was not beautiful, but she was appealing, and attractive in the way that smiling young people were.

"Good work, Maron, getting these photographs from the roommate. Both of you, study the series. She gave us fifteen, look closely at all of them until you know her like she's your sister. I'll be back in a moment."

Maron and Perrault moved to see the monitor, and Dufort quickly left his office and went outside. He tilted his face up to the sun and tried to take control of his breathing, feeling on the edge of hyperventilating. Seeing Amy on his monitor like that, smiling and happy—and then allowing what came next, the certainty that the girl was dead—all of it was making his anxiety ramp up faster than he could manage it.

Dufort looked both ways and saw that he was alone on the street save for an old woman pulling a shopping cart behind her. He stepped into the alley as though he had important business there, and pulled a blue glass vial from his pocket. He shook several drops under his tongue and counted to ten, looked up at the sun once more, and then headed back inside.

As he entered his office, the monitor gave a honk. "There's the video," he said. "We'll watch, and we'll keep watching, until we see something. You know who you're looking for now."

He tapped his keyboard a few times and the first video began to play. They were looking at the sidewalk, a blurry gray.

"This is one from a bank, I think it's the BNP."

Some legs went by, the trousers a bit too short, the shoes with run-over heels. No one spoke. Next they saw a flurry of legs, but they could not recognize anyone they knew, nor have any idea whether the legs belonged to strangers or old friends. The images were too fuzzy and people were not walking close enough to the camera.

The phone rang in the outer room.

"Maron, get that, will you?"

Maron took one more moment to watch the bank video, and then went to answer the phone. Dufort and Perrault could not hear his words, but they could guess from his tone that the call was something routine.

"How are we going to find her?" said Thérèse. "She looks...she looks like a million other girls. I don't see any way to describe her to make her stand out, am I missing something?"

"Almost makes you wish for an ugly tattoo on her forehead," said Dufort.

Thérèse smiled to herself but said nothing. She had a snake on her right butt cheek, the result of a wild weekend at the beach when she was nineteen. She rather liked having something private about herself like that, something that hardly anyone knew about.

"Let's look at the others," Dufort said, clicking the mouse. "Look at her body type, think about how someone who looks like her might walk, run—you're trying to get her physical reality into your mind, do you understand?"

"Yes, sir," said Thérèse. Amy was slender, and looked to be of medium height. Pretty enough, but so ordinary. It seemed impossible to find anything to separate her from the crowd of other women her age.

"That was Madame Vargas on the phone. Her husband has disappeared again."

Dufort blinked and looked away from Amy Bennett. "Ah. Hopefully we will find him in the usual place and set him back home. Maron, see to it, if you would."

Maron did not look pleased but he nodded and left without a word. Thérèse and Dufort spent another hour looking at the photographs Maribeth Donnelly had provided. They tried to make Amy Bennett come alive in their minds, tried to imagine the sound of her voice, what she liked and what she didn't, what made her Amy Bennett and no one else. They did not get very far with this exercise, but the investigation had only just begun, and they very much hoped there might be a break when they got through the rest of the video.

11

Perrault and Dufort watched the rest of the bank videos and the *Presse* video, but were still waiting to receive the one from Chez Papa. The rest of the day had been almost entirely taken up with the usual bureaucratic nonsense, apart from a few hours in the afternoon when all three gendarmes had taken to the streets and searched for Amy, by foot and by motorcycle. Now at least they had photographs they could show around, and a better idea of who they were looking for, even if they had yet to find a way to describe her in a way that would lead to someone saying, *Oh yes, I saw that girl!*

At the end of the day, Thérèse stopped by Chez Papa to ask what was holding up the video transfer, and to have a kir after a long and frustrating day.

"Bonsoir, Alphonse!" she said grinning.

"And what have you been up to today, *ma chérie?*" he asked, ruffling her hair as though she were six.

"You've heard about the missing girl?"

"Oh yes. I had Nico send the video, you got it this morning?"

"No, actually, we didn't." Thérèse worked to keep her naturally expressive face impassive. It wouldn't do to scowl at people now that she was a gendarme.

"Can't imagine why not, I spoke to him about it right when Ben called—first thing. I leave the computer stuff to Nico. I'm just too old for all that now! That camera has been nothing but trouble since I put it in, always on the fritz one way or another. Technology, bah!" Alphonse laughed and rolled his eyes. "So tell me, do you have any leads?"

"You know I can't talk about that," said Thérèse, but she shook her head. "So far, I haven't been able to figure out who she is, if you understand, what kind of personality she has. She's a talented painter, apparently, but that's all I've got. She looks totally average, like anybody really." Thérèse, like almost all the locals of Castillac, had known Alphonse since she was a baby, and it was easy and natural for her to talk to him about anything.

Alphonse nodded his shaggy head and said nothing.

"Ah, here's Nico!" he said. "Now we can get you your kir and straighten out this business of the video, all in one go. Come say goodbye before you leave." He ruffled her hair again and went around the bar and into the kitchen.

"Hey, Nico."

"Bonsoir, Thérèse." He smiled and leaned over the bar so they could peck each other's cheeks, once per side.

"You were supposed to send the video from the surveillance camera to us?"

Nico slapped his forehead. "Oh *mon Dieu*, I knew there was something I was forgetting! I will get that over to you right away, as soon as my shift is over."

Thérèse looked around at the nearly empty bar. It was barely five o'clock and there was no one else there but Vincent the taxi driver, drinking an espresso and reading the paper at a table in the corner. "Maybe you could do it now. There's nobody here, and my kir can wait."

"Oh no it can't," Nico said with a laugh. "Never let it be said that someone at my bar is going thirsty!" He pulled the bottle of cassis off a shelf and poured a small puddle into a white wine glass.

"Sparkling?"

Thérèse thought his smile looked a little forced. Why was he stalling?

"Sparkling would be lovely," she said. She had grown-up tastes but had never lost her appreciation of the things she had loved as a child such as fizzy Cokes and Haribo.

She took the glass, said "*Á la tienne!*" and took a sip. "Nothing better than a kir royale at the end of the day," she said, deciding to keep talking to Nico. Feed the line out a little and see where it took her.

"I couldn't agree more," he said.

"Do you ever try to guess what someone will order, I mean someone you don't know who comes into the bar? You know, matching what they're like at first glance to the drink?"

"Off and on," he answered, but Thérèse had the feeling he only responded that way to be agreeable.

"Generally," he said, "the locals drink the same thing all the time. Maybe someone will get a little crazy and order a cider instead of the usual beer, but on the whole...." He shrugged.

"And the tourists?"

Nico laughed. "Oh, they'll drink anything. Something about traveling makes people want to experiment. The other night, the woman who's living at La Baraque was in—Larry got her drinking Negronis. You can imagine that didn't end well."

Thérèse laughed along with him although she didn't find his story especially funny.

"Salut, Nico. Thérèse. Vincent," said a voice from behind her.

"Hello, Lapin," said Nico.

Thérèse sighed. She was in no mood to fend off the attentions of Lapin, and he was interrupting her attempt to interrogate Nico without his knowing it.

"Terrible about that girl," said Lapin.

"Awful," said Nico. "But maybe she'll turn up. People do run off, you know."

"They do," said Perrault. "Usually from bad marriages, mountainous debts, things like that. This case doesn't seem to fit that."

"Listen to our little *fliquette!*" said Lapin. "She's such a serious detective, now that she's all grown up. And into quite a woman, too," he added, running his eyes slowly from her face to her knees and back up again.

"Shut up, Lapin," said Thérèse with a sigh.

"Shut up, Lapin," said Nico, laughing. "You never give up, do you?"

"Persistence is the key to success," said Lapin with a wink. "Now pour me a pastis, will you?"

"And after you do that, go send that video," said Thérèse, watching Nico to see how he would react to her instruction. She was watching Nico so carefully that she did not see the way Lapin's face changed from jovial to a mask with no expression whatsoever.

❧

MOLLY WAS in a frenzy of cleaning. She had torn the cottage apart, even dragged furniture outside, hung carpets up and beat them, and attacked the windows with a ferocity that was on the verge of leaving her exhausted. That was one good reason for doing it—it helped calm her down, at least a little.

She had been feeling jittery ever since last night, when she had checked her email right before going to bed. Often inquiries from the States arrived then, and she had gotten in the habit of checking twice a day, always relieved to see more interest and get more business. But last night's inquiry was not simply a couple on holiday, easy enough to manage. It was the Bennetts, the parents of the missing Amy Bennett, asking to come for a stay starting on Tuesday, which was *tomorrow,* with an open-ended departure.

When Molly read the email, she got the wobbles.

She could not imagine what they must be going through. The depth of their fear. How in the world did they struggle with that kind of uncertainty? At least if you know what's happened, you can start to face it, however slowly; at least you know what you're in for. But what the Bennetts were dealing with was something else. Possibly a terrible loss, and also possibly a misunderstanding, a lost or dead cell phone, a secret lover, a letter that got lost in the mail.

Could be a hundred explanations. And no way to know when, or even if, they will find out which one is correct. Or some other reason they had never considered. It's possible they will *never* know, thought Molly, and a chill went up her spine.

Lunch on the terrace was some leftover quiche and some salad that was fairly wilted, but just this side of edible. She washed it down with the last of a bottle of rosé, and stayed sitting there after she finished, looking out at her wreck of a garden, not following any train of thought in particular. She was tired from the cleaning binge. Part of her wished she had told the Bennetts she was booked solid just to avoid being tangled up in the whole thing, but she couldn't have actually refused them. She had learned by now that uncharitable thoughts were perfectly fine as long as she didn't act on them. Hadn't she heard that somewhere? Perhaps during the mid-divorce, lie-on-the-sofa-all-day phase, when she had watched plenty of Oprah and Dr. Phil and anyone else who might toss a comforting word her way.

I wonder if there will be the kind of media frenzy there is in the States when a young woman goes missing, she wondered. I don't want newspeople trampling my garden and peering in my windows. I don't want...any of it. Of course I hope they find her. And if there's not a happy ending, if this isn't a misunderstanding,

I hope at least the Bennetts learn what happened. It's the least they deserve.

Molly suddenly stood up with the vigor that comes with just the right idea, and that idea was Pâtisserie Bujold—the almond croissant specifically. If anything was going to improve the day, it was going to be that almond croissant. No need for a hat, the day was cloudy and coolish, so she just picked up her bag on her way through the house and out to rue des Chênes, and was quickly on her way, mouth already watering.

The street was quiet. She hoped she was not too late and the shop wasn't closed, which would be almost unbearable; she wanted that croissant desperately. Taking a shortcut down the alleyway, she peeked over the wall and noticed the La Perla underwear out on the line again, at the same house. Who in the world wears La Perla all the time, she wondered. Just as she had the week before, she stopped and considered reaching over to touch some of it. But this time she kept her hands at her sides, and stood there for a moment contemplating it, imagining a life in which her underwear was always La Perla, her house was filled with the most coveted and brilliantly designed appliances, and her car—well, as long as she was fantasizing, why not get a little Austin Healy? Racing green, please. Or is that too cliché?

She took one last look at the house that the underwear belonged to. It was nondescript, really, not a dump by any means, but hardly the dwelling of someone used to sumptuous underthings, at least not from the outside. Curious, isn't it, how funny people are, the choices they make, and what they might be hiding?

At last she turned the corner and saw the enameled red outside of Pâtisserie Bujold. She breathed in the sugary vanilla aroma, and paused with her hand on the doorknob, wanting that croissant with all her being yet wanting to delay facing the proprietor. She took a deep breath, then another, and went in.

"Bonjour, monsieur," she said, glancing at him and then at the display case, always fantastically beautiful with its exactly ordered rows and its mouthwatering variety. Last week she had felt frustrated because she had already gotten in the habit of buying her few favorites over and over, and was feeling stressed out by all the morsels she wasn't choosing—and then she remembered that she lived in Castillac now. Neither she nor Pâtisserie Bujold was going anywhere, and she had all the time in the world to taste every last pastry eventually.

"Please, an almond croissant," she said, pointing. The proprietor was staring at her chest, same as the other times she had come in. He did not follow where she pointed but nodded and smiled enthusiastically, eyes still pinned on her. It occurred to Molly that his expression was the same one she had when she looked at the chocolate-covered creampuffs with whipped cream spilling out the sides—like he wanted to devour her on the spot.

Molly clamped her teeth together and rummaged in her bag for the right change. At least she knew what it cost and could avoid the extra time of back-and-forth by giving the exact amount.

"I understand your liking for the almond croissant," said the proprietor. "One of my favorites also. Award-winning," he said, gesturing to a yellowing document on the wall with some kind of fancy seal on it. "It is truly magnificent," he said, handing her the wax paper bag. "Just like you, madame." And with that, spoken in a low voice, he waggled his eyebrows in a way he must have thought alluring but that Molly thought was the funniest thing she had seen in days.

Like Groucho Marx! She laughed to herself on the walk home, stuffing her face as she walked with the indescribably wondrous pastry. The inside was layered with almond paste so that it was very soft, and almondy, and moist. The outside was the usual shattering butter explosion, with the addition of sliced and toasted almonds and a faint dusting of confectioner's sugar. Simple and spectacular.

She had finished the croissant long before she turned in at La Baraque, but the walk and the pastry and the waggling eyebrows had turned her mood completely around, and she felt no more yearnings for fancy undergarments or cars, and her worry about not being able to manage things with the Bennetts had diminished to something manageable. Perhaps the magic of France can be summed up in two words, she thought.

Almond croissant.

12

Dufort was up early on Tuesday morning. He went on a punishing run, taking a hilly route partly on narrow country roads and partly on trails through the forest, arriving back at his small house in town to shower before getting to the station by 7:30. A few days earlier, Gallimard had not been in his office or anywhere Dufort could find him, and the list of questions Dufort wanted to ask him was growing. He guessed Gallimard would not be at work that early, and so he strolled over to the Café de la Place for some breakfast first.

"Bonjour, Pascal."

"Bonjour, Chief, *comment allez-vous?*"

"I'm well, and you? How is your mother?"

"She is better, thank you. We are grateful for having a good doctor and she is healing faster than expected."

"Glad to hear it," said Dufort, keeping his thoughts about doctors to himself. "Petit café, please, and a croissant."

Pascal nodded and gracefully weaved through the tables on his way to get the order. The café was crowded with locals and families of tourists getting in a last holiday before school began. Dufort nodded to a few friends and then spent some moments observing. He had a nonchalant way of watching that did not alert the people who were being watched. It was quite a talent, actually, although Dufort did not realize this about himself.

Dufort closed his eyes and listened. At first he didn't try to hear what anyone was saying but tried to listen to the undertones, the emotions behind the conversations. He couldn't detect anything out of the ordinary. Then words began to clarify and he overheard a father getting angry at his son for losing a shoe, a young man telling his girlfriend that he was sorry but he was not going to stop playing video games, and an old woman complaining about a problem with her liver.

He wondered if anyone here had ever met Amy Bennett, or seen Amy Bennett, or had anything at all to do with the disappearance of Amy Bennett—the same thoughts that had been running through his mind ever since he first heard her name. For a fraction of a second, he was assaulted by the notion that he might never know what happened, might never find her.

The idea was horrifying and his heart began to race.

Carrying a tray on one hand over his head, Pascal came dancing through the crowded tables back to Dufort. He was a good-looking boy, Dufort noticed, and he could see several women at the café, of varying ages, following him with their eyes.

"*Merci bien*," he said as the espresso and plate with croissant were placed on his paper placemat.

Pascal smiled and nodded. "Oui, Chief. Anything else I can get for you?"

"Not a thing," said Dufort. "I speak for many when I say that the first coffee of the morning is possibly the best moment of the entire day, so I thank you." He bowed slightly, and they both laughed.

Dufort took a sip of his espresso, and then bit into the croissant. The café got them from Pâtisserie Bujold every morning, the best bakery in town, and he was not disappointed. The outer layer crackled and shattered, the inside was stretchy and almost sweet, and still faintly warm. Dufort let himself wallow in the sensations of the croissant, and then the bitter espresso, at least for a few moments free of thinking about Amy Bennett.

When he finished, he tucked a five-euro bill under his saucer and moved through the tables to the street, nodding at some people he knew but not stopping to chat. He wanted to use the walk out to Degas to think about what he knew about Gallimard, and try to come up with some questions that might throw him off balance just a bit.

Anton Gallimard. Has taught at Degas for nearly twenty years. Rumored to have quite a talent, had shown in Paris, won prizes, all the usual accolades, but his career had fizzled out in his late twenties. Has made no art (that anyone knows of) since coming to Degas to teach.

Dufort had never met Gallimard despite having several friends who were artists. It was somewhat surprising that their worlds had never overlapped, but not meaningful. He felt curious about the man, even apart from the business with Amy Bennett. Curious about why someone chooses to let a big talent go, to do nothing with it after such a promising start and so much encouragement and even acclaim.

Before long he was at the gates to L'Institut. This time he avoided the administration building and went to find the studios, hoping to catch Gallimard there. Of course he could have made an appointment, but he had found just showing up to be an easy way to put interviewees off balance, which is where every investigator wants them.

L'Institut Degas was a small school. The administration building was stately—eighteenth century, Dufort guessed correctly—and directly across a wide lawn stood the dormitory. It was three stories high but rather narrow; he figured the student body must number less than a hundred. He made a note to investigate the financial health of the school even though he did not at the moment see how there could be any connection to Amy Bennett's disappearance.

In between the two buildings, completing a U around the lawn, was a modern building of one story. It had dramatic cantilevered skylights, walls of glass, and a strange covering over some of the exterior that looked like it was made of jellyfish. To Dufort's eye, the building looked expensive and over-designed, although he did understand that artists required good light to do their work, and whatever else, this building would certainly provide that.

He heard and saw no one. Perhaps the young artists and their teachers were not up by 8:30. He found a door to the jellyfish building on the side by the dormitory, but it was locked. He looked through the side panels of glass, hoping to see someone who could let him in, but saw no one.

He was relaxed from his run, and the morning and the campus had been so tranquil, that he startled violently when the screaming began.

WHEN MOLLY WOKE up that Tuesday morning, she was not graced with the usual few moments of lazy stretching while her brain worked out who she was and what the day was going to bring. The instant she was conscious, she remembered the Bennetts' arrival and was slapped awake. Quickly she got up and put water on to boil. She longed for a pastry but had no time to go into the village to get one. Forgoing her usual time on the terrace with nothing to do but sip her coffee, she took her mug straight to the cottage with cleaning supplies under both arms. It felt important that the cottage was spotless and welcoming for the Bennetts. It was the least she could do.

She stuck her phone into a little portable speaker and clicked on the blues playlist. She paused, wondering if the neighbors liked

Percy Sledge, and then turned the volume up anyway. After an hour of scrubbing the floor and vacuuming up the hateful dust that poured out of the stone walls, she sat on the floor and leaned against the wall, draining the last of her cold coffee. Okay, she thought, make the place nice for these people who are going through something terrible. That's just being decent. But the cottage didn't need three hours of cleaning, it really didn't. Why is this whole thing making me so damn on edge? Why do I feel *afraid* for them to arrive?

She asked the questions but had no answers.

Earlier in the week, she had bought a cheap case of wine so that she would have welcome bottles for her guests, but when she went to get one, she wrinkled her nose at it, and picked a better bottle from her own stash instead. Then she roamed around the overgrown garden—an embarrassment, really—and managed to find some roses and artemisia to put in a vase. She put the flowers and the wine on the cottage's scratched-up dining table, took one last look around, and called it done.

At least this time she had started the work early enough that she wasn't rushed, and managed to be showered and presentable long before the Bennetts were due to arrive. But instead of picking up a book, planning dinner, or any of the other things she could have been doing, she started to pace, going from the kitchen down the narrow hallway to her bedroom and then back again. Movement didn't stop the bad feeling from intensifying but she kept on anyway.

Amy Bennett was dead.

Molly could sense it. She had no idea how, or whether she could trust the feeling, but it was undeniably there. It felt stony and real and implacable. She wondered if the Bennetts felt it too.

And if Amy Bennett was dead, what did that mean for Castillac, for the other women in the village? Was she killed by someone she knew? Somebody from the village? Somebody just passing through?

The village was large, by village standards—nearly three thousand people. Of course, Molly had barely been there a week. She had not even begun to understand the social webs that comprised the place, but it seemed to her as though the villagers were deeply connected to each other. That maybe you couldn't quite say that everyone knew everyone, but almost.

Not six degrees of separation, here in Castillac. More like two.

She smoothed a wild ginger curl back behind her ear and tried to steer her thoughts somewhere else. The Bennetts hadn't even arrived yet, there was absolutely no news about Amy that she knew of, she was totally getting ahead of herself. *Chill out, girl.*

Molly was not a big drinker, she really wasn't, not even when her marriage was falling apart, Negronis notwithstanding. But now that the Bennetts were due in moments, she had the idea of a little brandy, and the idea hit her with that feeling you get sometimes of Oh *yes!* That's just the thing!

She cracked the seal of some Martell and poured herself a finger and gulped it down just as Vincent's taxi pulled into her driveway. It burned her throat a bit but she felt the warmth going out to her fingertips, gathered herself together, and went out to greet her guests.

"Salut!" she called, waving.

Vincent pulled his bulky self out of the taxi and went around to open the trunk as Sally and Marshall Bennett got out. Sally looked dazed, so dazed that Molly immediately wondered if she was taking tranquilizers.

Marshall Bennett stood for a moment and blinked, then strode over to Molly with his hand outstretched. "Hullo! We're so glad you had space for us. Lovely place!"

"Thank you." Molly shook his hand and was suddenly overcome with wanting to sob. Surreptitiously she reached out of sight with one hand and gave herself a hard pinch, anything to focus her mind somewhere other than Amy.

"Marshall? You've got to pay for the taxi." Sally's voice was faint, as though she were in a thick bubble.

"Oh yes, what do I owe you?"

Vincent said "Ten euro," in English, then grinned, and held out his hand.

"See, I told you Sally, our lack of French was not going to be a problem!" Marshall smiled at Vincent and dug in his wallet for one of the notes he had just gotten at the airport. "We took a flight from London, then a train to Castillac," he explained to Molly. "I hate renting cars, it's a terrible expense—do you find it's very necessary here to have one?"

"Actually, I haven't been here long, but I haven't gotten around to getting one yet. I can walk to the village easily enough, and if I need to go farther, I can always call Vincent."

Vincent grinned again. "That's right, you call me," he said. "I can pick you up anytime you want."

The Bennetts had not brought much luggage. Molly picked up one of the small carry-ons and started toward the cottage.

"Let me show you where you'll be staying," she said, her nerves jangly despite the shot of Martell. How did one talk to people going through this kind of crisis? She didn't want to seem too sunny, or morose either.

Vincent waved and drove off, and the Bennetts followed Molly. Even their gaits seemed affected by what they were going through—Sally Bennett was unsteady on her feet, drifting off course, and Marshall stared at the ground and walked as though he were concentrating hard on where to place each foot.

"I don't know if you're interested in history," Molly began, as they came inside and put down their things. "I can't say this is verified, but I've been told the cottage dates from the early 1700s...." Then she stopped, shaking her head. "Oh, forget that. I just want to say—I know there are no words—but I am so sorry that the reason you are here is such a terrible one. I very much hope you get good news about Amy soon."

Sally Bennett dissolved into tears and Marshall put both arms around her. "Thank you, Molly," he said. They said nothing else and did not look in her direction again, so Molly mumbled some more welcoming words and backed out and closed the cottage door.

Well, I guess I put my foot in it already, she thought. My heart is aching for them, and I wish there was something useful I could do.

But nothing matters except their daughter. Of course.

13

The scream had come from inside the jellyfish building but the door was locked. Dufort ran to the other end of the building and tried that door—also locked. He stopped and listened. He heard several thumps, some talking, then another scream.

He considered breaking some glass to get in but instead ran to the administration building. The ground floor door was unlocked and he tore it open and burst through, calling out, "Hello! Police! This is Chief Dufort! HELLO!"

A secretary who always got to work hours before anyone else poked her head out of her office. "What's the matter? May I help you?" she said, taken aback.

"Unlock that middle building, someone inside is screaming. Can you open it? Hurry!"

The secretary disappeared into her office and came back with a card. "Swipe this," she said. "Do you want me to do it? Is someone hurt?"

"Stay here," said Dufort, grabbing the card and running.

He swiped once but the door stayed locked. Too fast. He tried again, swiping less frantically, and heard the lock click open.

Arguing was coming from down the hallway. Dufort trotted quickly and quietly toward the voices. He heard crying.

When he got to the right room, he stopped for a second to listen, then he eased around the corner. He saw a big man raising his hand, and a woman cowering before him.

"Stop!" cried Dufort, running into the room.

The man turned and stared at Dufort, his hand still in the air. "Who are you?" he asked, in a stunned tone.

The woman stood up. She looked oddly curious, not upset—she did not look like he expected.

"I am Chief Dufort of the Castillac police," he said. He turned to the woman. "Are you all right?"

The big man laughed. "We're doing a show. We're actors, just doing theater exercises and about to rehearse a scene!"

Dufort looked the man, then at the woman. Now that he was in the same room with them, he did not sense adrenaline, or fear. He believed them. "I'm terribly sorry," he said, trying to smile. "I was walking by, and heard you scream...."

"It's a violent play," the woman said, with a laugh. "My husband here, he's not a very nice man!"

"You'll pay for that remark," the man said, his eyes darkening.

"He's joking!" said the woman, seeing Dufort's eyebrows go up. "Really! Stop it, Marc, or he'll take you in." She laughed again, and Dufort could see the actress in her—how her laugh wasn't altogether genuine, but a bit of a performance, meant to charm him. "Hello, I'm Marilyn McKay."

"That's her character in the play," said Marc, rolling his eyes. She reached over and stroked his arm. Dufort wanted to leave this couple to whatever it was they were doing and get on with the interview he had come to do. But as long as he was here, perhaps they could give him some information. You never knew where the crucial bit might come from.

He looked around and saw they were in a large room filled with light. In the center of the room, where the couple was standing, an elevated platform stood about three feet off the ground. One wall, the one across from the hallway, was entirely glass, and the other walls were covered with drawings pinned to a strip that ran around the room just above eye level.

"I didn't realize that Degas has theater as well? I thought it was fine arts only?"

"That's right," said the woman. "We're just putting something on for fun. Not for the public, just the other students."

"I see," said Dufort, although he had never liked the theater and did not see, not really. The focus of his work life was on finding the truth, so traipsing about on stage pretending to be someone you're not...he had never seen the point. "Tell me," he said, "do either of you have classes with Professor Gallimard?"

Marilyn, or the actress playing Marilyn, laughed. "Oh, we all have Gallimard sooner or later," she said. "Is he in trouble?" she asked hopefully.

"Oh no. I was just wondering what kind of teacher is he, that sort of thing? If you have an opinion."

"Marc always has an opinion," said Marilyn playfully.

"He's okay," said Marc. "He gets a little over-focused on his female students, if you know what I mean."

Dufort nodded knowingly, as though he had heard as much before. "Is he good in the classroom? Knows his stuff and all that?"

"Very much so," said Marilyn. "Don't listen to Marc, he's a sculptor and never gives the painters any credit. Gallimard is an excellent teacher, he really is. And he's not shy about introducing his students to some of the influential people he knows, either. He makes an extra effort, outside of the studio."

"I'll say," said Marc. Marilyn elbowed him in the ribs.

"All right then," said Dufort. "I'm sorry to have barged in on you, I'm off—thanks very much for your help."

The pair nodded and watched Dufort leave the room. He walked briskly down the hall, not looking at any of the art hanging there, and headed back to the secretary in the administration building.

"Sorry, I'm Chief Dufort," he said, when he reached her office. "Thanks for your help, everything's fine." He handed the card back and nodded. He was calm enough now to notice that the woman was around his age, and quite attractive.

"I'm Marie-Claire Levy," she answered. "I was so worried after you took off that I followed you and listened in the hallway until I could hear everything was all right."

"I told you to stay put!" said Dufort, but he was smiling. Marie-Claire had dark hair pulled into a severe bun, but a warm expression in her eyes. And a lovely face, there was no doubt about that. Dufort smiled more broadly.

"Well, I know you did. And at first I thought if something bad was happening I would call the gendarmes, but then I realized you were already here. Silly of me, I know."

Dufort shrugged. "Theater exercises."

Marie-Claire laughed. "The students here are like students everywhere, always getting up to something, you know how it is!"

"Those days seem pretty far away to me now," said Dufort.

Marie-Claire nodded. "So, you are here about Amy?"

Dufort paused. With some effort, after taking one last appreciative look at Marie-Claire—her intelligent eyes and her slender form—he brought his mind back to work, and work only.

It was always a little tricky, deciding how much to say. He made a quick judgment that Ms. Levy was someone who might be useful in this investigation. An alert person in her job could be in a position to know more about what went on in the school than anybody.

"Yes," he said finally. "I am here about Amy."

SHE WAS a miserable chicken-hearted excuse for a hostess, Molly admitted that to herself. If she had even an ounce of courage, or the barest drop of the milk of human kindness, she would go over to the cottage and chat with the Bennetts, offer them a drink, take them some hors d'oeuvres, something. But no, instead she was holed up in her house leaving them to their own devices, because the whole aura of the Bennetts—their bottomless fear, their monumental, careening anxiety—was so deeply uncomfortable.

They had not left the cottage since Molly showed them in hours before. She realized she didn't have a lot of experience yet, but she was used to guests getting settled rather quickly and then wanting to have a look around La Baraque, or go into the village. Even the nutty Lawlers had not spent all day out of sight with the door shut.

I should be doing something to help them, she thought, but still didn't budge, staying on the terrace in her favorite rusty chair eating some bits of salami (wild boar with fennel, extremely tasty) and not moving in the direction of the Bennetts no matter how hard she flogged herself for not reaching out.

She checked her email, hoping to hear from some friends back home, but there was nothing besides some fresh inquiries about the cottage. She turned them down, having no idea how long the Bennetts would be staying. Will they live in the cottage until Amy turns up, one way or another? That could take months. It could take until...forever.

She shuddered. What I need, she thought, is some distraction. Hello, Lawrence Weebly! He's probably sitting on that same stool at Chez Papa this very minute.

She sailed into her bathroom, buoyed by a sense of purpose, however minor, and put on a bit of mascara and a swipe of lipstick.

I really do need to see about getting a car, she thought, turning down the driveway and heading for the village on foot as usual. Soon it's going to be cold, and dark early, and walking will be a lot less appealing. I don't want to spend a fortune on Vincent and his taxi.

Just as she guessed, Lawrence *was* at Chez Papa, on the very same stool, drinking a Negroni. Nico nodded when Molly walked in, and Lawrence hopped up and they kissed cheeks.

"My dear!" he exclaimed. "I was concerned that you had still not recovered from the other night. Sometimes the aftermath from Negronis is something of a steep climb. How are you? And I hear the Bennetts are staying at yours. Tell me everything."

"Bonsoir. Just a kir," Molly said to Nico. "Sparkling, please." She eased onto a stool and looked around, enjoying the friendly smell of Chez Papa: a mixture of duck fat, tobacco, coffee, and people.

"I don't have anything to tell, really."

Lawrence's face fell. "Oh come on, I'm not asking in an unkind way. Nosy, maybe, but not mean.'

Nico set down Molly's kir and gave her a wink.

"Thanks, Nico," she said. "Don't let me get into the Negronis, will you?"

"I only do what I'm told," he said, grinning.

Handsome boy, that Nico, thought Molly. He was dark and looked part Italian, and Lord knows the Italians hogged the market when it came to good-looking men.

"Oh, I'm not being huffy," she said to Lawrence. "I really don't have anything to tell. The Bennetts got here today, I took them to the cottage, and I haven't seen them since. I expect they'll be meeting with Dufort and the school, but as far as I know, none of that has happened yet. I'm just...I'm glad to find you here because I need to talk about this to someone."

Lawrence nodded encouragingly.

"For some reason, I'm going half to pieces about this Amy Bennett business, and having the parents right there, in my cottage...I don't know what it is...I feel so guilty, like I should be doing something for them, comforting them in some way. But I don't lift a finger. I let them sit over there by themselves all day, and here I am."

"Oh, Molly," said Lawrence. "I'd bet anything they want to be left alone. In their situation, the last thing you'd want would be to have to make chit-chat to a stranger, don't you think?"

"Yes. Of course." She sipped her drink. "You're right." Unfortunately, believing that Lawrence was right didn't do much to change her feelings. "Have you heard anything? What is the rest of the village saying about the whole thing?"

"Well, I have heard a few interesting bits. Someone told me Amy was here, at Chez Papa, the night before she disappeared."

Molly combed some unruly curls behind one ear, her eyes wide. "Really? Who was she with, friends from the school?"

"It's unclear. Apparently it was one of those nights when many who were here got a bit into their cups. My source tells me she was pretty drunk."

"Who's your source?"

"Not telling," said Lawrence, smiling and taking a gulp of Negroni.

"Hey Nico!" said Molly.

Nico sauntered over from the other end of the bar. "What's up, Boston?"

"Oh no, you're not giving me that nickname. Just forget that right now, hear me?"

Nico just winked at her.

"So Amy Bennett was in here right before she disappeared?" she asked him, her tone offhand.

Nico shrugged and looked away. "I don't know everybody," he said. "It gets crowded in here some nights. Tourists, students, locals, plus I don't know, random people from anywhere." He went back to the other end of the bar and wiped the surface vigorously with a bar rag.

"So he's not your source," Molly said to Lawrence.

"I do adore you," he answered. "But I never reveal a source."

"Well, okay, let's say she was in here the night before she disappeared. And let's say she was drunk. Where do those facts lead?"

"A fan of cop shows, are you?"

"Back in the day, I was obsessed with *Law & Order*, as any discerning TV watcher would be." Molly turned on her stool to get the wider view of the room, and spent a moment observing. It was a slow night at Chez Papa—a few couples eating dinner, a family with three children waiting to order. Molly couldn't help being impressed with how orderly the French children were, not clamoring or poking each other or looking at anything electronic, just sitting calmly in their seats and talking in quiet voices.

Molly turned back to Lawrence. "Tell me this, then. Is Dufort good at his job? I met him out on the road the other day."

"Hmm, I can't say really. Haven't had any dealing with him. But there are those other cases, you know. It's not like the crime ledger of Castillac is all clear."

Molly swallowed. She paused, wanting, for a few seconds at least, not to know anything more. One last moment to savor her ignorance. Then she asked slowly, "What are you talking about, 'other cases'?"

"Amy Bennett is not the first woman to disappear from Castillac, Molly. I know it looks rather serene and picturesque around here, but evil doesn't necessarily pay much attention to setting, now does it?"

Molly just stared at him, eyes wide and mouth slightly open. "Not the first?" she finally managed to say, but so quietly Lawrence had to lip-read to understand what she was saying.

14

It was Wednesday, the 17th of September. Amy Bennett had not been seen in over a week.

As the days ticked by, Benjamin Dufort's anxiety worsened no matter what combination of herbal tinctures he took or how far he ran in the mornings. He made lists of the steps to take in the investigation—people to interview, mostly, and other administrative details. And it was about time to go public and try to enlist the help of the entire community. But making the lists and planning weren't doing anything to diminish his feeling of dread. And on top of the dread was the constant sense that he was inadequate at his job, failing right in front of the whole village. Lawrence Weebly was not the only one thinking of the other women who had disappeared from Castillac. Of course Dufort was thinking of them as well, and had been, steadily, hourly, for years.

Three women. He had done *nothing* for them.

He wouldn't blame the citizens of Castillac if they began pressuring him to leave even before the gendarmerie ordered him to a different community as a matter of course.

The first woman to disappear had been Elizabeth Martin, a young British woman, a tourist, no connection to Castillac that

Dufort had ever found, beyond visiting one summer for a few days in the course of a ramble around France. All anyone knew was that Castillac was the last place she was ever seen—so the possibilities of what happened to her were practically uncountable. Wrong place, wrong time, and she was killed and never found? Or intentional disappearance, and she's living somewhere with a new identity, having cocktails in Ibiza with no looking back?

A million ways it could have gone. She had no family, no parents or relatives to keep the pressure on, and her case passed rather quickly into the dusty filing cabinets of unsolved files.

The next event had hit Castillac harder. Both because a second disappearance felt not twice as bad but more like a thousand times worse, forcing the villagers to admit that the first had likely not been random, not just one of those things, and that possibly the perpetrator has not gone away, but was there, present, *one of them*—and because the victim, if she *was* a victim, was a young local woman. Her name was Valérie Boutillier. She was eighteen when she disappeared six years ago. No one, including Dufort, thought there was any chance of Valérie's running off and never contacting home again. Her life in Castillac had been happy, family dysfunction only enough to keep from being boring, and she had been accepted into a top-notch university—her dream—scheduled to enroll a month after her disappearance.

There was absolutely no question in Dufort's mind that someone had abducted Valérie. Whether she was still alive somewhere, being held against her will...well, the chances of that sank lower every day, and there had been an awful lot of days since she vanished.

Dufort was back at L'Institut Degas, intent this time on following through with the Gallimard interview no matter what interruptions appeared. Marie-Claire Levy had told him where to find him and what hours he was likely to be in, and so Dufort was knocking on his office door following her suggestions exactly.

"One moment," said a gruff voice from inside.

Dufort heard some thumping noises, then a chair scraping a wood floor. Professors had their offices in the old administration building, and the smell of old books and wood and plaster reminded him of the buildings of his university up north.

Finally the door opened and a large man looked out. "May I help you?" he asked irritably.

"Bonjour, Professor. I am sorry to bother you. I am Chief Dufort of the Castillac gendarmerie. I'm wondering if I could have a moment of your time?"

Gallimard shrugged.

"I was hoping to speak with you briefly. I won't be long." Dufort saw that Gallimard was the kind of man who expected deference from other men, and so he gave it to him. On the surface.

Gallimard nodded and opened the door, gesturing for Dufort to come in. Inside was a wide desk covered with piles of papers and knickknacks, and what looked like an antique desk chair that swiveled. Beside the desk was a worn sofa, and at the end of the narrow room, a round window gave the only natural light.

Dufort wondered why there was no art on the walls, and realized that he had knocked on the door assuming the room would look a certain way. He made a note to think further about that, as he had found that his wrong assumptions could occasionally be very enlightening in unexpected ways.

"So," he said, playing a little disorganized, "It's a little surprising that we have not met before, isn't it? Let's see now...I'm here about the business with that student. Amy. Amy Bennett?"

"Yes," said Gallimard, and he glowered. "Awful. She is very talented. Not that her talent has anything to do with her disappearance. At least I don't see how it could. Anyway, what I can tell you is that she has a painting class with me on Wednesday mornings, and last Wednesday was it? So that would make it a full week? Yes, last Wednesday she did not show up. I haven't seen her since."

Dufort nodded. "That Wednesday morning class—how many students are in it?"

"Eleven."

"And how would you rate them, I mean to say, would you put Amy in the top of that eleven? The bottom?"

"Top. Very top. What does that matter?"

"I'm only...I'm looking to get an idea of who Amy was, that's all. Anything you can add, really anything at all, would be helpful."

A pause got a little longer than was comfortable, but Dufort did not speak.

"Well, I'm not sure I have much to tell you. She was quite a good student—talented, as I've said, and also hard working. Steady. I expected to make some introductions for her, sometime later, when she was just a little more developed, you understand. This was only the beginning of her second year. A ways to go yet. But the potential, yes, the potential was definitely there."

"Was?"

"Oh, I—I didn't mean anything by it. I say 'was' only because...because she's not here anymore, you see. Like she's on holiday or taken a term off or something, the way students do these days so often. Hard to keep track if they're coming or going!" he added, perhaps a bit too heartily.

"Can you tell me anything about her personal life?"

Gallimard pursed his lips. "Not at all. She seemed to get on with her classmates. Not a girl to stir up drama, you understand. Quiet. Not interested in posing as an artist, but in being one, if you understand me. Now, if there's not too much more? I have some papers that I absolutely have to grade this morning or my students will want to crucify me."

Dufort looked into Gallimard's face. He was perhaps in his early fifties, and his face betrayed a bit of rough living—too much alcohol, too many cigarettes, the bloat of too much of everything. His belly was round and his cardigan, buttoned twice, was strained to the point that Dufort guessed the buttons might not last the day.

"I understand, forgive me," he answered. "May I contact you again, if you do not mind, if anything comes up that I think you may be able to help us with?"

"Of course," said Gallimard, moving toward the door. Dufort definitely felt he was being rushed out. "I thought these days the police didn't investigate missing persons except for children?"

"That's correct," said Dufort. "I wouldn't call this an official investigation. Just trying to help out, when one of our community is in trouble. Possibly in trouble, I mean to say."

"Yes, of course. I expect she'll turn up. Young people—they get all sort of crazy ideas in their heads, you know. I had a student last year run off to Alaska, of all places. Got obsessed with some kind of animal, I don't remember, a marmot perhaps? And nothing would do but going to Alaska to see it. I believe he did get some rather good sculptures out of it!" Gallimard laughed, and for the first time Dufort could see his charm, a kind of knowing affability that drew you in, made you feel as though you were as cultured and urbane as he was, and that he really liked you very much.

Charm can be quite problematic, Dufort was thinking on his walk back to the village. It lulls people into thinking things are true that might not be true. It's almost like a spell, like magic, isn't it.

MOLLY COULDN'T STAND it a minute longer. She put on her grubbiest clothes, took a mug of coffee, and headed out to the overgrown garden with delusional plans for getting rid of the vines in the front border by mid-morning. It was the chilliest morning yet, and she had to go back in for a sweater, but quickly warmed up once she got going, digging down to get the roots and then flinging what she could tear out into a pile behind her.

In some ways, she liked this sort of gardening job best: it was mindless, it was physically demanding, and the detail work of trying to get up every last bit of root was detail that she could accomplish on auto-pilot. Maybe it would seem as though all kinds of anxious thoughts would come crowding into the empty space, but actually, they did not. During the weeding of vines, Molly's mind stayed blissfully empty, with no thought of the Bennetts, or of the stories Lawrence had told her the night before of the other two women of Castillac who disappeared and were never found. Nothing in her head but the look of unfamiliar dirt, the feel of the tough vines as she wrapped them around her hands to yank them, and maybe the odd curse under her breath when a root snapped off, leaving a hunk deeper down that would regrow if she didn't dig for it.

As the sun got higher, the day warmed up. The orange cat appeared and rubbed against Molly's leg, but she didn't deign to pet it.

"You think I'm that gullible?" she said to the cat. "My finger still hurts from the last time." The orange cat cried and rubbed against her leg again.

So many fantastic French rose varieties, Molly was thinking. Adore the damasks. Must have La Ville de Bruxelles, that deep pink gets me every time. And Duchesse du Brabant with the amazing fragrance. And Chapeau de Napoleon, can't do without that one, or De Meaux, and Fantin Latour. I better have constant bookings to pay for my rose habit, she thought, looking around, jarred by the clash between her vision of the garden, all abundant with cabbagey blooms and heavenly scents, and the prickly overgrown reality.

It was nearing lunchtime. Molly glanced over to the cottage but saw no sign of life. She wondered if the Bennetts could sleep at all—or maybe they're asleep all the time, with the help of some mighty tranquilizers? That's probably what I would do in their shoes, she thought. Drug myself into a stupor and pray that when I snapped out of it, everything would be okay again. How else to manage the helplessness and creeping gray horror of not even knowing what has happened, and nothing to do but wait and hope?

They probably aren't eating either, she thought. She nodded to herself and jumped up, left her tools sitting in the weeds, and went inside with the idea of making the Bennetts a decent lunch. She could do that at least, even if she never found the right words to say.

Shopping for food had become one of Molly's main pursuits in France. Back in the States, she had dragged herself to the supermarket once a week, and at least during the short summer to some farmer's markets, not convenient but with good produce, but mostly she had considered grocery shopping to be just another chore to be gotten through. In Castillac, it was a mixture of social occasion, culture, and art. Not to mention the logical complexity of working out what to get where in which season: one cheesemonger for fresh cheese and another for cheese of other regions; the man who sold organic fruit who only came on Tuesdays; the seafood truck set up in the Place on Wednesday evening. And on and on.

As the days passed and Molly chatted with various villagers, she got to know them a little and added bits and pieces to her knowledge of where to get the best of everything, and the result, at least for the moment, was that her larder was stuffed to bursting with a wide array of delicious ingredients. Surely she would be able to make something to please and fortify the Bennetts with so much bounty to work with.

She stood with the refrigerator door open, staring at wrapped parcels of meat and cheese, at lettuces, and a bottle of cream. If I were facing tragedy, she thought, what would I most want to eat?

At first she considered fancy, extravagant dishes, but then decided they were more appropriate for facing the guillotine than grieving. And while the Bennetts may feel rather as though they are facing the guillotine, maybe truffles and foie gras isn't the best gustatory direction to take. Something more comforting was called for.

She ended up making the simplest of dishes, a soupe Parmentier. Leeks, potatoes, and a splash of cream. There were some chives in the kitchen garden, there just had to be, and during the half hour she poked around in the rank overgrowth looking for them, the soup was done. The chives had been right by the back door after all, and so once the bread was sliced, lunch was ready. On a tray, Molly put a thick slice of some country pâté on a plate with a small knife, and the bowls of hot soup, along with rough country napkins and a bottle of Pécharmant from the Sallière vineyard down the road. Then she cut a few black-eyed Susans and put them in an old glass medicine bottle and squeezed that onto the tray as well.

And now—to face them.

She walked over to the cottage, her heart beating too quickly. Putting the tray on the ground, she took a deep breath and rapped firmly on the door, then picked the tray up again.

Silence.

"Hello?" she called. "I've brought you some lunch!"

Silence.

The orange cat cried somewhere close by, but Molly could hear no sound of anything else living. She knocked one more time, waited, and then placed the tray where the door would not knock into it, even though the cat would certainly make off with the pâté the minute her back was turned.

She sat on the terrace at the rusty table and ate a bowl of the soup, but did not taste it or even register what she was doing.

I'm not sure why I feel like it's my own daughter who is missing, she thought. Well, it's not quite that. But I'm somehow much more wrapped up in the Bennetts' problems than I have any reason—or right—to be. Maybe it's that I was a student in France, when I was Amy's age. I'm ridiculously nostalgic about it, and it seems like it ought to be a golden time for her, not...not this.

If they had not managed to leave without her noticing, the Bennetts were in the cottage, fifty yards away, but to Molly it felt emotionally as though they had set up in her living room, and their unmanageable feelings were running wild throughout Molly's house, and no bowl of soup was going to be able to keep them at bay.

15

1963

Seven-year-old Anton Gallimard tore through the salon of his expansive house waving a sheet of paper over his head.

"Do not run in this house!" his father shouted. "Go back!"

Anton held up his paper. "Papa, I want to show you—"

"Go *back!*"

The boy's head drooped. He turned and walked out of the room and back down the corridor, lined with paintings and etchings in gilt frames, many of great value. He sighed and turned back around, taking another look at his drawing. It *was* good, wasn't it? He had thought so, but now he was not sure. Maybe he shouldn't show it to Papa after all.

"Anton!" his father's voice boomed.

Slowly the boy made his way down the corridor, the sheet of paper flapping against his legs. He didn't want to show it now. He knew it was dreadful, and his father was only going to scream at him. The joy he had felt while the pencil was moving across the paper had evaporated. Meekly he approached his father and held it out.

A short pause. Anton could feel something happening in his brain, a clashing disturbance, and he put his hands over his ears before his father had even spoken.

"What sort of puerile scrawling have you given me?" his father sneered. He tore the paper in two, balled up the pieces, and threw them at Anton. "What is the matter with you?"

Young Anton had no answer.

16

2005

"Just remember," Dufort said to Perrault and Maron as they gathered in his office before the scheduled press conference. "The press can be very helpful to us. I don't want you to mind any of the rest of it—just ignore the criticism and the speculations. We need them to get the word out about Amy, to publicize her photos, and then we cross our fingers that someone comes forward with some information we can use."

"I've made a press kit," said Thérèse. "Some photos and a short write-up they can take with them."

"Good work," said Dufort.

"I'll bet there'll be bloggers, or citizen reporters, some like to call themselves. Any official way we can shut them down?" asked Maron with an edge of a sneer.

"We don't want to shut anyone down," said Dufort. "The more publicity Amy gets, the more it helps our investigation. We want her face to be recognizable. We want to get people thinking, remembering—you know how it can be, sometimes the little bit, the detail no one thinks about at first—sometimes that's the thing that unravels the whole case.

"So if some villagers or tourists or people from neighboring towns want to write about Amy online, I'm all for it. *Bon*, are we ready?"

Maron and Perrault nodded, and the whole of the Castillac gendarme force walked outside to the front steps of the station. There was not exactly a crowd waiting for them, only a woman from the regional paper and a handful of villagers.

"You did reach the TV station?" Dufort asked Maron.

"I did. They said they would send someone." He shrugged.

"Thank you for coming," Dufort said to the lone reporter. "As you no doubt are aware, a student from L'Institut Degas is missing. Her name is Amy Bennett, and she has not been seen since a week ago Tuesday night."

"Was she abducted by the same person who took Valérie?" asked the reporter.

"We are concentrating on Amy for the moment," answered Dufort with an inward sigh. He knew the subject of Valérie was going to come up, that was inevitable. But he did not expect it would be the very first question, right out of the gate.

It felt ridiculous, the three of them standing there, facing no cameras and no reporters save a single middle-aged woman. For something like this to work, you need bodies. Interested bodies. You need some *buzz*. The villagers had already moved on, and Dufort decided to cut this pathetic press conference short.

"Perrault, would you give—yes, here's a kit with all the information we can give out—"

Perrault jumped up to hand one over to the reporter, and smiled at her, trying to stay upbeat. Then the gendarmes nodded and said goodbye and filed back into the station.

"Well, that was a waste of time," said Dufort under his breath. He went into his office and closed the door, and immediately called up the television station to give whichever manager he could get ahold of a piece of his mind.

That done, he called Maron and Perrault into his office. "All right then," he said. "We've got to start looking for the body. As I've reminded you before, this cannot be an official investigation, so we're going to have to do it without looking like we are doing it. I'm going to spend some time in the morning, before I come to the station—I will take everything north of rue Gervais. Perrault, you check your family's neighborhood, up to rue Tartine. Maron, either ride your bicycle or take the car and look on the outskirts —farm buildings, garages, you know the drill. If anyone asks, make something up.

"We need to find her. I don't care if you look before work or after, but put the time in every day. We keep looking until we find her, is that understood?"

Perrault and Maron nodded, their expressions grim.

17

Dufort spent the last few hours of the workday walking around the village. He didn't stop to talk to anyone, but waved when he saw people he knew. He was putting himself in a sort of trance, the same sort of trance he went into when jogging, where the repetitive movement of his body settled his mind and allowed it to roam freely over the details of the Amy Bennett case and everything related to it. He was not judging the information, not trying to be objective, but rather the opposite—to sense the emotions underneath the facts.

But at this point, the facts were minimal. A young woman was gone. Third from this village. No apparent motive for leaving without telling anyone. No romantic entanglements that anyone knew of, and not a person who tended toward the dramatic or impulsive.

No sign of her. Her wallet, phone, and ID cards missing, her knapsack missing.

Amy Bennett: missing.

Dufort was walking down a narrow back street, his gait slightly uneven because of the cobblestones. He glanced in the villagers' back gardens, noting who kept things neat and who did not.

Coming the other way was a man walking a dog. He was a tall, spindly man with notably long feet. Glasses. Hair down over his collar. Dufort wasn't sure, but he thought the man was a painter who taught at Degas. Could this finally be a moment of serendipity, during a non-investigation that so far had been full of nothing but blockages and silence?

Ordinarily when he passed someone from the village he did not know, he did not speak but looked the other way so as to allow the person his privacy. But in this case he needed to speak, needed to see if the man had anything at all to tell him.

"Bonjour, monsieur," said Dufort, with a nod. He slowed and then stopped as the man and dog reached him. "I'm sorry to bother you, I don't believe we've met. I am Benjamin Dufort, of the gendarmerie."

"Bonjour, Chief Dufort. I am Rex Ford. Of course I know who you are, a leading light of our village," the man said deferentially. His French was perfect with only a slight accent.

Dufort made a quick, somewhat ironic bow. "I believe you teach at Degas?"

"That is correct. Six years now."

The dog, a dachshund, strained on the leash, wanting to sniff along the fence line of someone's backyard. Ford moved a few steps to allow the dog his pleasure.

"Do you mind if I ask you a few questions? I can walk along with you, so that you can accomplish walking your dog at the same time."

"You're very kind. Of course, ask away. I assume this is about Amy?

"Yes. It is about Amy." Dufort and Ford headed toward town, stopping every so often for the dachshund to sniff and lift his leg on any tuft of grass he could find. Dufort had been so deep in his trance that he was struggling to find a line of questioning for the teacher off the top of his head.

"So, did you have Amy as a student?"

"I'm afraid not. Although the school is small enough that we professors know the reputation of all the students. She's got quite a talent, I can say that without hesitation. And more important—she's a worker. Persistent. That's really what makes an artist successful, you know," he said. "Talent—eh, there are loads of people with talent. It's talent along with not giving up...that's what makes an artist who gets somewhere."

"Did Amy Bennett want to get somewhere?"

"I would say very much so. Quite ambitious, really. Almost like a businessperson, with thought-out goals and plans. Not a temperament we see often at Degas—the capacity or interest in long-range planning, that sort of thing. Of course, that makes it all the more out of character that—"

Ford kept walking but stopped speaking.

Dufort walked, made sure his body stayed relaxed, but he felt certain that Ford was about to say something interesting.

He waited, but Ford said nothing more.

"More out of character...?" Dufort prodded gently.

"I don't really like to say," said Ford, but Dufort had the feeling he actually very much wanted to say.

He waited, and tried not to betray his rising excitement.

After a few steps, Ford said hurriedly, "Oh, you know, typical stuff for young girls. They get infatuated, think the attention of an older man means something more than it does. Old story I suppose."

Dufort noticed a hint of bitterness in the man's voice.

"Would you be able to tell me...which older man was paying her attention?"

"Anton Gallimard, who else?" Ford said, and now the bitterness was out in the open, and when Dufort glanced at him, he saw a man who looked as though he had just eaten something spoiled.

"You must understand, the man never leaves the campus. I don't believe he even drives. He's always there, lending an oh-so-comforting shoulder for these young female students to cry on.

"That's how it starts," added Ford, but then he pressed his narrow lips together and was done talking. "I've got to get home, class this afternoon. I hope I've been helpful. And more than that—of course—I hope you find Amy."

He turned and tugged the dachshund along with him. Dufort watched them walk for a few minutes, the dog comically bouncing along on its short legs over the cobblestones, miraculously able to produce more pee as he lifted his leg four more times as Dufort stood watching.

Ford seemed to be hurrying away, and Dufort wondered about that. He could have been speaking from professional jealousy—after all, it was Gallimard who had the reputation for being a big talent, even if one never realized fully. No one had heard of Rex Ford as far as Dufort knew.

Or, if what Ford said was true, and Gallimard did take advantage of his students, Ford could be jealous of that as well. He could imagine a new flock of young women coming to the school every year could be quite the prize to fight over, for the sort of man who wanted that.

If Amy was so dedicated, so ambitious, would she have risked so much for a dalliance with one of her professors? A relationship like that could easily go wrong and lose her the support of an influential supporter.

Ah, thought Dufort, I am not so old that I don't remember how it was to fall head over heels in love. Or lust. Either one, he thought, smiling to himself at a particular memory, and then turning back toward town.

❧

It was really quite wonderful to feel like she was already

becoming part of the village, Molly thought, strolling along at dusk, on a back street, winding her way to Chez Papa. She felt sure that someone would be there to talk to, even if it was Nico behind the bar—someone who would look up when she came in, and recognize at her, and maybe toss out the odd tidbit of gossip.

Although these days, with the Bennetts staying in her cottage at La Baraque, everyone was looking to *her* for the tidbits, and so far she had nothing to tell.

"As far as I know, they haven't left the cottage even once," she said to Lawrence Weebly, who was installed on his usual stool drinking his usual Negroni.

"Well, what's it been, two days?"

"Yep. They got here on Tuesday. If your Negroni fog is not too thick, you know it's now Thursday evening."

"Negronis give me clarity, dear girl, not fog," said Weebly, lifting his nose in the air.

"So you say," said Molly, laughing, and taking a sip of her kir. "I understand that they wouldn't want to rush straight to the police. But wouldn't you expect they'd at least go over to the school, and talk to her roommate or something? And what about *meals?*"

"I find that people in deeply stressful situations often don't do what one would expect."

"I suppose you're right."

The two sat in companionable silence for several minutes.

"All of a sudden I miss smoking," said Molly.

"Ah, when did you give it up? I haven't had a cigarette in years. Seven years, actually. Seven years, three months, and seventeen days."

Molly burst out laughing.

"I'm joking. But really—if there were a way to smoke without ruining your face and lungs, wouldn't you go back to it in a second?"

"Nanosecond," said Molly. "Although despite what I just said, I almost never think of cigarettes anymore. It's sitting at a bar, feeling a little afraid, a little anxious—that's a prime smoking trigger, right there. I don't actually want a cigarette, I just remember how delicious it was to smoke at moments like this."

"Yes. They do pull a nice cozy blanket up over your feelings, don't they?"

"That describes it perfectly."

"Are you feeling afraid and anxious because of Amy?"

"Yes."

"Understandable. Sometimes I don't know how you women manage."

"That's not helping."

"Sorry," said Weebly, and patted her leg. "If you ever get worried being at La Baraque by yourself, just give me a call and I'll hop right on over."

"That's very kind," said Molly, moved by his offer.

It was a slow night at Chez Papa so far. Only one family was in for dinner, taking the corner table. Vincent was lounging at his usual spot near the door, nursing a beer. It did not have the makings of a wild night out, and for that, Molly was grateful. It was very pleasant to sit at the bar, not engaging in any shenanigans, and get to know her new friend better. It was calming, and her jitteriness over the Bennetts—parents and daughter—was slowly receding.

"Uh oh, incoming," murmured Weebly.

Molly spun around on her stool, not very subtly trying to see who Weebly was looking at over her shoulder.

"Bonsoir, *mes amis!*" said Lapin, clattering through the door. He was wearing some kind of boot that made a lot of noise on the tile floor.

"Oh jeez," said Molly under her breath. She crossed her arms over her chest and tried to arrange her face into something approaching neutrality.

"Always glad to see you, La Bombe," said Lapin, looking a bit peeved that Molly's arms were covering her chest well enough to ruin the view. "What, are you chilly or something? Nico, turn the heat up, man! Our Molly is about to catch a cold!"

Molly looked at Nico and saw him looking darkly at Lapin. She caught his eye and shook her head. Nico grinned at her and nodded.

"What have you been up to, Lapin?" Weebly asked.

"Oh, nothing much. Can't complain. You know Madame Louvier died last month, and I've been out to help the family."

"Lapin's a junk dealer," said Weebly to Molly.

"Junk? You affront me, Monsieur Weebly!" He turned to Molly, his eyes resolutely pinned to her chest. "I sell various valuable objects of antiquity," he said, "that I find occasionally in an attic or storeroom. Nico, get me a whiskey, will you?"

"He picks over the bones of the recently deceased," said Weebly drily.

"Would you rather I pluck them while they are still alive?" asked Lapin, with a guffaw. "Madame Louvier had some nice things, not that she ever let anyone in her house to see them. A chest of drawers I may take to sell in Paris. A few good rings...." From his expression Lapin appeared to be daydreaming about all the money he was about to rake in, but his eyes never veered from Molly.

Her arms were tired. She knew if she let them go to her sides, Lapin would stare, probably make a remark or two...but maybe then he would move on, let it go? It was worth a try. Slowly, trying to make the movement naturally so as not to attract attention, she let one arm and then the other drop away from her chest. She reached for her kir and took a small sip, holding her breath.

"Ah," said Lapin, "there now!" He was grinning broadly, and as expected, looking with wide eyes at Molly's bosom. "So happy to see the girls again. And may I say again, Madame Sutton, how very pleased I am that you have chosen Castillac for your new home."

"You're starting to make me rethink that," Molly said under

her breath, and turned on her stool to face Nico. She wondered why he had been giving Lapin the stink-eye when he first came in, but figured the various currents of village antipathy would take years to untangle.

"So what happens in winter?" she asked Nico. "Do people stay home, or is business brisk all year round?"

"Oh, it depends," said Nico distractedly. "We've got the regulars, of course, who come in every day—Lapin, Weebly here, usually Vincent. There's a German family that comes in for dinner every Tuesday, like clockwork. Almost no tourists once it gets cold. Sometimes we only serve dinner a few days a week, if business falls way off."

Molly got a pang suddenly, of wondering whether this move to France, to Castillac, had been a mistake. She hadn't known a single soul when she chose it—it had all been about the house whose photographs captivated her so. Of course she had understood that there would be annoying people—there were annoying people everywhere, after all. But this Lapin—he was annoying *and* standing right next to her, his eyes roaming over her body as though he wanted to take out a knife and fork and eat her. And he was *relentless*.

The prospect of spending a winter anywhere within fifty kilometers of Lapin seemed like a very long and unappealing winter indeed.

Weebly had ordered some *frites*, extra-crispy, which irritated the cook who maintained that *all* his frites were extra crispy. Molly shared them, delighting in every savory bite, thinking that fall must have arrived because now a dish of hot food was just the thing.

"The French don't really snack at the bar, like we're used to," said Weebly. "Even Nico thinks I'm an utter Philistine for ordering frites only and not the steak to go with it. But sometimes my digestion is not what it might be," he said, rubbing one hand over his belly.

"I am not a rule-follower," announced Lapin. "If you want to eat frites with no meal, then do it. If you want to eat frites for breakfast, do it. For myself—I do what I like. And I don't really give a flying fig what anyone else does either."

"That's quite a pronouncement," said Weebly. "Are you really willing to go against all of French tradition of what to eat when? I had no idea you were such an iconoclast."

"You think I don't know what 'iconoclast' means," said Lapin, looking angry. "But I do. And I am. So screw you."

Molly was not remotely in the mood for conflict. She ate one more frite, drank the last of her kir, and hopped off her stool.

"I'm going to say goodnight, fellas," she said. "Bonsoir *à tous!*"

"Oh don't let us scare you off," said Weebly. "Lapin and I are just play-fighting, right Lapin?"

"Sure," said Lapin, but Molly did not believe him.

"Honestly, I'm ready for bed. I can feel the chill coming in the door, and my book and a quilt are calling to me."

"*Bonne nuit* then, my dear," said Weebly.

Lapin nodded, still hoping to get a good look at Molly's chest before she left for the night.

"It's dark," said Vincent, lumbering up from his table by the door. "I'll take you home?"

Molly paused. The idea of getting a ride home seemed like an inviting luxury at the moment; she felt tired and completely done for the day. She couldn't really afford it, but....

"Sure," she said. "I don't feel much like the walk at the moment."

Vincent bobbed his head. His cab was right outside and he opened the door for her, grinning.

I've really got to save up the money to have these damn bags of silicone removed, she thought, and spent the few minutes it took to get home daydreaming about how soon she could start restoring the broken-down *pigeonnier*, so she would have another gîte to rent, and maybe double her income in one fell swoop.

18

The next morning, Dufort spent an hour searching for Amy before going to the station, but saw nothing out of the ordinary in the alleyways and dumpsters. Before going inside, Dufort stepped into the alley and took out his blue glass bottle. He shook a few drops under his tongue and closed his eyes. Turning his face to the sun, he took several slow, deep breaths.

Just do the next right thing, he said to himself. *Just do the next right thing.*

The situation with Amy was beginning to take over, the pressure to solve the mystery of her disappearance pressing down on him, threatening to trigger anxiety so rampant that he couldn't control it.

"Good morning," he said with forced optimism to Perrault and Maron who were already at their desks. "My office," he said, and they jumped up to follow him.

"Of course, we're not backing off from Amy Bennett," he said. "And we'll get to sharing where we are with that in a moment. But first I want to go through everything else, make sure we're on top of the rest of Castillac business. It's always tempting with cases like Amy's to run with them and get blinders to the rest of our responsibilities, and I want to make sure that doesn't happen.

"Maron, you went after Monsieur Vargas, uh, was it Sunday? That taken care of?"

"Yes, sir," said Maron. "He was not in his usual place, the bench in the cemetery behind the church. I walked all over the village looking for him and asking if anyone had seen him. Nothing. Then I thought, okay, if he usually goes to the cemetery, maybe I should look in the other ones—and sure enough, he was in that small cemetery on the edge of Salliac, sitting on the tombstone of a Monsieur Pierre Duchamp, eating a baguette with ham, happy as you please."

"He came with you without a problem?"

"None, Chief."

"Nice job," said Dufort.

At that moment, they heard the door to the station open, and Perrault went to see who it was.

"He's just gone and I can't *stand* it!" an old woman said, her voice loud and quavering.

Dufort went through to the front room and put his arm around her thin shoulders. "Bonjour Madame Bonnay, it's nice to see you. Yves is missing again, eh? Run off to chase the ladies?"

Madame Bonnay let out a sob.

Maron and Perrault exchanged looks of surprise, wondering at Dufort's brusqueness.

"I keep telling you, if you get that fellow fixed, he won't run off so much," said Dufort.

Maron's eyebrows shot up.

"But I cannot mutilate him like that," the old woman cried. "It seems so cruel! Oh Yves, where have you gone?" and she collapsed against Dufort with a fresh barrage of tears.

Dufort winked at Perrault. "Yves belonged to her husband Raimond, who was a skilled hunter," he explained. "He has distinguished bloodlines, doesn't he Madame Bonnay? A sought-after sire for hunting-dog puppies?"

"He is a Grand Bleu de Gascogne," she answered, drawing herself up. "He's been *very* popular," she said, wiping her nose with a lavender-scented handkerchief. "And I would hate to deprive him of that enjoyment, you understand."

All three gendarmes laughed.

"But on the other hand, every time he gets a whiff of a bitch in heat, he's off like a rocket. Could be any cur from the alley, you understand—selective he is not. I'm so afraid he will be hit by a car, or stolen."

"Of course, I understand," said Dufort. All three of us are going out in a matter of minutes, and we'll keep an eye out for him. And he does find his way back sometimes, yes?"

"Sometimes," Madame Bonnay said, almost managing a smile. "He's such a sweet boy. Now that Raimond is gone, I don't think Yves has enough to do. Well, thank you for looking for him. I'll let you know if he turns up. I was going to make him liver for dinner, his favorite."

"My favorite too," Dufort said, walking her to the door. "I'm sure when he gets the smell of that in his nose, he'll run right home."

"All right," said Dufort to Perrault and Maron once they were alone again. "Perrault, go over to Chez Papa and get that video from Nico. I don't know why they're dragging their feet, but put a stop to it."

"Yes, sir," said Perrault brightly, and left.

"You have anything?" Dufort asked, turning to Maron. "Thoughts? Ideas?"

Maron did not want to admit he did not. He put off answering, hoping something might occur to him quickly, but finally just shook his head.

"I would like for you to go out tonight, out of uniform. Chez Papa, or anyplace else you see students from Degas congregating.

Obviously this isn't exactly undercover work, and I don't mean for you to pretend not to be a member of the Castillac force—not that anyone would be fooled anyway—but I do hope that some informality might help with what I want you to do. Which is: find out what you can about Anton Gallimard. What do the students really think of him? What's his reputation with the female students?

"Be charming," said Dufort, with something of a brittle smile since he couldn't exactly imagine Maron having that sort of magic in his repertoire. "See if you can get them to loosen up and tell you some stories...."

"Yes, sir," said Maron. "And for the rest of today, any particular assignment?"

"Take a stroll through the village and see if you can find Yves," said Dufort. "Black and white mottled coat, long black ears sort of like a Basset Hound."

Maron showed no expression but nodded and softly said, "Yes, sir," as he left the station.

Dufort stood by his desk staring out of the window, his eyes glazed. Well, she may be able to help with the investigation, he rationalized, pulling out his cell, and tapping in the number for L'Institut Degas.

"Marie-Claire," he said, and his voice had a little of that charm he disparaged in others. "This is Ben. I wanted to thank you for helping me track down Gallimard—I found him in his office just when you said I would."

"I'm so glad. Anything I can do to help."

"And also I wondered—would you like to have lunch with me? Perhaps the day after tomorrow, Friday? I have a few questions for you about Amy," he added.

There was a slight pause that Dufort started to interpret but stopped himself.

"That would be fine," said Marie-Claire.

"I'll come for you at noon," said Dufort, and they said their goodbyes and hung up.

He slid his cell onto his desk, still looking out of the window, but in his mind he was seeing Marie-Claire, with her slim waist and intelligent dark eyes.

Perhaps this is a mistake, he thought. But sometimes making a mistake can be the best thing you can do.

DUFORT RAN a shorter route than usual on Friday morning. He was in a hurry to get to the station, hoping that the day was going to bring some news in the Amy Bennett case.

He was not disappointed.

Nico finally came by with the streetcam video from Chez Papa. He was apologetic—it kept slipping his mind, he was busy, he couldn't figure out how to send a digital copy—a boatload of excuses, none of which was at all convincing to Maron, who knew Nico to be anything but scatterbrained or inept.

Nico explained that finally he had made a copy off the DVR with his phone, and then copied that onto a CD since the file was too large to send by mail. He had contacted the security company that serviced the camera, but according to him, they were unresponsive apart from telling him to manage it himself if all he wanted was a copy and there was no break-in or evidence of wrongdoing.

"I tried to tell them that evidence of wrongdoing is exactly what you guys are looking for," said Nico with a shrug. "But eh, they didn't want to bother. Customer service isn't what it used to be."

Maron flexed his shoulders and said nothing.

Cold fish, thought Nico.

"All right then, if there's nothing else I can do for you?"

"Not at the moment. We may want to question you at some

point," said Maron, although he knew of no plans to do so. He liked putting people off-balance.

Nico nodded. "See you later then," he said, and left the station.

Thérèse Perrault came in just as Dufort and Maron were slipping the disc into Dufort's desktop.

"Bonjour, Perrault," said Dufort. "Whatever you said to Nico must have had an effect—he finally got himself over here with the video. Good job. It's the last one we know of, and the others have been useless, as you know. I will admit, my expectations are low."

Perrault squeezed in next to her co-workers and they waited for the image to appear. First the sound came on—the sound of a rollicking party, with someone singing, pop music playing, shouting in the background, the clinking of dishes and glasses—all happy enough, the sound of people cutting loose and having fun.

They did not have to wait long. "There she is!" said Perrault, pointing to a corner of the screen.

From the back, you could just make out the head and shoulders of a young woman, standing in a group by the bar.

"Are you sure that's her?" said Maron.

"I'm sure," answered Perrault. I've been looking at those photographs her roommate sent pretty much every minute. I feel like I practically gave birth to her at this point."

Dufort shot her a look and Perrault looked back at the screen.

The noise of the video was loud, and it was impossible to distinguish what anyone was saying, but every thirty seconds or so, someone let out a loud whoop. It all sounded very celebratory. And then the people in Amy's group clapped, and someone moved into the frame and put his arm around her.

"Looks like Lapin," said Perrault. "Always got his mitts on somebody."

They kept watching. The tape was twenty minutes long; it was not entertaining to watch a party's slow progress that way, unable to hear what anyone was saying, and only seeing the blurry drunkenness of everyone increasing as more drinks were ordered, more drinks thrown back.

"What were they celebrating, I wonder?" said Perrault.

All three officers were studying the video intently, watching Amy, and also scanning the rest of the frame for anything, anything at all that might be helpful.

At about seven minutes in, Amy turned toward the camera. They could see her blurry face, and all three of the officers were struck with how strange it was to see her there, smiling, and throwing her head back laughing, when almost certainly she was dead.

This many days out, what other options were really possible? You can't ignore the percentages, Dufort would always say.

The camera was just over the door to Chez Papa, so it recorded the tops of heads as people came and went. At about seventeen minutes in, the eyes of all three gendarmes widened as they saw Amy Bennett put on a sweater and walk unsteadily toward the door.

They saw the top of her head disappear as she left the restaurant, with Lapin Broussard's arm firmly around her waist.

19

"I don't really know Lapin," Maron was saying to Dufort as they drove out to Lapin's house. "Was that a surprise, seeing him leave with the girl?"

"Yes and no," said Dufort. His face looked grim. "He's notorious for bothering women. Putting his hands on them without any invitation, being rude. Lascivious. But at the same time—he's part of the village, Maron. People here grew up with him, they feel like they know him. That's why Perrault looked so stunned when we saw him leave with his arm around Amy.

"To be honest, I always thought he was more talk than action. That he got off on harassing woman in front of other men but wasn't actually trying very hard to get alone with one."

Dufort was quiet for a moment. He glanced to the right, not wanting to miss Lapin's house. "I thought he liked to look, and to talk, but not to act," he said softly. "Several years ago, there was an incident...."

Maron waited. Dufort did not elaborate. He wanted to jump in and press Dufort but restrained himself. Maron squeezed his hands into fists and counted to himself, at the same time wondering if he would ever be able to tolerate the hierarchy of the gendarmerie. Dufort could be so taciturn, and one day it might push him right over the edge.

Finally Maron said, "So...do you consider him a suspect?"

"Not precisely. I might call him a person of interest," said Dufort, running a hand over his brush cut. "I want the two of us to talk to him. I have known him for years—all my life, I guess. So it falls to you to be the tough one."

"Understood," said Maron.

Lapin Broussard's house was right off rue des Chênes, about two kilometers out of town as the road left Castillac heading south. It felt like the deep countryside even though it was walking distance to the village. Fields of fading sunflowers lined both sides of the road. Dufort noticed the forest stretching back behind Lapin's house, up a hill and over it.

They turned into Lapin's driveway. No car in front of the house.

Dufort and Maron got out, both of them feeling a tingling excitement, trying to anticipate how this was going to go. Would Lapin have a believable story to tell them, perhaps how he had gotten the girl back to school safely? Would he seem nervous, like he was hiding something?

Was he even home?

"Lapin is not known for being the first rabbit out of the burrow in the morning," said Dufort.

Maron did not smile and Dufort regretted the mild joke. He wished he were alone so he could take some of his herbal drops in privacy.

The two men strode up to the door and knocked. They listened.

No sound but birds, and the distant grinding of a tractor.

"His place is neater than I'd have expected," said Maron.

"It's important not to conflate qualities," said Dufort. "Just because the man is a bothersome lech doesn't mean he's a slob."

Maron gave a short nod.

They rapped on the old wooden door, harder.

"Lapin!" shouted Dufort.

Nothing.

"You stay here, in case he comes out," said Dufort. "I'll check around back."

As well as he could remember, the house had been left to Lapin by his father, who died when Lapin was still a teenager. Lapin's mother had died when he was a baby, and he had made his own way after his father's death. Lapin was older than Dufort by around ten years, and so what Dufort knew about his life was mostly from overhearing tidbits when he was young.

He remembered the women of his family feeling sorry for the orphan, and that villagers had pitched in to help him out at first, when Lapin was still a teenager and figuring out what kind of work he could do. And he thought he remembered hearing that the father had been something of a tyrant, and that people believed Lapin was probably better off without him.

The house was small but well made. In the cloudy light of the morning the golden limestone almost glowed, and the building looked infinitely sturdy and solid. It was old, probably seventeenth century. Dufort noticed that the roofers had done a thorough job; there were at least four layers of orange tile, and all the masonry work looked neat and well done.

Dufort saw there was no kitchen garden out back, not even a pot of herbs, just a patch of scraggly overgrown grass and encroaching underbrush from the forest.

Dufort walked up the hill behind the house and looked around. He looked at the roof, at the windows, at the garage. He turned and looked at the forest behind him, dark even in the daylight.

People are capable of anything, he reminded himself—he felt that he had to remind himself because he didn't want to believe it was so. He had no particular feeling for Lapin Broussard, apart from the fact that the man was part of village life, the only life

Dufort knew. But that was not nothing, and it made him sad to think that Lapin could have done something to that girl.

He dug in his pocket for the blue glass vial and shook a few drops under his tongue, and walked back down the hill.

For form's sake he knocked on the back door and peered in, and took a look in the garage, but it certainly looked as though Lapin was not home.

Whether that meant he had taken off, they could not know yet. But as Dufort came around the house and waved to Maron to get back in the car, he was making a list of other places they might go to look for him. He had not forgotten his lunch date with Marie-Claire Levy, and he couldn't help that a small, egocentric voice inside wished that he could arrive at lunch with some real news to tell her.

❧

HE KNEW it was probably the wrong move, but Dufort wanted to counteract the upswell of melancholy he felt on seeing the tape of Lapin going off with Amy Bennett. So he reserved a table at *La Métairie*, the best restaurant in the village, for his lunch with Marie-Claire. Wrong move, because this was supposed to be a sort of working lunch, and besides that, going to the best restaurant put too much pressure on the first date (because that's what it was, no matter how hard he pretended it wasn't).

He drove his own car, a Renault that had seen better days, to L'Institut Degas and arrived just a few minutes after noon. Before going in to the administration building, he looked around the campus, trying to get a feel for the mood of the place. He saw a group of students walking from the modern building to the dormitory, a young woman sitting against a tree with a sketchpad, an older man raking leaves. The scene felt normal, everyday. He stopped and closed his eyes, listening, opening his perceptions, but sensed nothing out of the ordinary, not even any particular tension.

He supposed at a campus that small, there was no need for rallies or a lot of public brouhaha. The faculty and the students were all aware that a classmate was missing. And presumably, everyone knew Amy personally, with varying degrees of intimacy. Everyone knew everyone, without exception—one of the great benefits and drawbacks of such a small, insular school.

Amy Bennett was by all accounts a seriously talented artist. Dufort wondered how the school handled issues of jealousy. Did they leave the students to work things out on their own? Make efforts to get the students to compete with themselves and not each other? Or the opposite—did they fuel rivalries, push them, incite them to competitive fervor?

Dufort could remember how it was in the gendarmerie training, how ruthless some of the cadets had been, stepping on anyone they could to get ahead and claw their way to the top. He didn't see any reason why it should be any different with artists. It's human nature, he thought, wanting to stand out and be noticed, to *win*. And when you add the financial divide between a very successful artist and one not so successful...he could see that the bucolic setting of Degas might seem more serene on the surface than it might be to experience as a student.

He wondered how Lapin had gotten anywhere with Amy. Level-headed, a planner, an ambitious and talented young woman—she did not sound like the type of young woman who would respond to the coarse attentions of someone like Lapin. Was it simply a matter of drinking too much, and making herself vulnerable that way? Amy did not seem to be someone who would drink too much, either.

Lapin was the last person to be seen with her, and she had now been missing for eight days. Yet Dufort felt decidedly mixed about the break in the case. He did not understand why Amy had left with him, and on top of that, he did not see Lapin as someone capable of doing something so terrible.

Discreetly, Dufort reached for his blue glass vial. He had used the day's allotment already, but ignored that and shook a few drops under his tongue—a mixture of lavender, lemon balm, and ashwaganda this time—before going in to the administration building to find Marie-Claire. It had been months since he had been on a date and he felt a not-unpleasant agitation. But when he saw Marie-Claire sitting at her desk, her brows furrowed as she typed something and stared at her computer monitor, his unease fell away.

She looks so intelligent, he said to himself. So intelligent, and also...sexy.

"Hi, Ben," said Marie-Claire. "Just give me half a minute," she said, still looking at the screen and typing furiously. Then she smiled at him and stood up and smoothed her skirt. "I don't know why I have this job," she said, shaking her head. "I absolutely loathe filling out forms and doing paperwork. And yet...that is eighty-five per cent of what I do."

She came around her desk and she and Dufort kissed one cheek and then the other.

"What's the other fifteen per cent?" asked Dufort, helping her with her coat.

"Listening to people bitch and moan," she said, laughing. "I'm sort of the resident pseudo-therapist, for both faculty and students."

They walked outside together and climbed into Dufort's car. "I make a lot of pots of tea, and do a lot of listening," she added.

"And do you like that part?"

"I do. The students here—and the professors too—they're interesting, engaged people, for the most part. Most of them are very ambitious. Not necessarily for money, not that kind of success. But for art. There's a kind of purity in it, you know? An innocence. And I like being around that, being part of it, helping in a small way."

When Dufort turned toward La Métairie, Marie-Claire said, "Ben! La Métairie, really?" but her tone was of happy surprise.

"I've got some news, I'll tell you when we're seated," he said. "I don't know, something about it—it made me want something very good to eat. Like a talisman? I don't really know what I mean."

Marie-Claire looked at Dufort, her expression serious. She did not ask him what he meant but waited until they were inside and had given their orders to the waiter.

Dufort hesitated. Strictly speaking, he should not disclose to anyone outside of the officers on the case what the video had shown, but he thought perhaps Marie-Claire could shed some light on Amy's movements that night. Would Marie-Claire think it possible Amy would go off with Lapin willingly? And for what reasons? Aware that this line of thinking was partly rationalization, he decided to go ahead with it anyway.

"I asked you to lunch to talk about Amy," said Dufort. "And I'd like to go ahead and do that. There has been something of a break in the case."

Marie-Claire sat very still and waited.

"We got video footage from around the village, hoping to find something, some clue about who she was with or...just anything, we didn't know what we were looking for. *Anything*."

Marie-Claire nodded.

"And video after video was useless. No Amy, nothing at all of interest. But the last one we looked at, just this morning, did have Amy. Many minutes of Amy, apparently celebrating with her friends and some people from the village. Amy left with one of those people. She looked rather inebriated, and his arm was around her as they left the restaurant."

Marie-Claire had her hand over her mouth and her eyes were wide. "I'm surprised to hear Amy was drunk," she said. "She...

wasn't like that. Not wild at all that way, I would have guessed. All business, that girl."

The waiter brought a small tray with tiny cups arranged in a line and explained in some detail what they were, but neither Marie-Claire nor Dufort paid any attention, though they looked at the waiter while he spoke and pretended to listen.

"I can tell you what they were celebrating, at least," said Marie-Claire. "Amy had just won a contest, the Marfan Prize. It's not one of the really big ones, but any prize brings a great deal of prestige at her age. And I believe there was a cash award, more than just a token. I'd have to check to tell you how much, but I'd guess around 5,000 euros."

Dufort cocked his head, then took one of the tiny cups and drank the contents. "Mmm," he said. "I have no idea what I just ate, but it is extremely good. Do you know if she had received the money?"

"No idea. I doubt it, because her winning had just been announced, and usually with these things, the check is a little slow in coming."

Dufort nodded.

"So are you going to tell me?" said Marie-Claire, smiling.

Dufort liked Marie-Claire's smile. It was warm, it was enticing, and part of him wanted to shove work to the side and get to know her better, instead of the endless talk of work, revolving around something horrible someone had done to someone else. With an effort he dragged himself back to the moment.

"I'm sorry, tell you what?"

"Whom did she leave with?"

Dufort nodded but did not speak. He really shouldn't tell her. But he did want to know several things: Had Lapin been hanging around the school at all? Had Marie-Claire perhaps seen him around, either before Amy's disappearance or after?

He took a breath before he spoke. "A man from the village,

known to many, including me. Lapin. Real name's not Lapin of course—it's Laurent. Laurent Broussard."

Marie-Claire shook her head. "Every woman within a hundred kilometers knows Lapin," she said, and took a sip of water.

The waiter brought wine, local and very good, and then starters and main courses and coffee and a pair of the most exquisite crèmes brûlées flavored with lavender. But unfortunately, the pall of Amy's disappearance, possibly at the hands of a man they both knew, cast such a deep shadow over their lunch that they barely tasted a thing. Their conversation was not what either of them would have hoped, but rather drooping and lacking in wit.

It's the constant not-knowing, thought Dufort later, going out for a second jog that evening. The whole village has been waiting over the course of years for this abductor to be caught. Yet to hear it might be someone we've known our whole lives—that does not bring any comfort either.

20

Lapin? Lapin?! *No.*

Thérèse Perrault had known Lapin Broussard since she was a baby. Everyone in Castillac knew Lapin. Because he was friendly, a *mec* who liked to socialize more than anything, who knew all the latest gossip because in the course of his junk collecting, he was up in everyone's private business, and he delighted in passing on what he saw and heard.

Really, if someone was going to get killed, Thérèse thought it more likely to *be* Lapin, not at the hands of Lapin.

Of course she didn't approve of the way he pawed the women he came in contact with (or hoped to come in contact with, she thought wryly). Of course she'd seen him behave like a total creep, no doubt about it, and it wasn't infrequent behavior either.

But that didn't make him an abductor. A possible murderer.

He used to do these silly tricks, like making coins rain out of my nose at Sunday dinner, she thought, and the memory made her angry.

Dufort and Maron had gone to find Lapin, and Thérèse was left at the station with nothing to do but sit by a phone that rarely rang.

I'm going out to Degas, she thought. If I had to pick someone guilty here, it would be that blowhard of an art professor, Gallimard. Let's see what the students have to say about him.

She had no police vehicle to take, and since this plan of hers was not directed by Dufort in any case, she figured she was better off on foot. She could always say she was out looking for Madame Bonnay's dog, who was still missing.

As she set off, Thérèse made a list of questions about the case in her head.

Why did Nico take so long getting us a copy of that video? Was he protecting Lapin? Does he know something?

For a moment, she considered stopping off at Chez Papa to interview him, but thought rightly that she shouldn't take that step without talking to Dufort first. He might want to question Nico himself.

Thérèse had struggled in school and in office jobs because she had real difficulty following the rules. The gendarmerie, of course, had even more rules—of protocol, of procedure—but the work was so meaningful to her that she had managed to stay in line so far.

And now that the pressure was on, she was determined not to get carried away by her own ideas and stick to doing what she was supposed to do. Probably hanging around Degas wasn't Dufort's idea of sticking to the rules, but she didn't think it would be enough to get her in real trouble. Hell, maybe Lapin would be able to tell Dufort something useful, if he had been with Amy so late in the evening.

Had Amy really left with him *voluntarily?*

Well, at least from the tape, it looked like she had. She hadn't appeared to be struggling or resisting or anything at all like that. Just walking calmly, if a little woozily, out of the door of Chez Papa, with Lapin's arm firmly around her waist.

Thérèse loved Lapin, sort of. Or at least, she loved the fact that he was a village institution, a presence she was used to. He had been a fixture at many of those Sunday family dinners since her mother had taken pity on the "poor orphan" and invited him countless times, even though he was a grown man. But still—to *leave* with him? A young woman Amy's age? It didn't make any sense.

Thérèse thought about it for a good stretch of the walk to Degas, and she could not remember any woman ever leaving with Lapin. Because let's face it, he may be a semi-beloved village character, but he's an unattractive boor when he's trying to seduce someone.

If he's even trying to. Thérèse had always had the feeling it was all a bit of a show, not meant for anyone to take seriously. She certainly hadn't.

It was nearing noon when she turned into the driveway to L'Institut Degas. It was a little chilly, but a few students were outside with sketchbooks. She wondered whether there was any sort of food service on campus, or whether they had to troop into Castillac for all their meals.

Deciding to start by going into the modern building that looked oddly like a sea creature, she started down the path heading to it, when out of the corner of her eye she saw Dufort leaving the older building on an adjacent side of the commons. He was walking with a woman Thérèse did not know. She wasn't sure, but something told her Dufort was not, at that moment, working.

So had he and Maron found Lapin? Was Lapin in custody?

More than anything, Thérèse wanted to rush over and ask those questions along with about ten others that popped into her head, but she was learning to hold back, difficult as it was.

Dufort did not see her. She watched them get into his car, saw Dufort smile in an especially warm way she had not seen him smile before, and that answered at least one of the ten questions.

The door to the sea-creature building was locked, so she

headed over to a group of students talking on the commons, wishing she were not wearing her dorky gendarme's uniform, and mentally rubbing her hands together at the prospect of digging up some dirt on Gallimard.

❧

THIS REALLY SHOULDN'T BE a big deal, Molly was thinking, sitting out on the terrace in the chilly morning, drinking her second cup of coffee. Okay, so the Bennetts don't want to leave the cottage—that's their business. If I can't get in there to clean, that's also their business. I can't go busting in there and tell them what to do, they're paid up and not bothering anyone. And really, a clean floor doesn't matter much in the grand scheme of things. Or even at all.

They must be thinking...what does *anything* matter, anything at all, in the face of their daughter missing, precious as all daughters are.

Of course I don't know, having no daughter myself. But it's not hard to imagine, is it, she thought, throwing back the last of her cup and feeling a surge of determination, having just come up with what she thought might be an excellent idea.

I will hire someone to clean the cottage while the Bennetts are here. Can't afford it long-term, not yet, but at least if someone else did it now, just while they're here, I can take that load of worry off.

It feels to me like there's this aura of fear around them, and I get the wobbles when I step close.

I'm a horrible person, really. Complaining about my feelings when it's not even my tragedy.

Thinking that perhaps her neighbor might know of someone she could hire temporarily, Molly got dressed and brushed her wild hair, even trying (and failing) to tie a scarf around her neck in the French way.

It was nine in the morning, a time when Molly often saw Madame Sabourin in her garden, but that morning she didn't see her, so she walked around to the road and came down the stone path to her front door and gave it a hard rap.

Please let my French be adequate, she prayed to the gods of language. I'm not asking for fluency, just let me be understood and not completely humiliate myself. That's all I ask.

Her neighbor answered the door dressed in a dusty housecoat, her hair covered by a scarf.

"Bonjour, Madame Sabourin!" said Molly, a bit too heartily. "Excuse me for making you bother, but I looked for a girl who cleans?"

"Ah," said Madame Sabourin. "Come in, Madame Sutton. Can I offer you a coffee? I am cleaning the house myself at the moment, as you can see." She gestured first to her clothing and then to a bucket and mop leaning against the wall of the foyer.

"Yes," said Molly, grinning because she understood. "Thank you but no coffee anymore." She looked into her neighbor's kindly face, thinking how beautiful she was with her wrinkles and bright brown eyes. Something so warm about her, so solid in her life, with its regular chores and no doubt regular meals.

Molly was struck suddenly by the desire to confess what she was up to.

"You know the Bennetts? The parents of the girl who is gone? They are here, in my cottage," she began, and Madame Sabourin nodded encouragingly. "And I do not understand myself, but...I am fearful with them, do you know this?"

"They make you nervous? Because they are so deeply upset?"

Yes, that is it," said Molly, relieved. "And I would be easy if a girl came and cleaned the cottage now. Not after the Bennetts, but during the Bennetts."

"I understand," said Madame Sabourin with a small smile. "I'm trying to think...but I'm afraid no one is occurring to me at the moment. I will consider it, though, and let you know if I come up with anyone."

Molly nodded. "Thank you," she said, feeling pressure to say more, but not able to find the words. "Thank you," she said again. "I will go now," she added awkwardly. "See you later!"

Perhaps Nico will know someone, she thought, and went straight down rue des Chênes to Chez Papa, although she had no idea whether it would be open so early in the morning.

She pulled her sweater tight as she walked, feeling the chill in the air and wishing she'd worn a coat. Glancing at gardens along the way, she saw that there had not been a frost the night before, but she bet it had been close. The village felt half asleep, as though with the cold air everyone had decided to take a few extra hours in bed where it was warm and safe, before venturing out to begin the day.

Chez Papa was indeed closed, and Molly could see no one inside when she peered through the window.

Now what?

Well, perhaps she might as well go by Pâtisserie Bujold since she was practically next door anyway. Croissant *aux amandes*? Yes, definitely. And she would pick some up for the Bennetts while she was at it. Of course it was always a trial going there, with the lecherous proprietor to contend with. Worth it, for pastry.

But then, almost anything would be worth it for pastry.

MOLLY HAD NOT BEEN able to resist the duck legs at the market, and she was braising six of them for lunch. After several hours in a low oven, the carrots, onions, celery and tomatoes had made the most delicious, unctuous sauce imaginable, and the duck meat was falling off the bone.

No one could possibly resist this, she thought, first inhaling the scent of rosemary and onion, and then arranging two legs per plate along with a big spoonful of the thick sauce, and a small heap of rice on the side.

Tentatively, she walked over to the cottage with the tray.

I'm probably making a real annoyance of myself, plying them with food all the time. Or maybe they're grateful because even though I understand some people do not eat when they're upset (strange creatures, if you ask me) even so, you can't keep that up for days on end. You just can't.

She set the tray down and knocked, bracing herself against the turmoil and fear that she felt swirling around the cottage, determined to press on regardless.

"Hello!" she called out. "I'm sorry to bother you, but please answer!"

Quickly (had he been watching her approach?), Mr. Bennett opened the door.

"Are we behind in payment?" he asked. His face was pale and drawn, and his eyes glassy.

"No, no, nothing like that," said Molly. She stooped and picked up the tray. "It's just that I've brought lunch. May I come in? I won't stay."

Marshall Bennett paused, a too-long pause, and finally opened the door wider.

Sally Bennett was sitting on the sofa, perched on its edge like a sparrow on a branch. She turned her head toward Molly but did not change her expression, which—Molly was not sure how she would describe it—it looked like her face had fallen in on itself somehow, as though the bones and cartilage had turned soft, or melted.

"I'm sorry to intrude," Molly said softly. "But I'll be honest, I'm worried about you. You don't know anyone here, you've got no support, and...well, you need help. It's far, far too much to try to deal with something like this all by yourselves."

Well, that was more than she had planned to say. So much for keeping it light.

She placed the tray on the round dining table. "I made some

braised duck. I'm sure eating is not the first thing on your minds, but I'll tell you, when I've gone through some bad times, a good hearty meal often gave me the strength to keep going."

Okay, now she sounded like a TV ad or someone's over-zealous grandmother. "I don't mean to be pushy," she added.

The Bennetts just looked at her, blinking slowly. Molly had the clear idea that they were on tranquilizers.

Who could blame them? Molly had thought a few times after the news about Amy broke that she wouldn't say no to a handful of them either.

"Well, maybe I *do* mean to be pushy," she added. "Come on then, have a seat. I'll get some napkins and forks. The duck is so soft I don't believe you'll even need knives."

She almost went to get a bottle of wine but then thought mixing that with tranqs was a bad idea, so she filled two glasses with water and set them next to the plates.

The Bennetts had taken places at the dining table and were staring dully ahead, eyes unfocused.

"All right then," said Molly. "Pick up your forks, stab a bit of meat, and onward!"

Ridiculous, talking to them like that, but the Bennetts appeared to need that level of instruction. Fleetingly, Molly wondered if they were taking something other than tranquilizers and were actually drug addicts of some sort, and out of it like this even before their daughter went missing.

No, that isn't it. It's got to be grief plus a bit of understandable self-medication.

"Have you had any contact with the police?" *Might as well dive all the way in, now that I'm this far.*

Marshall shook his head slightly. Sally picked up a fork and looked at it like she wasn't sure what it was for.

"Well, I can understand not wanting to start down that road, I absolutely can. But I've met Benjamin Dufort, the chief of police.

He's quite a nice man, and intelligent, from what I could tell. Not cold, or anything like that."

Marshall blinked at her. Sally seemed to wake up a little, and ate a tiny forkful of sauce with a bit of rice.

I should never have left them alone this long, Molly thought, trying to hold back a crashing wave of guilt.

"Come on, Marshall," she urged. "Eat!"

The Bennetts began to use their forks, lifting food to their mouths and chewing it, but the effect was something like watching a display of automatons, circa 1910. They were so disconnected from the present that it felt spooky and lonely to be with them. Molly began to feel their fear again, and her knees got shaky.

"Well, I'm glad you've been eating something at least," Molly said, gesturing to a bag of McVitie's Digestive Biscuits and another of horrible-sounding salty licorice on the table.

"Oh no," said Sally, her voice sounding far distant, like she was down in a basement instead of five feet away, "Those are for Amy. We brought them for her. Her favorites." Sally's voice cracked and she covered her face with her hands.

"How about this," Molly said, wanting to change the subject. "I could be a sort of go-between, if you like. I can understand how the logistics of any of this, and talking to strangers, especially in another language— would be overwhelming. So I would be happy to call up Dufort and make an appointment for him to see you. I have no doubt he'd *like* to see you."

There was another long pause, longer than people under normal circumstances would allow. Finally Marshall spoke. "All right," he said. He did not make eye contact, but looked at the closed door, as though he were expecting someone.

Molly wondered if the Bennetts spoke any French, but she didn't want to ask. Getting them to eat a few mouthfuls was enough progress for one visit.

"All right then," she said, heading gratefully for the door. "I'll call Dufort. And I'll just text you with the time, if that's all right, so I won't have to bother you again. And we'll go together."

The Bennetts made no sign of hearing her but she stumbled outside anyway closing the door firmly behind her, and feeling terrible for wanting so badly to get away from them.

21

Molly was up early the next morning, unable to do anything but wait for the Bennetts' appointment with Dufort at nine. She wandered around the garden, looking at how the night's frost had changed the way everything looked: every leaf, every stalk, every withered blossom was brushed with white. There was no more clinging to the idea of summer, not anymore.

She tried to tell herself it was beautiful. She knew—objectively and subjectively—it *was* beautiful, the way the almost infinite number of colors were all variations of green and brown, and even the way the frost was melting in the path of the sun.

But to Molly, it just looked like death. She was not a lover of fall.

Finally she decided to walk quickly to the village and back, so that she could give the Bennetts some croissants before it was time to go to the station. They probably wouldn't want to eat anything, but at least on the off chance they had any appetite, she could offer something fresh and tasty.

And more than that, at least they would feel like someone was looking out for them, even if only for breakfast.

Molly went quickly down the rue des Chênes after only one

cup of coffee. It was cold and her breath sailed out in plumes, catching the sun. A deep breath before entering Pâtisserie Bujold, which opened at six.

"Bonjour, monsieur," she said.

"Your accent, madame—it gets better every day," said the proprietor, staring as usual at her chest.

Molly gave a curt nod and asked for four croissants and three croissants *aux amandes*.

Well, she was feeling peckish, what with everything so unsettled.

On the walk back, her mind zigzagged back and forth from empathizing with the Bennetts to feeling anxious about the fact that the person who had taken their daughter was still loose. With a sudden stab she wondered if she should even be out walking alone, when it was so early hardly anyone was around?

How was it possible for this man—for certainly it *was* a man, assuming the world hadn't turned completely upside down—to continue to abduct women from this small village and not be caught? She was very much looking forward to hearing whether Dufort had made any progress on the case and she hoped he would be forthcoming.

At 8:30 she called Vincent and asked him to come give the Bennetts and her a ride into the village. It was a short walk, not even twenty minutes, but Molly figured bundling them into Vincent's taxi would be a lot easier than herding them down rue des Chênes. She imagined they might stop in the road and inexplicably refuse to walk, or wander off down side streets. The Bennetts, as far as she could tell, were not firmly attached to reality, and who could blame them?

After making the call, she took a tray over to the cottage with coffee and the warm croissants. She was surprised to find the couple dressed and ready to go.

"Past time to get this over with," said Marshall, pouring himself a cup of coffee.

"Maybe he has some good news?" Molly said, and then wanted to bite her tongue off. Her words of hope sounded so false to everyone; the Bennetts had the grace to ignore them.

Sally nibbled at a plain croissant while Molly ate one plain and one with almonds. She closed her eyes as her teeth broke through the outer crispy layers and into the sweet almondy softness inside. She managed to stop herself from groaning, it tasted so good, the perfect counterpoint to the bitterness of the black coffee.

All three of them looked up at the sound of a car pulling into the driveway. "That would be Vincent. I thought it would make things easier—and it's quite chilly too—"

The Bennetts took a last sip of their coffee and slowly put on their coats. Their movements, their expressions, everything about their demeanor suggested they were preparing to go to the guillotine, as though Vincent were arriving with their tumbrel.

"Good mornings to all!" said Vincent amiably, opening one of the back doors to his somewhat crumpled Peugeot.

The Bennetts said nothing but got into the car, and Vincent backed around and headed for the village.

"Please excuse the whorehouse," he said, turning back to look at them and alarming Molly who would rather his eyes stay on the road.

A long silence while the three English speakers tried to make sense of what he said.

"Oh!" said Molly. "He means the mess. '*Bordel*'—it means whorehouse, but also disorder, a big mess. Am I right, Vincent?"

Vincent turned around again and smiled. "Yes, madame," he said. "I am pleased for the opportunity to speak English, and I thank you."

"*Pas de problème*," said Molly. She pushed some of the food wrappers on the floor under the seat in a vain attempt to neaten up for the Bennetts, though she guessed they hardly cared. Marshall and Sally looked out of the car window, their eyes unfocused, not saying a thing.

Maron showed up at Chez Papa well after lunch, hoping to catch Nico when bar business was slow. The restaurant was empty and Nico was leaning up against the bar reading a tattered paperback.

"Bonjour, Nico," said Maron, sliding onto a stool.

Nico startled but tried to pretend he hadn't, just as someone who's been woken up will pretend he was not asleep, even though no one is ever fooled.

"Bonjour, Gilles. I'm afraid the kitchen is closed," said Nico. "Would you like something to drink?"

"Petit café."

"Certainly." Nico turned to the espresso machine and began the process. Maron saw him take a deep breath. "So," said Nico, his voice not altogether natural, "any news about that girl, the art student?"

"We have not found her," said Maron slowly, rather enjoying the idea of toying with Nico a bit. Nico was too handsome for his own good, was Maron's opinion, though he understood there was nothing specifically criminal about that. "But I suppose you looked at the video before we did? So you saw what we saw, yes?"

Nico's face flushed. "Yes," he admitted. "I saw her."

"With Lapin."

"Yes."

Maron wondered why Nico looked so guilty. It was almost as though the video had shown him leaving with Amy, not Lapin.

"Listen, Gilles—I know how it looks, I saw her leave with Lapin that night and I don't mean only on the video. But I don't for one minute think—I mean, come on, we've known him all our lives, here in the village. Don't you think we'd have known long before now if he were that twisted?"

"Not necessarily," said Maron, spinning slightly on his stool. "There've been numerous cases of people getting away with all kinds of heinous crimes for years, right under the noses of their families and neighbors. I don't know why Lapin should be automatically excluded from that group. But of course," he added, "I am not from the village. Perhaps I see him a bit more clearly than the rest of you. Without benefit of nostalgia."

"He paws at all the women, sure. He's obnoxious. But he wasn't even doing that to Amy that night. He just got caught up in this big group, all celebrating some prize she won. You know how it can be—a burst of excitement, it's like a match on gasoline or something, and suddenly the whole bar is whooping it up. I honestly don't think for one second he did anything to her."

Maron looked at Nico and cocked his head, but said nothing.

"What does Dufort think?" Nico asked.

Maron did not answer. He found silence put people off balance and was more productive in getting them to say things they might not have otherwise. The truth was that he didn't believe with any certainty that Lapin had something directly to do with Amy's disappearance. In Maron's mind, the perpetrator field was wide open, though so far, Lapin was the clear leader by default. And he still had not managed to find out about what Dufort called "the other incident," when Lapin had done *something*, but apparently not been formally arrested.

"Dufort has not forgotten the previous incident," said Maron, imagining his words as a juicy bit of wriggling shrimp on a fishhook that he was casting over to Nico.

With a satisfying splash, the fish hit the bait.

"Oh, that wasn't anything, not really," said Nico. "Lapin is like a child in some ways, you understand. Yes, he'd bought himself some fancy camera on the internet and was trying to take some snaps up women's skirts. Of course he was caught right off the bat. You've got to be a little sorry for him, is how I feel, you know?"

Maron shrugged, feeling resentful that Dufort hadn't just told him the story when they first saw the incriminating video. "Is that how you'd feel if it were your skirts he was peering under?"

Nico blushed and looked away, shaking his head.

"I'd be interested to understand why you dragged your feet about getting the video to us," said Maron, trying and failing to sound easy-going. He knew that his manner tended to make people defensive.

Nico looked uncomfortable, almost as though he were going to cry.

"Were you really only protecting Lapin? Or someone else?"

Nico shook his head. "No, it's not like that. It's just...I feel so guilty. I served her too many drinks. I knew she was drunk, I should have stopped her. And then...then maybe she wouldn't have...."

Maron did not speak. He felt a wave of sudden disappointment, as though Nico were a horse he'd placed a bet on and lost his money. It would be so satisfying to haul that handsome face into jail. And so very annoying that Nico had an understandable, even a moral reason for being so slow with the video.

Nico finished fiddling with the machine and put a cup of espresso in front of Maron and stepped back. "Well, if you're interested," he said quietly, "there is...there is someone else I'd be looking into, if I were you."

Maron sipped his espresso and waited.

"You know about Gallimard?" asked Nico.

"The art professor? What about him?"

"Well, he doesn't come in here," said Nico. "It's too crowded with people who might know him. But I have a friend who works at a bar outside the next village, sort of an out-of-the-way place, you understand. And he told me Gallimard comes in there all the time, with all sorts of women. Young. Students, most of the time. They leave totally shit-faced."

Maron was interested but kept his expression impassive. "So you're suggesting...what?"

"That he's sleeping with half the student body at Degas," said Nico, his voice barely above a whisper. "Don't you think...?"

Maron shrugged. "I'll look into it," he said, acting as though doing so would be a tedious chore unlikely to make any difference at all. "But I don't see what a few affairs has to do with a girl disappearing."

Nico's voice rose. "No? You don't see how jealousies, ambitions, alcohol, and sex can come together to make an explosion?"

Maron shrugged. "Like I said, I'll look into it. The question then would be at what point did Amy leave Lapin and end up with Gallimard? Because so far, the last person to see Amy alive was Lapin Broussard. Right after you, that is."

Nico recoiled, his face flushing again. Maron noticed that the blush made him look more handsome, and he forced himself to smile after he tossed back his espresso and said his goodbyes.

22

The Bennetts climbed out of Vincent's taxi as though underwater, their limbs under pressure. They moved so slowly that Molly's impatience surged, and she wondered if they would ever get all the way out and close the door. Quickly she paid Vincent and went up the steps to the station, feeling all the anxiety the Bennetts had displaced with tranquilizers as though it had been deflected off them and leapt onto her.

Chief Dufort was just inside the door.

"Mr. and Mrs. Bennett? Chief Benjamin Dufort. I am pleased to make your acquaintance," he said, shaking Marshall's limp hand. He turned to Molly, "And thank you for this help taking the parents of Amy here," he said, and then winced. Turning back to the Bennetts he gestured to his office, then back to Molly. "By any chance do you have some extra minutes? My English..." he shrugged and shook his head.

"You want *me* to help translate?" said Molly, stunned that anyone could think her rudimentary language skills were useful. "Chief, I'd like to help, but really, my French is *absolument* worse than your English, believe me."

But he looked at her so imploringly, and he was quite good-looking, there was no dodging that. "All right," she heard herself saying. "I'll try." And so Molly unexpectedly found herself in Dufort's office for the first meeting of the chief with the parents of the missing girl.

"Thank you for seeing us," said Marshall. He at least seemed to be awake, if a little shaky. Sally Bennett looked as though she might doze off at any moment. Molly added concern about an overdose to her long list of worries about the Bennetts.

"Thank you very much for coming," said Dufort. "I wish deeply that the circumstances of our meeting were easier."

He continued with various reassuring words, and to her surprise, Molly found that she understood Dufort quite well, and she managed to get what he was saying across to the Bennetts, if rather clumsily and imprecise.

There was little news. Several times Chief Dufort told them that the Castillac force was doing all it could to find their daughter, and he detailed some of the things they were doing to accomplish this—the phone calls to airports, that kind of thing—but he stayed well clear of giving them the idea that they were, at this juncture, looking for a body, even though in fact, that was a critical part of the investigation. It was the job of police to cover all the bases and so that is what they were doing, with rigor and attention, no matter the anxieties it might provoke, but Dufort saw no need to alarm the Bennetts further, when their distress proved they already suspected the worst.

Once Molly got over her panic at having to translate—which made it easier than she would ever have imagined—she was excited to be there in the middle of everything, then disappointed that Dufort was either absolutely nowhere on the case or not telling any details.

Handsome men are so often slow-witted, she thought, but I don't think that's the case with the chief. He has a smart look about him, but skittery. A little nervous. Is it because he knows more than he's telling? Or because that's simply his way?

"Yes, she has had boyfriends, but none serious," Marshall was saying. "Art was everything to her, you understand. She wasn't going to allow a boy to get in the way of her success."

"That worried me," Sally said, her voice barely above a whisper.

"How so?" asked Dufort.

"Well," said Sally, but then paused, and the pause went on and on.

Molly stood on the balls on her feet as though she were playing tennis, waiting for Sally's next words so she could hit them softly over the net to Dufort if he gave her the signal she needed to translate. But Sally did not continue.

"It's that...Sally has always thought that perhaps Amy's single-minded pursuit of a career in art might end up making her unhappy," explained Marshall.

"Alone," added Sally. "It's not like a painting is going to love you back, even if it's a masterpiece."

Everyone in the room considered that statement. And then Sally let out a heartrending wail, because the clear image of her daughter spending her last moments with someone who did not love her was so painful that her tenuous self-control evaporated. She wobbled, and Marshall reached his arm around her to hold her up.

"I do understand," said Dufort, feeling the parents' agony acutely.

Molly wondered if he was married and had children. Although it probably made no difference—it's not like it took a huge leap of imagination for her to understand the Bennetts' pain. She guessed anyone in that room felt it deep in their bodies, as she did, fighting back tears and her legs none too steady. She glanced at Dufort and saw that his handsome face was pale and his lips were pressed tightly together.

"Molly, can you make sure the Bennetts get back to your place all right?" he asked.

She nodded, her throat still closed up.

"Please," said Sally, reaching a hand out to Dufort.

"We're doing everything we can," he said, his voice cracking. "Everything."

❧

MOLLY'S NEIGHBOR Madame Sabourin had found her a cleaning girl, although she made no particular recommendation as to her skill. The girl was the daughter of the man who repaired furniture in a little shop on a back street of the village, and Madame Sabourin talked at length about the armoire he had fixed up for her: he hadn't charged too much and his workmanship had been more than adequate, especially on a tricky bit where the lacquer was worn.

So after a deeply awkward phone conversation during which Molly struggled to get out even a few words of understandable French (she found it ridiculously difficult to speak French over the phone, and all her progress seemed to evaporate on the spot), Constance agreed to come that very day. Molly wasn't particular; all she wanted was a body. Anyone can run a vacuum cleaner, right?

With some trepidation, she knocked on the door to the cottage to alert the Bennetts that the cleaner was coming that afternoon. Perhaps they wouldn't mind sitting in the garden or going for a walk while their place was spiffed up? And would they like anything from the village? Molly was going to catch the tail end of the Saturday market.

The Bennetts were amenable, as they always were, untethered to any reality beyond their missing daughter. Molly wasn't absolutely sure they understood about the cleaner—they appeared even more tranqued up than before, even Marshall—but she took them at their word, waved, and headed into the village with her market basket over her arm. She wished for tomatoes but saw none she liked, and hoped she would come home with something besides lavender soap. And croissants *aux amandes*.

The first person she saw when she got to the Place was Manette, reigning over her beautifully arranged harvest like a queen of légumes.

"Bonjour, Manette," said Molly, a little shyly, unsure whether Manette would remember her.

"Hello, Molly!" Manette cried, her English accent so wrong that Molly burst out laughing. "Tell me," she said, continuing in French, "Have you figured out where Amy has gone?"

"Me?" said Molly. "Oh no. I'm not...that's not my line, I don't think. Because..." she cocked her head and looked up to the sky. "How can you guess what people will do, when we're all of us capable of anything?"

Manette nodded solemnly. Molly didn't know what it was about her that brought on these fits of philosophy.

"It is true," said Manette, "that people lie. About anything! And to ourselves most of all. Now look," she said, gesturing to a heap of artichokes. "They're imported, I won't lie to you,"—she winked—"but see how beautiful they are? A bit of butter sauce, just a squeeze of lemon?"

"I'll take five," said Molly, and waited for Manette to weigh them. "Do you have children, Manette? I'm sorry if that is too personal a question."

Manette waved off her apology. "No, no. Yes, I have four! I'm in the center of chaos! The eye of the hurricane!"

Molly smiled. It was so easy to picture, rosy-cheeked Manette laughing in her kitchen with children everywhere. She felt a stab of envy and forced herself to keep smiling anyway.

Then she went to find that attractive organic farmer Rémy,

hoping for some tomatoes. He had none, but she talked with him for about fifteen minutes about the weather and then about Lapin Broussard. His English was extremely good, and she relaxed into speaking English herself.

"I'm not sure I give intuition any weight," she said, "but honestly, Lapin is incredibly annoying, and I've considered moving to another village to escape him—but a *killer*? Or at the least, a kidnapper? I just don't get that from him."

"My wife slapped him once, at Chez Papa. Right across the face. He stopped bothering her after that," Rémy laughed.

Molly took a quick breath. She had been flirting a little with Rémy—he had a sort of hippie farmer appeal, broad-shouldered and capable, with a smudge of dirt on his chin—and now felt embarrassed that he was married.

"My ex-wife, I should say," said Rémy, with a smile, as though reading her mind.

Molly smiled back. And although all in all she was finished with that part of her life, and she was more suited to a single life, she really was...her next thought was about how lovely his smile was, and his mouth, and how if at some point in the future he wanted to kiss her, she wouldn't say no.

And then he had been saying something and she had missed it entirely with her daydream of kissing.

What, am I fifteen?

"So sadly you must wait until next July for real tomatoes," Rémy was saying. And then a last-minute crowd of customers surged up behind her, and it was time to go home to La Baraque.

She went straight to the cottage to see how far along Constance had gotten, sure that the Bennetts would be anxious to get back inside as soon as possible.

"Constance!" she called, seeing a bucket filled with dirty water and a mop leaning against the wall. Molly walked into the tiny kitchen and saw a pile of dustrags on the counter. "Hello? Constance?"

But Constance was gone. The cottage was not particularly clean, and the implements of cleaning were scattered upstairs and down, so that Molly spent her last ounces of energy straightening up after her cleaner so that the Bennetts could leave the garden and go back into seclusion.

23

This was a terrible idea, thought Dufort as he tried to straighten up his living room on Sunday evening. He had invited Marie-Claire over for an *apéro*, forgetting that the Bennett case had thrown him off his usual routines, and his small apartment in the gendarmerie was not really tidy enough for company—especially for company he was hoping to impress. Quickly he tossed back ten drops of tincture and dashed around the living room, neatening and straightening, shoving things under the sofa and into drawers.

Marie-Claire drove up in her ancient *deux chevaux*. Dufort watched her check her makeup in the rearview mirror, which made him smile. He went to the kitchen and took out a bottle of pineau and then out the door to welcome her.

"Bonsoir!" he said, very glad to see her. She was wearing pants, which Dufort was sorry about because he liked to have a look at her legs. But the pants were snug and showed off her fit body, and he grinned like a schoolboy as she walked toward him.

"Bonsoir, Ben," she said, smiling back. They kissed cheeks, Ben noticing how nice she smelled, and headed inside.

"I've never been inside the gendarmerie before," said Marie-

Claire, looking all around. "It's not bad, is it? Do you mind being moved around from place to place?"

"If I had my way, I'd stay in Castillac indefinitely. I'll probably be off to a new posting sometime in early January. It's not that I don't like new places...more that I'm just attached to this one. When I am away from the golden stone for too long..." He looked up suddenly and smiled. "How about a drink? Would you like a kir? Pineau?"

Marie-Claire nodded. "A kir would be lovely." She looked around, trying to see what she could learn about Ben from his place. It was neat enough. One pile of books was on a side table and another pile next to the sofa. She tried to peer into the kitchen without being obvious about it.

"Perhaps a thoroughly unsurprising question, but you know we detectives have to cover the background," said Dufort, handing Marie-Claire her drink. "I don't think you've told me where you grew up and how you managed to end up in Castillac."

Marie-Claire smiled and sipped. "An unsurprising question with an unsurprising answer," she said. "And I will ask the same: you are Castillac born and raised, I take it?"

Dufort nodded.

"Seems to be the case for most of the village. I've been here close to two years now, and not sorry at all I came," said Marie-Claire.

Dufort noticed, of course, that she did not answer either of his questions.

"So Ben, forgive me—I should not ask about your work. It's the height of rudeness, and ordinarily..."

Dufort sighed inwardly. "Amy."

"Yes. Amy." She looked at him hopefully. "Any news at all? Of course I understand if there are things you can't tell me, but I just...I just want something...."

Dufort opened a packet of nuts and shook them into a glass bowl. "We're still collecting evidence." Inwardly he cringed at that little lie, since there had been precious little evidence—actually, zero—to collect.

"And Lapin? Have you interviewed him, if that's what you call it?"

"No. We don't know where he is. And we've not narrowed it down to him, in any case. Just someone we want to talk to."

"Is it difficult to be objective, since he's your friend?"

Dufort swallowed a sip of his drink. Marie-Claire was making him uncomfortable; it felt almost as though she had agreed to come for a drink just so she could get the latest gossip. Or was he being overly cynical?

"I wouldn't say friend, not exactly," said Dufort. "I've known him all my life, like a lot of people here. He's...I guess you would say he's a fixture of the village. A pain sometimes, especially to women...."

Marie-Claire nodded. "Apparently I am not his type—I don't think he's ever given me a second look."

"Hard to believe," said Dufort with a hint of a smile, which Marie-Claire found very charming. "In any case, fixture of the village or not, we have to look at the evidence, obviously. The fact that we've not been able to find Lapin to question him, that is actually more worrisome than the video itself."

"If he had a good explanation, then why not march into the station and give it?"

"Right," Dufort nodded. "But not everyone is capable of that sort of practical directness, taking an action that might seem obvious to you or me."

"But I think...excuse me if I'm coming too...close in. But I get the feeling from you that you do not believe Lapin took that girl. That you will go down the list and ask the questions, etc. and etc. But your intuition says no."

Dufort shrugged, smiling again. He liked this woman. Liked that she said what was on her mind, and that she obviously had some decent intuition herself. When she reached for her drink, he let his eyes roam over her for just a moment, and when she put her glass back down, he touched her cheek with the back of his hand, then put a lock of hair behind her ear. The movement felt impossibly intimate and he took a deep breath and stood up.

"It's gotten so chilly, I thought I would light a fire," he said, rummaging in a drawer for some matches. He was grateful for the old building, which still had fireplaces in most of the rooms.

Marie-Claire hugged herself and shivered. "It is rather damp," she said, watching him with an animated expression. The fire he had set earlier caught beautifully, and the couple sat on the sofa next to each other gazing at the flames. They had another drink, they ate some nuts, and soon enough they were sitting close enough to touch, and then close enough to kiss, and at least for a precious few hours, Benjamin Dufort did not think about Amy Bennett even once.

THAT NIGHT MOLLY did not go out. The interview with Chief Dufort and the Bennetts had been absolutely harrowing, and then on top of that, her new fiasco of a cleaner. So she worked in the garden with headphones on, then drank half a bottle of Médoc and went to bed early. The next morning, she decided to go on a long walk using one of the maps of trails she had found at the *Presse*. It was one more thing to love about France, how apparently landowners large and small not only allowed perfect strangers to go traipsing across their property, but encouraged them to do so by allowing the trails to be marked on very detailed maps found at any *presse*.

She chose a route that would take her through the forest, then across several pastures, and loop back around to rue des Chênes and home. It will take hours, she thought, and I'll come home so beat I won't have any energy to worry.

It did occur to her that being alone in secluded places might not be completely safe with an abductor on the loose, so she took along a canister of mace she'd managed to get past security at the airport—a holdover from the old neighborhood back home. It had given her a real sense of safety then, even though she'd never actually pulled the trigger. But anyway, surely whoever took Amy —and the others, she thought with a shiver—wasn't roaming around the forest. Probably not where you'd go on the prowl for young women.

Part of her brain knew that she was rationalizing, which is likely a mistake when you're trying to guess what a murderer might or might not do. But the other part trampled all over those objections and she set off anyway. And there is always hope there has been no murder, the rationalizing part whispered.

The first section of the walk was down rue des Chênes, away from the village, but she had walked that way before and so it did not offer enough distraction to keep her from obsessing about the Bennetts and about Amy.

I wonder if the Bennetts *know*, she wondered. Is there a particular sixth sense parents have, so if their child is dead they can feel it?

I sort of bet there is. And that's why Sally is so undone.

Molly consulted the map and found the path off the road to the left without trouble. It was wide enough for a car, and in minutes, she felt as though she were miles and miles from civilization. Except for the path, there was no mark of humanity in any direction, and she was far enough from the village that there was no human sound either, nothing but the chatter of birds and the rustle of branches in the light breeze.

It wasn't until the first twinge of hunger hit that she realized she had left her lunch behind. A neatly packed lunch that included a very nice cheese and a water bottle filled with ice—sitting on the kitchen table. She considered turning around but thought she would lose any sense of accomplishment, even though she knew that was silly. But it did feel good to exert herself, and to be outdoors, far from gendarmes and the Bennetts and poorly done housework. No duties save putting one foot in front of the other.

The path turned and went around a hillock, then came out into a small pasture. Molly was increasingly aware of the sound of her footsteps and her breath (a little labored as that last part had been uphill). It was lonely where she was, the trees in the midst of shedding their brown leaves, the sky low and gray.

If someone wanted to find a private place to do something bad, this would do pretty well, she thought, stopping to catch her breath. No houses in view, no roads. There's not even any livestock to watch what you're doing...just woods and pasture, empty of everything but the odd vole.

Suddenly she felt a kind of chill. An emotional chill, as though her body sensed something wrong though she could not consciously see what it was. She turned to look behind her, wondering if someone was coming.

There was no one.

She was alone on the edge of the woods, and as far as she could tell, there was no one for miles, or close to it. Nevertheless she felt endangered somehow, as though there were something lurking in those woods, something she could not see but could sense, and its presence was large and dark and not going to back off just because of a little canister of mace on her keyring.

Her fear was absurd and she felt foolish. Molly jogged back the way she had come, running away from all the feelings, all the way down the path to where it popped out on rue des Chênes, trying hard to focus on the lunch that was waiting for her, and not give in to the impulse to look behind her, into the dark woods.

24

It was Gilles Maron who found him. As well as checking several times during the day, Maron had been driving by the Broussard house at least once or twice every night since seeing the incriminating video. Finally, on Monday night, eleven days after Amy Bennett had disappeared, he saw a small light on in the kitchen, barely visible from the road.

Lapin did not run when Maron came in the back door. And he did not protest when Maron packed him into his car and then into the small cell at the station and locked him up, although there was not nearly enough evidence to justify doing so.

"We're going to want a DNA sample," Maron said roughly, handing Lapin a blanket that did not smell fresh.

Lapin merely nodded. His head drooped as though something had gone wrong with his neck. His eyes were glassy.

"So what did you do with her?" Maron asked. He had alerted Dufort but hoped to get something out of Broussard before the chief got there.

Broussard did not answer. He just shook his head, pulled the blanket over his lap, and leaned his big body against the wall, his eyes on the floor.

❧

"WELL, what I heard is that he gave them a DNA sample. Doesn't even have a lawyer." Molly sipped her kir and put her elbows on the bar at Chez Papa, her voice low despite the noise of the bar.

"Disappointing in a way, isn't it? DNA has taken all the fun out of detective work."

"Lawrence!"

"Oh, you know I'm kidding. At this point, what good is a DNA sample going to do anyway? What do they have to match it with?"

"I'm sorry to say it, but no one else is saying it: they've got to find the body."

Lawrence nodded. "You've clearly watched far too much *Law & Order*, but...I'm afraid you're right. Doubtless Dufort is looking. He has never struck me as a man who shies away from...from what needs to be done."

"But what about the other cases? You don't think...I mean, *two* other women have disappeared, right? Cases unsolved? Yes, Dufort seems like a good guy when you talk to him. But he's not exactly got a winning record."

"No," said Lawrence, taking a long pull on his Negroni. "He does not. Though I'm not sure you can look at the situation like it's a baseball season or something. Maybe this person he's up against is more devious and smarter than the rest of us, Dufort included. Maybe more evil that we can comprehend."

"Or lucky."

"Could be that too."

"Or maybe...maybe the three cases are unrelated. Could be that one of the women is living incognito in Mexico, another is happily married in Gdansk, and only poor Amy is really lost...."

"I wonder if a detective has to have a rather dark side to be any good. I mean, to understand the whys and hows."

Molly thought about it. She hadn't spent that much time with Dufort, had only seen him in action that one time at the station with the Bennetts. "My main impression of Dufort is that he really is a very decent man. A little nervous, maybe? I can't really say because honestly, being around the Bennetts makes me want to jump out of my skin, so I'm not the best judge."

"Are they still hunkered down in your cottage?"

"They've never left, except the one time. But really—what is there for them to say? What is there for them to do?" Molly rubbed the back of her neck. "It's so heartbreaking. They brought a bag of things for her, you know. Her favorite cookies from home. Like they were visiting her at camp."

Lawrence just shook his head. "And how are *you* doing? Does it make you nervous, living alone in that big house?"

Molly considered. "I'm not lying awake at night, but I admit I don't feel totally at ease either. I went for a walk this afternoon, and I...I don't know. I got creeped out, being in the woods alone. Might be nice to have a big burly guy living with me at La Baraque."

"Didn't realize your tastes ran in that direction," said Lawrence, teasing.

"I'll probably get a dog," said Molly.

"Are you relieved at least that Lapin is in custody?"

"I would be, if more people thought he was guilty. But so far I haven't found a single person who says, 'Oh yeah, now that I think of it, that Lapin Broussard for sure could have taken that girl away. I always knew he had a dark side.' What I find is a village of apologists and defenders."

Lawrence laughed drily. "Who?"

"Rémy, for one. Manette. You."

"Oh," said Lawrence, his eyebrows shooting up. "You've met Rémy, have you? Good-looking man," he added, pretending to inspect a bit of non-existent lint on his sleeve.

"Oh, stop," said Molly, remembering Rémy's mouth, and

thinking that the idea of being under someone's protection was really very appealing. Just let those strong arms and back take care of everything, she thought dreamily.

"...still young," Lawrence was saying.

"Who's still young?"

"You are, my dear! Though apparently a touch deaf."

"Pshh. I'm in my declining years, but I've made peace with it," she said, glancing down the bar at Nico.

"Liar. And let me say quite unequivocally that you haven't lost your *je ne sais quoi*, Molly. I've no doubt the men of the village have noticed your arrival with enthusiasm and interest, and I'm not just talking about the chumps leering at your fake ta-tas."

Molly turned to Lawrence with a soft smile. "You're very kind to say that," she said, and then steered the conversation elsewhere.

She hadn't entirely given up on love, it was true. Although she very much believed she would be happier if she did.

25

Thérèse Perrault was first to the station on Monday morning. She went straight downstairs to the solitary cell to see Lapin, but he was lying on the cot with his face to the wall, the mildewed blanket pulled up to his neck. When she whispered to him he did not respond.

She could not believe this complete travesty of justice was taking place right here in Castillac. Lapin Broussard was no more capable of taking some girl and hurting her than flying to the moon. It was that idiot Maron's fault, she thought darkly. Always trying to do anything to curry favor and get in Dufort's good graces. Well, she didn't think incarcerating Lapin with no evidence was going to help his career any.

She hoped the chief would have something productive for her to do today. Some lead to follow that would get Lapin out of jail and the real perp in handcuffs. It was so hard for her to be patient, to wait for her orders, when what she wanted to do most of all was drive back over to L'Institut Degas and get the goods on that jerk of a professor. If anyone in the village was capable of doing something to Amy, it was him. And this ridiculous detour with Lapin was only going to slow down their progress in nailing him.

When Dufort came in with Maron on his heels, Thérèse had mastered her impatience more or less, or at least hidden it. The three said their bonjours and went into Dufort's office and shut the door.

"I'm not going to talk right now about whether you did the right thing by bringing him in," said Dufort. "Not at the moment. And—" he said, shooting a look to Perrault—"we don't actually know yet whether it was a good move. Lapin may give us something or he may not.

"But one thing I want both of you to think about. Something like this, and I'm talking murder now, let's be frank if only in here with the door closed—something like this doesn't just happen out of nowhere. People don't lead ordinary lives and then boom go out and kill somebody. There is a context in which the action makes sense. And it is our job to look under the surface of what is going on, to look back at what has historically taken place, so that we see that context. We are lucky enough to live in a village small enough that we are not without some measure of detail.

"Do you follow what I am saying?"

Perrault and Maron nodded. Dufort narrowed his eyes at them. "Don't nod just because you think that's what I want you to do. I'm asking if you really understand what I'm saying, what I'm asking you to do. You cannot look at Lapin Broussard and think: Well, he was the last person seen with the girl, and he annoys women all the time, plus there was that peeping Tom incident a few years ago. And so all that adds up to guilty for doing away with Amy Bennett and we'll spend our energy proving that because in our minds the case is closed."

"But Lapin—" said Maron.

"I'm not saying it cannot be Lapin," interrupted Dufort. "I'm saying: Let's look at his context. He grew up without a mother. His father was by all accounts, brutal with him. Physically, I believe, as well as emotionally. Belittling, pushing very hard, far beyond what a child could manage—that sort of thing. Does that make a murderer?"

"It could," said Thérèse. "But I still don't think—"

"Thérèse," said Dufort softly, "you must learn to separate your childhood self from your detective self. That does not mean cutting off all you know, all your life experience—those things are valuable, especially in a village such as ours. But you must find some *objectivity*."

Thérèse nodded. The chief was right. It was as though having Lapin in the cell had sent her back to being eight years old, with all the blind outrage at unfairness that comes at that age. Lapin had spent many Sundays at her house, throughout her childhood—and she should be combing through those memories instead of childishly railing at Maron.

"Yes, Chief," she said. "But may I ask, are we still looking at anyone else?"

"We are not at all considering this case closed," said Dufort. "First, I'm going to talk to Lapin. Maron, I'd like you to be there as well. Perrault, stay in the office and deal with whatever else comes up. If I'm not mistaken, it's getting to be about time for Monsieur Vargas to take off, am I right?"

Thérèse laughed though she did not think having to stay in the office was at all funny. If she had to go wrangle M. Vargas today instead of being in on the most important case of her career, she might just lose her mind.

DUFORT STEPPED outside the station before going down to see Lapin. He ducked around to the alley and tipped a few drops of herbal tincture under his tongue. It had been helping lately more than usual, and he made a note to go see his herbalist and thank her. The stress of a case like this could eat a person alive, and he was grateful for the support.

Then, leaving an unhappy Perrault by the phone, he and Maron went down the short stairway to the cell in the basement of the station. The cell was used infrequently, and it felt unusual to both of them to be undertaking an interrogation down in the damp stone room where they hardly ever went.

Lapin was still lying down with his face to the wall. For a frightening moment, Dufort thought he might be dead, but after repeated and increasingly louder bonjours, Lapin rolled over, clutching the blanket close.

"Can't a fellow get a decent night's sleep?" he said, with a little smirk.

"You're not in any position to joke," said Maron roughly.

"Come on, then," said Dufort. "We've got a few questions, let's see if we can get this thing straightened out. I'm hoping you can tell us something helpful."

Lapin sat up and rubbed his eyes. "How about a coffee?"

"This isn't a hotel," snarled Maron.

Dufort took out his mobile and texted Perrault, asking her to bring down a cup of coffee. Maron glared at him.

Dufort spoke. "As Maron has told you, you're here because the video surveillance of Chez Papa shows you leaving with Amy Bennett on the night of the 22nd, and no one has seen or heard from her since. I'm sure there's an explanation, and that's what I'd like to hear this morning. Anything you can tell us about where she might be, anything at all?"

Maron understood that the chief was being so friendly partly as a tactic, but it grated anyway. He narrowed his eyes at Lapin.

Lapin scratched his armpit. "If I had anything to tell you, I'd have come in when I first heard she was missing," said Lapin.

Maron rolled his eyes.

"All I know is that there was a big group celebrating at Chez Papa, something about an award or a prize or something the girl had won. She had too much to drink and so I helped her outside to get some fresh air. That's it."

"Some fresh air," said Maron sarcastically.

"So you went outside with her, and then what?" asked Dufort.

"Then nothing. She said she was fine and I went home." Lapin looked up at the corner of the ceiling and then down at his lap.

He might or might not be lying, thought Dufort, but for sure he was holding something back.

"You say she'd had too much to drink. If you were going to help her, why not get her home? Were you too drunk to drive?"

"No, I...I was not drunk, Maron. Look, she told me she was fine. Her exact words. I'm not one to push myself where I'm not wanted, you know?" Lapin winked at the policemen.

"Lapin," said Dufort, "you know I'm on your side here. But you do not help yourself by making light."

"I'm not making light," protested Lapin. "And honest to God, I would tell you if there was anything to tell. All I know is what I've said already—she was a little tipsy, I walked outside with her, she told me she was fine, I went home. End of story."

Some people are terrible liars, and luckily for the gendarmerie of Castillac, Lapin Broussard was one of them.

"Did you drive yourself home?" asked Maron.

"Yes."

They could hear Perrault coming downstairs with a cup of coffee. "*Salut*, Lapin," she said to him, her tone perfectly professional, not friendly and not cold either. She handed him the coffee, nodded to the chief, and went back upstairs.

"Perhaps you drove Amy home as well? Degas is right on the way to your house from Chez Papa."

"No, I did not drive Amy. She said she was fine, and I went home."

Dufort took a long, deep breath. He considered Lapin, wondering what it was that he knew that he did not want to say. "And did you happen to see, as you were leaving to go home alone

—did anyone else stop to talk to Amy? Was anyone else on the street?"

Lapin paused. The answer was right there, in that pause, thought Dufort. The story of what happened to Amy, almost physically palpable.

"No," said Lapin. "I went home, I didn't see anything. End of story."

Dufort stood up. He moved his chair back against the wall and gestured to Maron to leave the cell. "All right," said Dufort. "You keep thinking, keep trying to remember. It could be the littlest detail that opens this up, so please, continue to try. We will be back."

It was odd, thought both Dufort and Maron, that Lapin did not ask to be released. They had no justification for keeping him, and surely Lapin knew that.

"He's lying," said Maron, once they were upstairs.

"I know," said Dufort.

26

Monday morning. Molly woke up to pounding on her front door. Groggily she slipped on a robe and went to see who it was.

"Bonjour, Sally?" she said, opening the door wider once she saw who it was. "Is something wrong?"

"I need you to come with me!" Sally said, her face ablaze with emotion. "I must speak with Dufort right away, and I'm afraid of getting lost in those crazy narrow streets. Will you take me? Now?" Her arms were stiff at her sides, her hands clenching and unclenching.

Molly blinked, still only half-awake. "Of course," she said. "Just...just give me a minute to get dressed. Come in," she added.

"No, thank you," said Sally. "I'll wait here."

Molly managed to find some clean clothes and put them on, and give her hair and teeth a quick brush. She looked longingly at the coffeepot on her way to the front door and Sally.

"Has something happened?" she asked, as they walked quickly through the yard and out to the rue des Chênes.

"Marshall went into town last night, by himself," Sally said, her voice shaking. "I'm...I'm not sure I can talk about this," she said, stopping, and then bending over and putting her hands on her thighs as though out of breath.

Molly put her hand on Sally's back. She couldn't imagine what could have happened to Marshall to make his wife so upset. "Is Marshall all right?" she asked. "Tell me how I can help!"

Sally stood back up. She no longer looked drugged, but alive, and for Molly it was almost as though she were meeting her for the first time.

"Did you know that this Broussard guy has been in trouble before? *Sexual* trouble?" Sally's lips trembled as she spoke, with rage not sorrow.

"I...no. What do you mean, 'trouble'?"

Sally began walking toward the village again. "I mean he was caught trying to take photographs up girls' skirts! A peeping Tom, that's what!"

Molly was mildly surprised. "Hmm," she said. "I wouldn't have guessed that. He's known for..." she cast about, trying to think of how to say the truth without making Sally feel even worse. "He can be sort of aggressive with women," she said quietly. "He's never touched me or anything like that," she was quick to add. "But he leers. Makes a lot of comments, that kind of thing. Annoying."

"*Aggressive?* Wonderful," said Sally acidly. "Well, if there's a man who is known to the village as being sexually aggressive, and he's already gotten into trouble, and then a young woman goes missing—why was he not picked up a week ago? Even if just for questioning? That's what I want to ask Chief Dufort." Sally was walking so quickly that Molly had to trot to keep up with her. "Although the answer is pretty clear, isn't it? The village is protecting their own. I don't know why I ever had any hope that the police here would actually do something. They aren't going to give up a villager in order to get justice for an English girl who's only here as a student, who has no connection with anyone outside of school."

"I'm...I don't know about that, Sally," said Molly breathlessly, feeling defensive about her new home and simultaneously yearning for a cup of steaming coffee with cream. "At least I haven't gotten the idea from anyone that people here would behave that way. Sure, it's a close-knit place, and the connections are deep and maybe sometimes tangled. But it's a big jump to say they'd cover up for m—" She almost said murder but clamped her mouth shut just in time.

"*Murder!*" shouted Sally. "You think I haven't thought of that? You think by not saying the word, the idea won't be out there, in the air, suffocating me?"

Molly didn't answer because she understood there was nothing to say. No way to comfort this woman, no way to soothe her. Not unless her daughter came back, alive and unharmed.

"Dufort is going to have to explain to me why this Broussard wasn't brought in first thing. And why we, the parents, had to find out he was in custody from strangers in a bar!"

They were a block from the station. Molly figured she might need to translate so she pressed on, and the two women entered the station just as Maron and Dufort got back upstairs from talking to Lapin.

"Chief!" said Sally, grabbing his sleeve. She began talking so fast Dufort was instantly lost, and looked to Molly for help. Molly opened her mouth and closed it again. Sally was screaming now, and crying. Maron looked deeply uncomfortable, and Perrault came out of the office. She took Sally's hand and pulled her into the room, and got her a drink of water.

"She hears about Lapin with the camera," said Molly to Dufort. "And she wants to know why so long for him to have questions." Now that she said it, Sally did seem to have a point. Molly herself had momentarily daydreamed about moving to a different village once Lapin had started pestering her—it was that bad. It felt as though she couldn't go anywhere without having to fend him off and listen to his growly insinuations. But now it was impossible to tell whether she had wanted so much to get away from him because he was annoying, or because she had sensed something else.

Something much, much worse.

"And you *know* whoever took her has raped her!" Sally was shouting. "That's what always happens and you damn well know it!"

Molly saw Thérèse Perrault blanch. Dufort remained calm, and he reached for Sally's hands and held them. Then he spoke in halting English.

"I tell you, Madame Bennett: We look, and we find out what happened. We will not stop until this."

Sally sat down and put her head in her hands, but was finally quiet. Molly saw the pain in Dufort's eyes and liked him quite a lot for it. Then she touched Sally on the shoulder and they left the station, both of them feeling wrung out.

"I have to make a stop before we head back," said Molly, steering for Pâtisserie Bujold. She couldn't fix any of the things that were so terribly wrong, but at least she could get a box of cream puffs.

Which was not nothing.

MOLLY SUPPOSED it was better to just go, even though her feelings were mixed and she couldn't begin to imagine how the Bennetts would manage. L'Institut Degas had a yearly gala at the end of October, and the school was moving ahead with it despite their star student having been missing for nearly two weeks. Lawrence had insisted she go with him—everyone in the village will be there, he'd told her, *everybody*—but she took her time getting ready, the usual uncertainties about what to wear snowballing into almost frantic indecision, quite uncharacteristic for Molly.

It's my first village party, she thought, and I have no idea whether to dress up or down. Or way up.

Or...maybe she shouldn't go. In fact, she was pretty sure she felt a headache coming on.

Right, you're going to skip the first party in your new village because you don't have a headache but you think you might, sometime? Could you be any lamer?

And with that little self-slap, she pulled herself together and thought the problem through. One of the few pearls her mother had left her with was: Always err on the side of overdressing. So she went with a black cocktail dress, because really, how could that ever be too far wrong? And a good pair of heels, plus more than five minutes devoted to hair and makeup.

She had been so taken up with the move and culture shock and getting La Baraque ready for guests that she had sort of forgotten about her appearance. She dragged out a curling iron, found an adapter, and tamed her wild red hair. It took a half hour to get the eyeliner right, but she had started the whole process early and so was ready when Lawrence came by to pick her up.

"Who *are* you?" he said, laughing. "I wondered if there was a glamor puss hiding somewhere under all that tangled hair. I'm glad to see there is."

"Um, thank you?" Molly smoothed on lipstick looking in the mirror by the front door. "Damn," she said, having drawn outside her lip line. She used her thumb to correct the error.

"So the burning question..." Lawrence said, leaning against the doorway while she put things in her bag and took them out again. "Is whether whoever took Amy will be there."

Molly looked up sharply. "You look positively gleeful about the idea."

"No. Well, yes. Everyone has a Sherlock Holmes fantasy deep inside, don't they? I mean, come on, Molly. Wouldn't you like to be in the midst of the crowd and suddenly point at...someone... and say: *It's him. This is the man who took Amy.*"

"You're sure it's a man?"

"Of course I'm sure. You disagree?"

"No. I don't. Just asking."

As they walked to Lawrence's car, Molly gave a fond glance back to La Baraque. The house looked so beautiful in the moonlight, so mysterious yet inviting, with one light showing in the kitchen and the grosser imperfections hidden by darkness. She felt a sudden strong urge to turn away from the car, to go back inside and get in bed and read a book.

She stood with her hand on the car's door handle, not opening it.

"You've never struck me as the shy type," said Lawrence, but his tone was soft.

"I'm really not shy," said Molly. "But I...I don't know...I'm feeling..." She shook her head quickly and got in the car. "It's dread," she said quietly as they drove into the village. "That's what it is. And it's not about the party. It's that...something is going to happen, and whatever it is...it's bad. It's bad, Lawrence."

He took his hand from the gear shift and rubbed her arm. "I don't want to tell you to ignore what you're feeling," he said. "But I do think having the Bennetts so close by, and depending on you, might be having...an effect. I'm not at all convinced anything awful has happened. There's no proof. No evidence at all except for her absence."

"I'm not claiming to be clairvoyant or anything. But I...and maybe...oh, I don't know."

"Look, this is usually the best party of the year. The food will be amazing, and as I said, everyone will be there. So, dear Molly, try to put the Bennetts out of your mind just for tonight. They will be waiting for you in the morning, after all.

"Rémy will be there," he added, with a twinkle in his eye so bright Molly could see it in the dark.

She had figured he would be. Not that she was the least bit interested one way or the other.

27

1990

Benjamin was in his room, polishing off the last of an apple tart and pretending to do his homework.

He heard his mother scream, and it sounded to him not like her usual screaming about his eating habits or ants in the kitchen, but this time as though something was seriously wrong. He ran downstairs to help.

In the living room, his mother was lying on the sofa with an arm over her eyes, and his father knelt beside her, his hand on her shoulder. "It's all right, isn't it, Marine? It's going to be all right."

Ben stopped short, feeling as though he was intruding on something private. He saw his mother take her arm away from her face, saw the gratified look she gave his father—and with a flash of understanding he realized that his mother had fabricated the upset in order to get his father's attention. And now that she had it, all was well.

He crept back upstairs to his room and ate the final bite of tart. Why would his father be so solicitous, when he was obviously being manipulated, he wondered. And if Maman wanted his attention, why not just ask him to go somewhere with her, or play a game of cards?

He wanted to understand why people did the things they did. But at that moment, his parent's actions seemed so inscrutable, he was not confident he would ever comprehend them.

28

2005

Lawrence parked on the road, at the end of a long line of cars. "I'd say our timing is perfect. Never want to be among the first."

"No," Molly agreed. She took Lawrence's arm to steady herself, her heels threatening to turn her ankles on the uneven side of the road. "Do you really think he'll be here?" she said in a low voice.

"Rémy? Almost certainly."

"No no, I mean...the person who took Amy."

Lawrence pressed his lips together and shrugged. "I was just messing around before," he said. "I make fun because I don't know what else to do. Of course it's highly unlikely we'll have any sort of Grand Unveiling of the Murderer, like we're living in the middle of Agatha Christie-ville. But still...I would say, all kidding aside, that it is likely that *someone* here knows *something*. Is that vague enough for you?"

Molly nodded. The thought creeped her out, but she agreed with him. She wondered if Dufort would be here, and if he was thinking the same thing. She wished she'd put the mace back on her keyring, even though she wouldn't be alone and certainly not in any danger. It was just that the thought of it was reassuring.

The party was in the big modern building that looked like a jellyfish, in a large room that jutted away from the road. Round tables dressed in white tablecloths lined a dance floor, and servers scurried around with platters of drinks. A small band played on a stage at one end. It looked to Molly as though half of Castillac was there. She caught a glimpse of that pretty gendarme, Thérèse she thought her name was, and saw Alphonse of Chez Papa going wild on the dance floor with a woman she recognized but hadn't met. She got a glimpse of her next-door neighbor, Madame Sabourin, talking animatedly with a man who stood with his arms folded across his chest, nodding at whatever she was saying. The band finished the song, and the crowd cheered.

This was her village. Her life now. It was time to jump in and enjoy it.

Lawrence was quickly swallowed up by the crowd, and Molly made her way toward the bar, enjoying the high energy of the room. Pascal, the handsome server from Café de la Place, was bartending, and she felt buoyed up by his dazzling young smile.

"*Merci*," she said to him, taking her kir and moving away. The music was insistent with a good beat. She heard shrieking laughter coming from one end of the room, someone nearby talking very loud and insistently about politics, and the hum of a party with momentum. She stood on tiptoes and ran her eyes over the crowd, looking for anyone she knew.

"Bonsoir, Molly," said a voice behind her. She turned to see Dufort smiling at her.

"Bonsoir, Ben!" Awkwardly they kissed cheeks, Molly at first turning the wrong side. Dufort kept smiling and Molly thought again that she liked this man. He just seemed so decent. "I am glad to see you here."

He nodded. "Would you dance with me?" he asked, surprising her.

"Of course!"

He took her hand and led her to the dance floor. Just then, the band switched tempo and started to play disco, of all things. Molly and Ben laughed and moved their hips to the beat and Molly sipped her kir and felt younger and happier than she had at any moment since her divorce. At the end of the song, Ben made a small bow and an excuse, and disappeared into the crowd.

Well, that was a little abrupt, she thought. I wonder....

Then she saw Rémy. She felt herself flush at the sight of him; without thinking she had expected him to appear as he always did, in jeans and a shirt streaked with mud, sometimes a battered hat. But of course, he had dressed for the occasion like everyone else.

And my, he did scrub up good.

Molly walked straight to him and said hello. They kissed cheeks, not awkwardly, and Molly got a whiff of his masculine scent.

"You look fantastic," said Rémy, looking into her eyes.

Molly's face got redder. "Not so bad yourself," she answered.

Lawrence staggered off the dance floor and joined them. "How am I supposed to stay in shape if there's only one party like this a year?" he asked, mopping his brow with a monogrammed handkerchief. "I don't think I've been dancing since last year's gala."

"I had no idea Castillac was such a hotbed of disco," laughed Molly, raising her voice to be heard. The three of them went to a table and sat down. Molly slipped her feet out of the torturous heels and took in the scene. Three older women were dancing together, doing a creditable version of the hustle. A group of men at the next table were huddled together, talking with serious expressions.

Lawrence leaned close to Molly and said, "The guy in the pink shirt is Jack Draper, head of the school. American. Nobody much likes him."

Molly nodded. "Doesn't look like they're having a very festive conversation."

Rémy scraped his chair over closer to Molly's. "Okay, let me in on it. What juicy tidbit are you telling Molly, Lawrence?"

"Ha—I wish I had a juicy tidbit," said Lawrence. "I bet if we could hear what they were talking about—" he tossed his head in the direction of Draper, Rex Ford, and Gallimard "—it would be...interesting."

"So come on, Larry, give us the dirt!"

"Says the farmer," laughed Lawrence. "I don't know why you think I know anything. Draper's okay, as far as I know, although he thinks very highly of himself. Don't we all, deep down," he shrugged. "Gallimard, the one next to Draper, with the big belly —he's a bit of a sad case, in my opinion. One of those people who peaked way too early and so has felt a failure most of his life." He paused to consider.

"So what do you think," he continued. "Which is worse: to show tremendous promise and then fizzle, or never to have any glory or promise in the first place?"

"Fizzling is worse," said Molly. "Because your failure is on everyone's minds all the time. I mean, look at us. We don't even know him, at least Rémy and I don't, and yet we sit here judging and thinking about how he had something big and then lost it. Pitying the poor man for his failure. But when anyone looks at me, they're not thinking about blown potential, but just...taking me as I am. Whatever that is," she shrugged.

Rémy nodded. "I would have to agree with the American," he said, with a little smile.

"I suppose for Gallimard there are compensations," said Lawrence thoughtfully. "From all reports, he pretty much runs the school. Draper is more a figurehead and promoter than anything. It's Gallimard who decides who's in and who's out."

"Amy Bennett's teacher, I suppose?" said Molly.

Lawrence nodded.

On the dance floor, Dufort came into view, dancing with Marie-Claire Levy. It was a slow song and Dufort was holding her close. Molly watched them, unable to suppress a pang of remembering how very pleasant it was to have a man hold her like that. She shook her head as though to wipe those thoughts away.

"Lawrence, come on!" she said, dragging him out to the dance floor as the band started the next song, and hustling like it was 1975.

❧

ON THE OTHER side of the room, Thérèse Perrault appeared to be partying with a group of her oldest friends, but in fact, she was working. She laughed at her friends' jokes, she danced, she ate and drank—and every minute she was thinking about Amy Bennett, and looking at the crowd thinking that somebody there knew something, and how in the world was she going to figure out who.

He's got to be here, she was thinking. He's probably laughing at us, knowing we're lost. Maybe even sizing up his next victim.

She tried to follow along in a line dance while scanning the room for suspects. Even though she had been well trained in police work, she couldn't help holding on to a slice of hope that something less rational, less by the book, might point her in the right direction. Like if she happened to look into the man's eyes, she would *know*. She would be able to see down into his rotten core, see what he was capable of and what he had allowed himself to do. After that, justice for Amy would simply be a matter of walking backward and collecting evidence along the way.

"Come on, Thérèse, you're not listening to a word I say," said Pascal, putting his warm hand on her cheek. He was so charming that he managed to make even a complaint sound inviting.

"She's off in the clouds," said her friend Simone, bumping hips with Thérèse.

"No, I'm listening," she said, reaching for Pascal's hand and squeezing it, and looking past him at the group of men who ran Degas, who were huddled together as though sharing the best gossip ever.

But Pascal saw that she was not listening, not to him, and so he gave up and walked away, wanting to spend his few minutes of break with someone who was interested in his company. If she wanted to work undercover, he thought, bartending would do pretty well. He was always amazed at the things people would say as they waited for their drinks, as though he weren't an actual live person with ears standing only a few feet away.

29

Rémy was dancing with his sister, and Lawrence had disappeared who knew where. Molly didn't mind. She loved being in the swirl of the party, officially part of her village, talking to whomever she happened to be standing next to. She remembered all the big parties she had gone to when her job was fundraising, and how dreary they had been because of it. She was free now, and her new life in France was rumbling along very well indeed.

Or perhaps her feelings of expansive optimism were the result of three kirs, Molly having developed a mighty thirst thanks to so much disco dancing. At any rate, she was enjoying herself, with thoughts of the Bonnetts not entirely absent, but in some sort of manageable perspective. Always there, but not running the show at the moment.

At her elbow, a man appeared, so tall that Molly had to look up to meet his eyes. "I wanted to introduce myself, Ms. Sutton. I am another American living in Castillac." He held out a hand with preternaturally long fingers and they shook instead of kissing cheeks. "My name is Rex Ford."

"Hi Rex, nice to meet you," she said, by now almost used to

strangers knowing who she was. “I’ll ask you what everyone always asks me—how did you end up in Castillac?”

“Ah, yes. I teach at Degas. Painting. I’ve been there many years now.”

Molly’s brow wrinkled and she nodded. “Did you....”

Ford smiled at her but his eyes were flat. “Are you asking about Amy? Everyone’s asking about Amy. No, I haven’t taught her. You see, as I said I’ve been teaching there for many years, but my focus is on the art and on my teaching, not on playing politics, you understand? So when the other professors are fighting over the students, trying to get the best ones for themselves—I don’t allow myself to get involved with that sort of thing.

“At any rate, no, I’m afraid *Gallimard* was Amy’s painting teacher. Anton Gallimard. You have heard of him?”

“I’ve heard his name. He’s here, I suppose?”

Rex Ford raised his eyebrows and jutted out his chin to point him out. Gallimard was on the dance floor, his face florid and his belly shaking, doing The Bump with a pretty student, both of them laughing.

“Ah,” said Molly, nodding and looking back at Ford. She saw hatred in his eyes as he looked at Gallimard. Saw how he couldn’t take his eyes off him, in fact. “So tell me about teaching at Degas. You’ve been there a long while, so you must like it there?”

Ford nodded. “Well, I like parts of it. I like living in France.”

Molly nodded enthusiastically.

“And art...art is my life,” he continued. “When I reached the point in my own career where I could see I would progress no further, teaching was the only possibility that made sense.”

“I understand,” said Molly. “That must have been a difficult moment.”

Ford was looking over Molly’s head, not at the crowd but still at Gallimard. “Yes,” he said.

Molly started trying to think of a graceful way to get away from Ford. She moved her hips, eager to be on the dance floor, then stopped because she didn't want to get stuck dancing with Rex.

"It is never easy to have desires that cannot be fulfilled," Ford pronounced, and then looked down at Molly with an expression of such tangled emotion she stepped backward. "Take Gallimard, for example. He was supposed to be the next Pollock, the next Chagall. And now he's nothing but a fat nobody. What do you think that might drive a person to do?" Ford asked, bending his head down and breathing in Molly's face.

"Drink too much?" she said in a small voice. "And I don't know. Who doesn't have to confront failure in middle age? Almost nobody ends up being what they imagined they would be."

Rex cocked his head and swiveled his attention to her. "Perhaps. Perhaps. But you see him out there, right now—do you think it's an accident that he's dancing with the best-looking girl in the school? Do you understand? He's like a parasite, wanting to suck her youth right out of her nubile body."

Ford licked his lips. Molly saw a bead of spittle in the corner of his mouth, and decided that maybe it was Rex Ford himself who wanted to suck on nubile bodies. His intensity was making her feel more than a little uncomfortable.

"They've got that junk dealer in jail," Ford leaned in close and whispered in Molly's ear. "But it's a mistake. They've got the wrong guy."

The fact that Molly agreed with him did not make the conversation any less awkward. Where had Lawrence disappeared to?

And Rémy? Not that she cared.

Really.

❧

IT WAS DISGUSTING, thought Maribeth Donnelly. The way everyone just goes on as though nothing has happened. Amy disappears and it's like she's been dropped into the sea, without a single ripple. Maribeth had a quick image of a painting—the ocean, abstract and dark, a small figure lost—and then felt a little sick at having turned Amy into art, just like that, without meaning to.

Maribeth did not fault the police, who at least seemed to be making some effort to find her. At least they had somebody in custody, from what she'd heard. But L'Institut Degas, that was another thing altogether. Bunch of old white men looking to line their pockets and their beds, was her assessment. She had already made arrangements with her family to go home after the semester was over, which was no small thing since she had begged to come to the school, and had had to admit she had been wrong about her choice.

But at the same time, confusingly, her work *was* better. Deeper, more accomplished technically. She had learned much from Gallimard, and from the other students as well. But this... this *gala*, not two weeks after Amy was taken...it was more than she could stomach. She looked around hoping to see Officer Perrault, so she could thank her. But if she saw that Maron guy, she would avoid him. She did not like his vibe. Not one bit.

SHE FELT SO good in his arms, and it made Dufort happy the way he could feel her laughter ripple through her body as he held her. He wanted to pay attention to Marie-Claire, and only Marie-Claire, and leave all of the mess of L'Institut Degas and Amy Bennett behind. If only for a few hours.

But after one dance, Marie-Claire gave him a serious look and pulled him toward the door. "Something I need to tell you," she said mysteriously in his ear. They threaded through the crowd, Ben nodding at various people along the way, until they got to a side door of the big room and let themselves out.

The night was cold and their breath made twin plumes, illuminated by the light of the party. Dufort stood up straight and breathed deeply, the air tickling the inside of his nose and smelling of pine. "Why are you intent on freezing me to death?" he asked Marie-Claire, smiling.

Neither wore a coat and they shivered in the cold. "I have to make sure no one hears what I'm about to say," she said. She was not smiling. Ben looked at the way some of her hair had escaped her chignon and wreathed her head like a halo. "It's about the school. Something I've found out. It's probably nothing to do with your case, and I would be fired if Draper knew I was telling you this—"

Ben took her hands. He waited.

"—the thing is, I was poking around where I didn't belong. I handle much of the school's correspondence, emails to parents and that sort of thing, but a couple of things had happened that got me curious...anyway, to get to the nut of it: Degas is in serious financial trouble. I'm pretty sure Draper has been siphoning funds away for his own personal use. Maybe Gallimard as well."

Ben looked into her face and thought how serious and lovely she was. He put the back of his hand on her cheek and she startled, his fingers were like ice. "And what do you think this might have to do with Amy?"

"I don't know. Like I said, probably nothing. But I suppose I thought, well, here are some people pretending to be one thing—upstanding citizens, leaders of a prestigious school—when in actuality, they are nothing more than hustlers. Nothing more than thieves. And isn't that true of whoever took Amy? If it's someone we know, someone in the village? He's a liar? A faker?"

"How did you find this out?"

Marie-Claire did not answer. She had managed to guess Draper's password (people are so much more predictable than they think they are) and read his private emails. But what had seemed like a good idea at the time, in retrospect was a clear violation.

She had even, she somehow did not realize until that moment, broken the law herself.

"Now that I've said it out loud, I can see I was being ridiculous," she said, looking down at her feet in her favorite black ballerina flats. "Just because someone's a thief doesn't make him a killer."

"It doesn't," said Dufort. "But you've done the right thing to tell me. We still don't know if what happened to Amy has anything to do with the school. We don't know if it was random or had something to do with who she was, her relationships and so forth. But without as much information as we can get, what hope do we have of finding out?"

When Marie-Claire realized he was not going to press her for how she found Draper out, she relaxed a little. "Smells like winter," she said, lifting her face to the moon.

Dufort leaned in and kissed her on the neck, then on the lips. He wanted to be simply standing outside in the dark with Marie-Claire, kissing her. That was all.

All the rest of it could wait, at least for now.

30

Twenty-two year old Simone Guyanet was walking home alone from the gala, a little tipsy and ready for bed. Just that week, she had finally moved out of her parents' house and gotten her own place near the center of town. As she passed the *Presse*, something flashed to the side, a quick movement, a furtive shape in her peripheral vision.

She faltered.

Then she walked faster, looking forward to getting to the apartment that was all hers and climbing into her freshly made bed. Out from the space between two buildings, a man stepped just after she went by. Silently he followed, and in a few strides had reached her, put his hand over her mouth, and tried to pull her into the darkness, down the alley next to a clothing shop.

Simone wrenched her body violently to one side and his grip loosened. She ran. She had always been the fastest runner in her class and she was in good shape despite her office job, and her attacker was quickly blocks behind, empty-handed.

"WELL, I did have a good time, yes. But now, I don't know, I'm sort of let down, now that it's over," said Molly, making sure she had her handbag as Lawrence was pulling into the driveway of La Baraque. "I see the Bennetts are asleep, or at least their lights are off."

"I wonder if anyone invited them. Not that they'd have wanted to go, but it would be weird not to invite them, don't you think?"

"I guess. I didn't see them before I left. Where's the protocol manual for handling parents with missing daughters?" They sat in the warm car, thinking about the Bennetts. Finally Molly spoke. "Want a nightcap?"

"Oh, you're sweet. But maybe this once I'll be good and go home and put myself to bed. I hope your let-down feeling doesn't stick around too long."

"I'll be fine. It's that—I had this feeling when I was getting ready that something was going to happen tonight, you know? That little tingle you get before something really dramatic happens?"

"Hmm, little tingles," said Lawrence. He seemed about to say something teasing but changed his mind. The friends kissed cheeks and said goodnight. Molly walked down the flagstone path to the front door, pulling her coat tight around her against the cold. She turned to wave at Lawrence as he backed out and drove off.

And as she went to pull the latch on her front door, she felt fear come rumbling at her, slow and suffocating as an avalanche. Fear that someone—someone *bad*—had broken in some way, and was waiting for her inside. Fear that whoever was taking young women wasn't going to stop. Fear that she had been clinging to the idea that she was safe but had been terribly, horribly wrong.

I need a dog. Like now.

Molly slipped off her shoes and left them just inside the front door. She did not turn on the light, partly because she was afraid of what she might see. Walking as silently as possible, she headed for the end table in the living room with its one drawer, where she had put the mace.

She listened hard but what she heard was the coursing of her own blood through her ears.

Maybe it's a little narcissistic to think the killer would come after me, right? I'm not so young, for one thing. And...

By the time she reached the side table Molly had worked out three rationalizations and was working on the fourth. She slid open the drawer and grasped the mace. *Much better now.* Without worrying about noise, she turned on the table lamp and the spooky dark shapes instantly transformed into familiar pieces of furniture. She let out a long breath.

A crash behind her.

Molly whirled around, her right arm extended, thumb and finger on the trigger of the mace canister. The orange cat streaked over the back of the sofa and out the French doors to the terrace. Molly shook her head, trying to summon a laugh at herself, but she couldn't quite manage it. She put the mace on the kitchen counter and poured herself a big glass of Perrier and drank it down. Then she put the lamp back on the side table, locked the French doors and the front door and the little door in the pantry that she never used, and went into the bathroom to wash her face before going to bed.

Castillac may have turned out to be a terrible choice, she thought to herself, wiping her face over and over with a hot washcloth. But I'm not ready to say that yet.

Not yet.

31

Simone kept running even though she heard no footsteps behind her. She was trying to get somewhere less solitary, somewhere with so many people she would be safe, and then she could call the police. But on the night of the gala at L'Institut Degas, everything was closed. Everything. She ran past Chez Papa—dark. Same with the other bars and restaurants on the Place. It was nearing midnight and she could think of absolutely no place to go except back to the gala.

She stopped abruptly and looked behind her. The street and sidewalks were empty. The street dark, the pavement damp from a brief shower. The shapes of buildings deeply familiar as she had lived in Castillac all her life.

She waited until she had caught her breath. Still no one.

And then, because she didn't know what else to do, and now going alone to her new apartment was about a hundred times less appealing than it had been ten minutes earlier, she started running down rue des Chênes, back to Degas as fast as she could go.

THE GENDARMES of Castillac were at the station early Wednesday morning.

"I had my eyes and ears peeled last night," Thérèse was saying to Dufort and Maron. "I was thinking most of the village was at the gala. So the chance of our perp being there was pretty decent." She bowed her head. "But instead he was roaming the streets and almost got Simone."

"I should have had you patrol since you weren't going to be at the gala," said Dufort to Maron.

Maron shrugged. "We can't be everywhere at once. Did your friend give a description?" he asked Perrault.

"Unfortunately not," answered Dufort. "It was dark, he grabbed her from behind. All she could say was that she was pretty sure it was a man, and that he was somewhat hefty."

"What does 'somewhat hefty' mean?"

Dufort gave a brittle smile. "I asked that very question. Ms. Guyanet said only that the person was substantial, not slight. She would not hazard a guess about weight."

Maron nodded. The three officers were quiet, all of them trying to have the breakthrough thought, the inspiration that would finally lead to some progress.

"You could say that Gallimard is 'somewhat hefty,'" said Perrault. "Too bad he was at the gala, surrounded by a hundred witnesses."

"Professor Ford spoke to me about him again," said Dufort. "Definitely has a personal grudge against Gallimard. But maybe there is something to what he says."

"Might be, if he didn't have an alibi," said Perrault.

Maron glared at her. "He could have slipped out and gotten back in ten minutes. You can't prove every single minute was accounted for."

"I'm going to talk to Ford again," said Dufort.

Perrault glanced at Maron, and gave him some grudging credit for keeping his gaze steadily on the floor and not shooting her a glance of victory.

The feeling in the room was not one of optimism or energy. They wanted a lead, a clue, a body. And in the absence of all three, it felt as though they were going through the motions of investigation. Plodding along a treadmill, never advancing.

Lapin had been let go, since there was no legal pretext for keeping him, and of the three gendarmes, only Maron thought there was any chance he had anything to do with Amy's disappearance. Perrault and Dufort had tried talking to him again, but neither had succeeded in getting anything new out of him. Whatever he had held back, he was still holding back.

They were at square one. Exactly two weeks since Amy went missing.

Dufort stood up and walked to the window. He pushed down a slat of the Venetian blind and looked out. "Somebody in this village knows something," he said. He felt a hollowness growing in the pit of his stomach and knew it was time for a dose of his tincture. He closed his eyes and tried to take himself back to last night, to dancing with Marie-Claire, but stress had taken over and he got no relief from it.

"Maron, I'd like you to do some legwork on the financial picture for Degas. Find out what kind of endowment they have, if any. Find out how well tuition covers expenses. Find out—everything you can."

Maron nodded and went to his computer. Perrault looked at Dufort expectantly.

"Thérèse," he said quietly, "you and I will look for Amy's body, and we will make no effort to disguise what we are doing. You take the north side of the village, I will take the south. Look in every backyard. Every shed, every barn, every garden. Start in the center of town and move farther out."

"Yes, sir," said Thérèse. "Too bad we don't have a Bloodhound."

Dufort nodded. "Listen. The key to this whole thing is in the village, in our history," he said. "I can sense that it's right in front of us, and we just haven't been able to see it."

Thérèse waited to see if Dufort had more to say, but when he was quiet, she nodded and left to search, experiencing for the first time the deeply mixed emotions that come with wanting desperately to find a body so that the case could proceed, while at the same time, never wanting to give up on the hope that Amy was alive, somehow, somewhere.

32

The morning after the gala, Molly called Constance and asked her to come back and finish the job cleaning the cottage. No, she wasn't fired. Yes, she did have to mop after vacuuming. Yes, it would be better if she came this morning. Then Molly walked over to ask the Bennetts if they would mind leaving the place for a few hours, but when she knocked, no one answered.

Were they still asleep? Gone out before Molly was up? She walked around the side and peeked in a window, but she couldn't see much. She went back to fetch the vacuum cleaner and mop, then banged hard on the door. Silence.

Molly put her hand on the doorknob and slowly turned it. She wanted the cottage clean, really clean, even though she knew in the grand scheme of things it made no difference. It was just the one thing she could do something about.

"Hello?" she called out, stepping inside the cottage. "Bonjour? Sally? Marshall?"

No answer.

Then a clattering and whooping as Constance came down the driveway on her bicycle. She popped her head through the doorway, breathless and rosy-cheeked. "Am I late? I hope I'm not late. I was supposed to get a ride from Thomas but he's absolutely useless, always promising and half the time not showing up? Ever had a boyfriend like that, Molly? I should dump him."

Molly laughed. "You're not late. Here's the stuff you need, and this time, please—vacuum the entire cottage, including under the beds. And then mop. The whole place. These stone walls are the trouble, it's like they weep dust all the time. So we have to mop at least twice a week."

Constance was nodding but Molly had the distinct impression that she wasn't listening.

"All right then?" said Molly. "Any questions?"

Constance shook her head and lunged at the vacuum cleaner and plugged it in, and Molly retreated to her house, where coffee was waiting. It was a little too chilly to sit on the terrace, so she decided to indulge herself and climb back into bed with a novel. The coffee was strong and hot, the covers warm and cozy, and the book engrossing. Before she knew it, nearly two hours had slipped by. Better go check on Constance, she thought. And where on earth have the Bennetts gone?

As she walked on the path leading from La Baraque to the cottage, Molly heard giggling. Mystified, she walked faster, pulled open the door, and found Constance on the sofa, her shirt half unbuttoned, and a young man with his arms around her, kissing her on the neck.

"Excuse me?" said Molly, her eyes wide.

The couple broke apart. The young man jumped up and smoothed his hands down his shirt. "Bonjour, madame," he said, with the good grace to look embarrassed.

"Molly!" said Constance, who on the other hand had the serene expression of an angel. "Look who turned up after all! This is Thomas. Thomas, this is Molly, the actual owner of La Baraque!"

She made the introduction with such a grand flourish Molly

had to fight back a smile. “Have you finished cleaning? Any sign of the Bennetts?”

“Nope, haven’t seen ’em,” said Constance, stretching out her legs and making herself more comfortable on the sofa. “I’m nearly done, just have the bathroom to do. Hate the bathrooms,” she said to Thomas, who nodded, still looking embarrassed. “I don’t know, maybe what happened to Simone got the Bennetts upset,” she said, turning back to Molly.

“Simone?” Molly asked, a chill running through her.

“We were in school together, you know. She’s sort of a know-it-all, if you want to know the truth. Thought she was better than everyone else just because she got good grades.”

“You were just jealous,” said Thomas, smirking at her.

“Wait, what happened to Simone?” said Molly.

“You didn’t hear? She was attacked last night. Just walking along by herself, right on the Place.”

“What? Is she okay? Did she call the police? Details, Constance!”

“Okay, okay. All I heard was that she was walking home from that thing at the school, and she was alone. And somebody tried to grab her, but she got away. She is a really fast runner, that Simone. I’ll give her that. Used to always win every race during recess.” Constance’s expression darkened and Thomas slipped his arm around her and gave her a squeeze.

Molly stood with her mouth hanging open. Another attack. Another attack in the charming, beautiful village she had moved to, looking for safety and calm.

“Do you think it’s someone in the village?” she asked in a low voice.

“Oh sure, it’s gotta be,” said Constance breezily. “I mean, it keeps happening here in Castillac. Doesn’t make sense that someone from somewhere else would travel here every few years just to...to take someone and disappear with them.”

"Actually, that seems like a smart way to keep from getting caught," said Thomas.

"Oh okay, now we're seeing how the criminal mind works," said Constance, digging into his ribs and grinning at him. "Hey, I heard that teacher at the school is kind of a...what's the word... well, kind of a jerk anyway. I've got a friend who cleans for him. Says he's got girls in there all the time, it's like total drama, you know?"

"What girls? You mean at his house?"

"Yes, his house. And I don't know exactly. Students, I'd guess. Like he's practically got a harem, if you believe my friend."

"Her friends?" said Thomas, looking at Molly and circling a finger around his temple to make the sign for crazy.

Molly took a deep breath. Her head was so full of questions she thought it might burst. She paid Constance in cash without remembering to walk through the cottage to check on her work, and then threw herself into yanking vines out of the garden with such intensity her arms and legs got all scraped up. She discovered all manner of noxious weeds new to her, and thought how foolish she had been to think that moving to France would solve everything. She had had this rosy picture of *parterres* of herbs and flowers in her front yard, and freedom from upset and violence.

And what she had found, now that she was settled in, were weeds just as bad as the creeping Charlie back home, and women disappearing and being attacked. Right on the Place, which already she felt so attached to that the thought of something bad happening there brought tears to her eyes.

I don't know how I could have been so stupid, she thought. Of course there are murderers everywhere, no matter what country or village you're in. The world is apparently crawling with them.

DUFORT WAS glad to get out on the street. His head felt like it was in a vise when he was inside—movement and fresh air gave some relief, though not nearly enough.

He was sure Amy Bennett was dead. It was not statistics and probability that told him that; it was his heart. And all he could do was try to find her, even though it was too late to save her. He left the station and started down the main road, then turned left on the first side street, heading south. He wished he had a dog. He wished he had a force of fifteen that he could put to work with gridded maps, leaving no stone, no trashcan, no pile of leaves unturned.

But all he had was Maron, Perrault, and himself, and they would have to do, at least until they found a body.

If they ever did.

The street was unusually quiet. It was Wednesday, the day children had off from school. At this point in the morning, they were normally streaming through the streets, on their way to the grocery to buy candy, or to the soccer goal in a dusty square on a back street. Maybe the mothers are keeping them in, after what happened to Simone, he thought.

They must be thinking I am useless at my job. And I would be inclined to agree with them.

Dufort went in a side door to an old stone garage. It was filled with junk and the dust was thick; no one had been in there for at least a year. He shone a flashlight around to make sure the dust was undisturbed everywhere, and then moved on. He stepped into gardens and looked under row covers, where cauliflower was growing vigorously in the chilly air. He looked under porches, behind compost piles, in the bed of an old truck up on concrete blocks. He looked in sheds, in shrubbery, in dumpsters.

But nowhere was there any evidence of Amy Bennett, or of anything besides everyday, ordinary, unexceptional life.

Eventually, he found himself on rue des Chênes, and quickly walked the kilometer to Degas and the office of Anton Gallimard.

"Bonjour, *Professeur*, I hope I'm not intruding," he said, when Gallimard answered his knock.

"No, no, not at all," said Gallimard, waving his arm grandly as though inviting Dufort in to the salon of a *château*. "Tell me what I can do for you?"

Dufort smelled alcohol and saw a glass on the corner of the desk, with about a half-inch of clear liquid. He glanced at his watch and saw that it was 10:30 in the morning.

"Oh, I'm simply out and about," said Dufort, putting on an expression of dull-wittedness. "Asking if anyone knows anything about Simone Guyanet getting grabbed last night."

Gallimard's eyebrows flew up. "Simone Guyanet? What happened?"

"She was walking home, around eleven, I think—wonderful gala, by the way, I enjoyed myself immensely—and somebody came up from behind and tried to take hold of her."

"Is she all right? Did she give a description?"

Dufort had wondered how long it would take Gallimard to ask that.

"Simone is fine. She's a fast one, you know—got away and outran him like that," said Dufort, snapping his fingers. "Now I wanted to ask...you were at the gala until when, exactly?"

Gallimard turned away and sank into his chair. "Oh, let's see." He drummed his fingers on his desk, then straightened a pile of papers. "I do love the gala, you know—we raise quite a lot of money every year. It's very important to the school. And we're so grateful to get the support of the village," he added, smiling at Dufort.

"And so you left when?" Dufort closed one eye and then wiped at it distractedly.

"I admit I don't wear a watch, so I can't be as precise as you might like," said Gallimard. "But I stayed quite late—say, close to midnight?"

"And did you attend alone?"

Gallimard laughed. "Chief Dufort, I'm beginning to think you are interrogating me!"

Dufort smiled. "I'm asking the same questions all over town. I'll be honest," he said, leaning forward as though letting Gallimard in on a secret. "I don't have the first idea what to do about this case. I'm completely mystified!"

Gallimard narrowed his eyes slightly at Dufort. Surely the gendarme of the village was not the buffoon he was pretending to be.

Or perhaps he was.

"I'm hoping you can tell me more about Amy," Dufort said, blinking and wiping his eye again.

Gallimard nodded. "Certainly. Anything at all, as I've said. I'm happy to help."

The two men sat in silence for a few moments. The building gave off a sort of sigh, and the radiator under the window hissed. Dufort had the patience of a tortoise and could wait out anyone.

Finally Gallimard stood up and took a bottle of pineau from a shelf. "Thirsty?" he asked Dufort, pouring a splash, and then another, into his glass.

Dufort shook his head. What interested him was that it looked as though Gallimard had been drinking since fairly early that morning, as well as hitting it hard the night before, at the gala—but without the smell and the glass to give him away, Dufort would not have guessed the professor to be under the influence. Dufort had the distinct impression that Gallimard wasn't drinking to get drunk—he was drinking just to stay on an even keel. Drinking because *not* drinking was no longer an option, physically.

Finally, Gallimard spoke. "As I told you a few days ago, Amy is very talented. And a hard worker, which is the most important thing, really. The young ones think it's all about how much talent you have." Slowly he shook his large head. "But that is wrong, hopelessly wrong. I'm perfect proof, Dufort. I had all the talent in the world, you see. And it was not enough."

With effort Dufort kept his eyes from widening in surprise, as he had not imagined that Gallimard would open up like this. Perhaps he was drunker than he appeared.

"It must be difficult," Dufort said, his tone gentle, "to have students who might become great successes. With all the attention that brings. And money."

Gallimard poured another finger of pineau into his glass and took a long pull.

Dufort continued, "Not only to watch them succeed, but through your teaching, be part of the reason for their success. I'm not sure I could handle that." He watched Gallimard carefully. His graying hair swept back from his temples in dramatic fashion, his eyes were tired and red. Deep dark circles under them.

Dufort waited.

Gallimard took another sip of his drink. He pressed his lips together. Then he spoke, his voice low and gravelly. "I am nothing but pleased when my students do well," he said. Then he opened a drawer of his desk and took out a pack of cigarettes—Gauloises Bleues. Slowly he shook one out. "I'm not going to ask if you mind," he said. His mouth was in the shape of a smile, but there was nothing warm or friendly about it. "It's my office, and I can do what I like." He struck a match and lit his cigarette, sucking on it hard and then blowing a plume of smoke over Dufort's head.

Inwardly Dufort was grinning. He made sure to keep his face looking as stupid as possible without going too far. When a charming man stops being charming, he thought, that's when things get interesting.

33

As far as Molly could tell, the Bennetts had disappeared. She kept reminding herself that they certainly didn't have to keep her abreast of any plans they had, they were paid up and free to come and go as they pleased. Yet still, it felt odd. *They* were odd. Or no, it was only that Molly had no experience with people going through something like this. Who knows what any of us would do?

She decided to have dinner at Chez Papa, hoping for some distraction. Probably Lawrence will be there, and thank God Lapin seemed to be laying low. She was not in the mood for his drooly expression and wandering eyes, not tonight.

As she walked into the village, she had one of those moments when she wasn't worrying about something or making plans or thinking over what happened. She was simply walking down the road, seeing what was in front of her. The air was chilly and the stones of the buildings no longer looked warm but rather forbidding. The sun had burnt off the frost but everything looked cold: the bare trees, the tiled roofs, the neat stacks of firewood in backyards.

She went down the alley and looked to see if the La Perla

woman had hung out her wash, but the line had been taken down. Molly supposed she could ask around to find out who lived in the house, but she rather liked the mysteriousness of not knowing. At last night's gala, she had found herself wondering, when she met women of the village—are you the La Perla woman?

She stood by the back gate trying to understand why this stranger's underwear was taking up more than a moment of her thoughts. It's that...all of us have this face we show the world, but there is so much we don't show, so much of who we are that is underneath. The La Perla woman would appear to be chaste, and sober, and moderate in her behaviors—but underneath, she is extravagant and sensuous. Perhaps she shows that side to her intimates; of course, Molly couldn't say.

The man who took Amy is more than likely a person Castillac knows. We see his public face and don't suspect what is underneath—his need to hurt, to control.

Molly walked faster, looking forward to the particular smell of Chez Papa, that heady mixture of coffee, tobacco, and people.

"Lawrence! I was hoping you'd be here!" she cried, seeing her friend on his usual stool, Negroni in place.

"Hello, my dear," he said. "I hope your let-down was brief?"

Molly slid onto the stool next to him and waved at Nico at the other end of the bar. "Well, no, actually, I'm still in the grip of it. Kir, *s'il te plaît*," she said to Nico.

"It's not the party," she continued. "I'm officially totally creeped out by the Amy situation. It's going to be someone you all know, Lawrence, someone among us. I've just been thinking about how we make friends, we go to work, we socialize—but how well do we really know each other? Aren't all of us keeping things back, maybe even the biggest things?"

Lawrence smiled. "So, you first, Mollster. What are *you* keeping back?"

"I'm serious, Lawrence. But all right. Here is the...the undercurrent I don't talk about with anyone. I'm thirty-eight years old.

I always thought I would have children. I don't mean just because it's the expected thing—I mean, I *wanted* children. And here I am, running out of time, well, not even that, it's not going to happen, now that I have no one to have the children with—"

Lawrence put his hand on Molly's shoulder. "You're *not* too old," he said.

"Maybe not right this minute. But I'm single with no prospects. So figuring that in—I'm done. And I think about it all the time, or it's not even thoughts, really, more like the knowledge of it is woven through my consciousness 24/7, even though I've more or less made peace with it because what other choice do I have?

"But this thing with Amy, and having the Bennetts with me—it's made it ten times worse. Brought back the yearning, the disappointment, and the desire to figure out a way to make it work when I know there is no way."

Lawrence listened. He did not jump in with advice or instruction, but simply squeezed her shoulder and listened to Molly pour her heart out. She talked about the children of friends and how much she enjoyed playing with them, how annoying and demanding they could be. How deeply she wished to have that in her life, including the annoying and demanding parts.

"I don't talk about it because I know it makes me sound so self-pitying. Maybe I'm one of those people who is never satisfied," she said. "I mean, look, I moved to France, for crying out loud. My dream. And I love it here even more than I could have imagined. I should be happy. So why do I have to go back to this old scab of no children and keep picking at it?"

Lawrence shrugged. "It's what we do," he said.

They sat for a while drinking their drinks and not talking, lost in their own thoughts.

"You do know I'm gay," Lawrence suddenly blurted out, and Molly burst out laughing.

"Well, I didn't expect that to be a punchline," he added drily.

"No, it's just...of course I know that," she said. "Do you really think I'm that clueless?"

Lawrence cocked his head and considered. "Hmm, not usually." He sipped his Negroni. "And to go back to your original point —it's true that I don't go around with my sexuality announced on a sandwich board, but I don't think that means no one knows me or I have some dark private self that's capable of running around doing evil deeds while I pretend to be Mister Rogers.

"And the fact that you don't blather on about your personal regrets—that just means you're polite, Molly. Not false. Not a potential axe murderer."

"Another?" Molly said to Nico, pointing at her empty glass. "But do you feel you really *know* the people of the village, the ones you see nearly every day? Or are you just interacting with façades?"

"I'm willing to accept that if someone I know is indeed abducting women and murdering them, then yes, Molly dear, I have been ignorant of who they really and truly are. But for everyone else? I'm satisfied that I know enough. Not everyone needs to know everything."

Molly spun on her stool and looked around. Two families were eating together at a long table—four parents and a pile of children, including a baby in her mother's lap. Three young women sat together talking about makeup, sipping drinks that were an arresting color green. Nico took coffee to an old lady sitting with her poodle. Vincent read the newspaper at his table by the door. Thomas, Constance's boyfriend, walked by outside and waved at Molly through the window.

This was her village and she realized she loved it more fiercely than she ever would have thought possible. Whatever this evil was that lurked here—she wanted it gone.

THE NEXT DAY Molly put on a heavy sweater riddled with moth holes and attacked the garden. She slammed the Dirt Devil into the soil and pried out the long roots of the vine whose name she still didn't know. Before long, she was warm enough to toss the sweater aside. She worked for several hours, but the border still had a long way to go.

Wandering around her property, checking the bark on a few fruit trees along the back for insect damage, Molly thought about where to plant the bulbs she'd ordered. In the darker corners of her mind lurked the Bennetts and Amy's abductor, but she was reasonably successful at blocking them all out.

By lunchtime she was starving, and sat at the kitchen table slicing bits of salami and eating hunks of bread and cheese.

She was lonely.

She felt like a long walk but wished for someone to take it with. Lawrence had told her he was allergic to exercise, and she didn't have any other prospects she'd feel comfortable asking. So with a shrug, she laced up her walking boots, slipped the keyring with mace into her pocket, and set off down rue des Chênes, heading away from the village as she'd done before, confident that once she got into a walking groove and into the forest, her mood would brighten.

Now that it was mid-October, all the houses along the way had smoke rising from their chimneys. The air smelled of cozy hearths and Molly imagined families playing board games in front of the fire, grandfathers napping, dogs stretched out in the heat. She remembered how the dog from her childhood used to sleep so close to the fireplace that his fur would be too hot to touch. With a pang she missed him, remembering how she used to call him Finkler for reasons forgotten, although his name had been Henry.

The lush banks of ferns had died back and only a few brown skeletal fronds remained. Once past the visible houses, she found the turnoff onto the wide path and in a few minutes, everything was different—the light was only the spangled light that filtered down through bare branches, the sound of her steps was muffled in the leaves, and she felt as though she were the only person for many miles around, though she knew it was not so.

Also it felt as though her hearing became more acute somehow, that she could hear each little mouse scurrying in the leaves, each bug rubbing on its cousin.

And then something louder. An animal. Snuffling, then whimpering.

Molly walked faster in the direction of the sound. It sounded like a dog and she was not afraid of dogs. She had to leave the trail to see where it was, and the underbrush was thick. Briars grabbed at her pants and thin branches whipped in her face as she fought her way along, not thinking, just knowing that she had to get to the dog.

She came through an especially dense bit of growth and the dog was not twenty feet away, a huge dog, dappled gray with large brown spots, and ears like a Bassett Hound. It lifted its head when it saw Molly, and barked. And kept barking, as if to say: Come look, person, look what I've found.

Molly stood absolutely still, her eyes wide.

The dog was digging at a mound of earth that looked loose and freshly dug. It swung its head around and looked at Molly, its long ears flapping, then went back to frantic pawing. Clods of dirt flew past her as she stepped closer. Then she stood still, a tremble of horror going through her body.

Molly could see a human hand sticking out of the dirt.

34

It had been a long three days at the Castillac gendarmerie. Dufort and Maron had brought the corpse to the morgue and sent multiple DNA samples to the lab. Dufort had called in favors to get the results as quickly as possible. The Bennetts had finally appeared and identified the body, after which, understandably, they went to the cottage and would not answer when Molly knocked.

"The results are not in yet," said Dufort in response to Perrault's hopeful look as he came in the station after lunch. "But I did get a bit of preliminary information, which is that there was recoverable DNA under the fingernails. At least that will tell us if Lapin was involved, although I think we'd all be surprised if that turns out to be the case." He looked at Maron and Perrault in turn, and they each nodded.

"The other slight bit of good news is that the flask found near the gravesite was not, according to the Bennetts, something that Amy owned. The roommate, Maribeth Donnelly, agrees. Of course those statements aren't definitive, but there is a decent chance the flask was dropped by the killer in his hurry to bury the body. It may produce some testable saliva."

Dufort lifted his arms up over his head, laced his fingers, and bent over to one side and then the other.

"Thank God for Madame Bonnay's dog!" blurted out Perrault.

Dufort smiled grimly. "Yes, so far Yves has been the best detective we have. Along with Molly Sutton."

"So now what do we do?" asked Perrault. "We still have Gallimard to look at."

Maron shook his head. "The body was a couple of kilometers outside the village, way up in the woods," he said. "Gallimard not only doesn't have a car, he doesn't even drive. How's he going to get the body that far, unless he's got an accomplice?"

Dufort stroked his chin. Perrault stared at the wall, her mind racing. "Are we sure he didn't have an accomplice?"

"Almost unheard of in a case like this. A sex criminal will want his victim all to himself."

Perrault persisted. "Do we even know it was a sex crime? And he could have stolen a car. Even just for a few hours. And then put it back and no one would be the wiser if he didn't get it messy. It's not like it takes a genius to drive an automatic car a few kilometers in the middle of the night with no traffic."

"You have a point," said Dufort.

Maron scowled.

"Most people don't lock their car doors. And again," said Perrault, "we don't absolutely know it was a sex crime, not yet. Not until the coroner says so."

"I don't know what's taking them so long," muttered Dufort. He straightened and walked toward the door. "I'm going up to Degas now. I'm going to talk to as many students as I can find—I want to see if all these rumors we keep getting wind of are true: Was Gallimard having affairs with his students, or wasn't he? If yes, does that include Amy? And one more thing. Maron, did you get anywhere with looking into the finances at Degas? I've gotten a tip that there's something shady there—might be something to it. If I could get you the books, could you take a look?"

"Right up my alley," said Maron with a rare grin.

"I don't know," said Perrault. "Excuse me, Chief. But don't you think, especially given the pattern with the others, that this isn't a murder about money. I know I was just saying we don't know yet, but still, it's most likely a sex crime, don't you think?"

"Make up your mind, Perrault. Maybe it's a financial crime made to look like a sex crime," said Maron.

"Hold on," said Dufort. "One step at a time. We have a body now, so we are much closer to solving this than we were before. But we have to stick to the basics and not get ahead of ourselves. Means, motive, opportunity. That's what we apply to every suspect, you know this from your training."

"I think we spent maybe an hour on this at the academy," said Perrault under her breath.

"Perrault!" said Dufort, rather harshly. "We are going to get to the bottom of this murder. We are going to find him, and arrest him, and gather the evidence to convict him."

"Yes, sir," said Perrault.

"Right now, we have nothing," said Maron. "We've got only the old circumstantial evidence pointing to Lapin we had last week, but nothing further. With Gallimard, all we have is a bunch of gossip. No evidence at all that he's done anything besides be a failure as an artist and a blowhard. We have *nothing*."

"Correct," answered Dufort. "But we are only getting started. We await the test results, we comb through the financial papers of the school, we keep talking to Amy's friends and teachers. We persevere, Maron. We persevere."

And then Dufort bowed his head. The emotional struggle of staying in a place of such uncertainty, with the threat of another defeat hanging so heavily over him—it was almost too much to bear.

Maybe I'm in the wrong job, he thought. Maybe I'm too soft to succeed at this.

He shoved a notebook into his pocket and nodded to

Perrault and Maron and left the building. He was out of his herbal tincture but did not want to take the time to visit the herbalist. He made sure his cell was charged up and jogged through the village toward Degas, and this time he was so focused on the case that Marie-Claire did not enter his thoughts even once.

❧

MOLLY HAD BECOME a village celebrity after finding Amy Bennett's body up in the woods. It was not exactly what she would have chosen to be known for, but she was glad to have helped the Bennetts find what the talk shows called closure, a horrible word that attempted to make complicated, ugly feelings tamer, as though one could simply shut a door on the chaotic storm of loss.

But surely it was better to face the pain of knowing than the relentless dread of not knowing.

Despite everything, the Bennetts had lovely manners, and they knocked on Molly's door after hearing from Dufort, wanting to thank her. They explained that they had been traveling around to all the churches and cathedrals within a hundred miles, lighting candles for their daughter. Hearing this, and enduring their thanks, was probably the most awkward five minutes of her entire life, not to make it all about her.

The other result of finding the body, also all about her, was that her phone went from always silent to ringing quite often. Her neighbor, Madame Sabourin, called to see if she would like to come over for tea the next day. Constance called wanting to know if her services were needed. And Rémy called to ask her on a date.

Well, he didn't call it a date. But what else is an invitation to dinner? Molly suspected all of them wanted a firsthand account of her discovery, but she didn't really mind. In fact, she was the sort of person who works things out by talking about them, and she didn't mind rehashing the story over and over, and remembering new details as she went along.

She was sorry that the dog had turned out to belong to someone else, a Madame Bonnay—she would have taken him in on the spot.

What does one wear on a date to a farm?

This was such a knotty question that Molly emailed several friends back in America. While waiting for them to answer, she tried on a few semi-nice things, then put on old ratty clothes and went wandering in the garden, an eye out for the Bennetts. A hard frost the night before, and all the plants in the front border were brown and sagging. This was one of her favorite times in the garden, when the only job was clearing out the dead plant matter and making room for the new.

Hearing the crunch of gravel on her driveway, she turned around to see a truck pulling in, Rémy at the wheel.

"Bonjour Molly!" he called out. "I had to make a trip to the feed supply store and I figured I'd swing by and pick you up since you're right on the way. I hope you don't mind my being so early!"

Well, no, she didn't. He was grinning at her and he looked so boyish and enthusiastic and, well, *hearty*—that she grinned back and hopped in his truck. "No problem!" she said. And even though she did wish she wasn't wearing that sweater with all the moth holes in it, and maybe could have used a shower, she had the feeling that Rémy wouldn't care.

And it was true that she was very glad to be leaving La Baraque for the evening, and the somber murk that emanated from the cottage.

Rémy's farm was up in the hills above Castillac, on a rolling piece of land he told her had belonged to his great-grandfather.

"We're all a bunch of dirt farmers," he said, and when she looked puzzled, thinking she didn't understand his French, he took off on a long and mostly interesting explanation of how his efforts were always directed at improving the soil of his farm, and the livestock and produce that grew there were actually a second priority.

Molly liked listening to him talk about his land. And she liked meeting the goats, dogs, and cats that followed him as he led her on a tour. If a goat approves of a man, she thought, he must be a decent guy, right?

He poured them a glass of red wine from a big plastic jug, and they sat outside on a little terrace where they could see the rooftops of Castillac in the distance and a flock of ducks in the front field. "All right," said Rémy. "You know I'm going to ask, but just tell me if you don't want to talk about it. You found the body?"

Molly nodded. She'd told the story enough times that it was almost starting to feel made up, or at least the distance between her and the event was beginning to feel quite wide. "I did find her," she said quietly. "I had been thinking about Amy almost non-stop, since they—her parents—have been staying in my cottage for over a week. But I wasn't out looking for her or anything like that, just going on a walk. I heard Yves barking, went to see what was the matter, and that was that."

"Is it giving you nightmares?"

Molly laughed a grim laugh. "No, no nightmares. But the sight of that hand sticking up out of the dirt is something I won't ever forget."

"I'm sure," said Rémy. He leaned back in his chair and stuck his rangy legs out in front of him, and turned his face up to the sky. "Gonna rain tomorrow," he said.

And with that little comment, Molly realized she had pinned an awful lot of unspoken hopes and dreams onto this date with Rémy, and they had absolutely nothing to do with the man himself, whom she hardly knew. But in that moment she knew this: She was not going to be marrying and having the children of Rémy, no matter how neat the solution would be to the sorrow she couldn't seem to let go of.

It wasn't that he spoke of the weather, or that he was a farmer, not at all. It was that a kind of connection she wanted, even needed, was not happening between them. For whatever reason. And in Molly's experience, despite what those same talk shows that went on and on about closure led people to think, if that spark isn't there, it's not going to appear sometime later.

She ate a lovely dinner of steak and vegetables that he had raised himself, and enjoyed talking to him about soil pH and nematodes and other gardening matters. And then she called Vincent for a ride home, and said goodnight.

When she climbed in Vincent's car she kicked the food wrappers under the seat, feeling irritated by the mess.

"*C'est un bordel ici!*" she groused.

"Oui, a thousand pardons," said Vincent, smiling at her in the rearview mirror.

Molly felt sad on the drive home. Of course, it was totally ridiculous that she had been starting to think of Rémy as her next boyfriend, before they had spent more than ten minutes alone together. She was too old for this nonsense.

The date forgotten, by the time she was home, Molly was making a list of who she needed to call to get the *pigeonnier* project started. It wasn't love or a new family, but it was making something that would hopefully be both beautiful and lucrative, and there was no small comfort in that.

35

"Lab reports are in," said Dufort, and Maron and Perrault left their desks to follow him into his office. "The sample from under the fingernails was good. Not degraded. They were able to get material from the flask as well, which matches the fingernail sample."

Perrault realized she was holding her breath, even though she knew Lapin would be cleared.

"Neither matches Lapin," said Dufort, and Perrault whooped and then tried to look serious.

"I thought Lapin was considered to be a giant pain by pretty much every woman in the village," said Maron.

"He is," said Perrault. "But he's our pain, you know?"

Maron shook his head.

"If we could narrow down a suspect, we have the DNA to arrest and likely convict. But we can't run around the village taking samples from everyone on the street. We still don't have means, motive, and opportunity pointing at anyone."

Dufort spread his hands on his desk and looked as though he was going to push them straight through the wood. Perrault, to her undying embarrassment, got a little teary. Maron was the only one of the three who did not look thrown by their lack of progress.

"Maron, anything on the financial angle?" said Dufort.

"Yes, Chief. Let me get the books." Quickly he stepped to his desk and returned while opening up a ledger with a red leather cover. "It was pretty easy, actually," Maron was saying, pointing to some fine print in Degas's accounting books. "You see this list of vendors that the school paid money to every week or every other week? Cleaning services, laundry, and the like. Well, I checked out each one to make sure they were legit. All of them were—except this one...." he pointed to Acmé Food Services, which appeared to be receiving 2,254 euros a week.

"It's a dummy," said Maron, gleefully. "There is no food service at the school. Vending machines, that's it, and the school doesn't pay for them."

"So that 2,254 euros is going where?" asked Perrault.

"Someone's pocket," said Maron. "The board of the school is more or less for show. Gallimard decides who gets hired and which students get admitted, and Draper takes care of the finances. Both of them have access to the books and to the school's bank accounts and investments. Either of them could be siphoning off this money, or they could be working in concert."

"That's well over 100,000 euros in a year. Something of a dent in their operating budget, I'd imagine, in a small school like that. Nice work, Maron," said Dufort, leaning up against a radiator and looking out the station window. "Unfortunately, I will tell you that I got these books through...a not entirely legal process. So for the moment, let's keep the thought of embezzlement under our hats, yes?"

Perrault's eyes were wide. She would never have thought Dufort capable of skirting the law. He was the chief!

"The important thing," Dufort was saying, "is that even with the embezzlement, there's no link to Amy Bennett. We would have to prove that Amy found out about it, that she either threatened to tell the police or they believed she would, and that the embezzler's solution to the threat of being caught was to kill her. I'm afraid at this point, that's simply a fairy tale that we have absolutely no evidence to support.

"So even though we've got the body, and we've got DNA... we've got nothing," said Perrault.

"Correct," said Dufort, and he looked so grim that the two junior officers unconsciously took a step backward.

"I was at Degas yesterday, talking to a number of people. Students and faculty as well as administration. It's a curious thing, but though I heard more of the wild womanizing rumors about Gallimard from several people, I could find absolutely no one who could confirm even one instance of it. I spoke to three people the rumors had linked to him and they were quite convincing in their denials.

"My conclusion is that Gallimard himself does what he can to promote the rumors, although apparently, there is not so much as a hint of evidence that they are true." He walked from behind his desk and glanced out the window to the street. "People are strange," he said.

Maron shrugged. "It's not so different from guys at university, bragging about what they had done with certain women. But all of it's just fantasies, you know?"

Dufort considered his words but did not speak. He rubbed his close-cut hair with one hand, he looked out the window, he twiddled the small glass bottle of tincture that was in his pocket.

"This crime," he said slowly, "looks more and more as though Perrault is right. We're dealing with a murder of a young woman likely to be the aftermath of a sex crime. So, a sociopath. He wants to hurt, to dominate, and he cares little of what damage or pain he causes in his pursuits. Actually, it might better be said that he is unaware of others' pain because other people are not real to him."

Perrault was looking intent, hanging on her chief's every word.

Dufort spoke softly. "The way to catch a criminal is to put yourself in his shoes. Think how he thinks. And it is abundantly clear that thus far, I have been unable to do this effectively. I know he is among us, probably someone we have at least some connection to, in a village this size. Yet so far—for *years*—he has acted with impunity.

"Let's get back to it," said Dufort, with a briskness that was almost worse than his anger. "Somebody in this village knows something, and we won't hear it hanging around the station."

AFTER A COUPLE of days in near-seclusion, Molly was looking forward to dinner at Chez Papa—extra-crispy frites, perhaps a hanger steak and sautéed mushrooms—and some company. The Bennetts had finally emerged from the cottage to tell her they planned to leave the next day. They were effusive in their thanks, which made Molly feel terrible.

"Lawrence!" she said, spotting her friend in his usual spot and opening her arms for a hug. He slid from his stool and wrapped her in a big hug.

"I can't believe after all that has happened that you didn't come tell me all the details, you minx!"

"I know," Molly said, feeling chastened. She realized in the moment that if the positions were reversed, she'd have stayed glued to her stool at Chez Papa until Lawrence showed up and told her all about finding the body. "I'm sorry, I needed a few days to hole up and get my feet back under me," she said.

"I understand. Sort of," he added, giving her a sideways look. "I suppose you don't want to hear the little tidbits I've gleaned in your absence?"

"Tidbits? What kind of tidbits? Does Dufort have something on somebody? Has anybody been arrested? Come on, Lawrence, don't be horrible!"

"Bring her a kir, Nico. She's overwrought."

Molly gave him a sharp elbow to the ribs and Lawrence filed away a mental note not to call her overwrought ever again. "Well," he said, after taking a fortifying sip of his Negroni, "what do you know so far?"

"I don't know anything. I called Dufort when I found her—or Yves showed her to me, more precisely. I took the dog down to the road and waited for the cops there, which, uh, I felt a little funny about. I mean, I knew she was dead and everything, obviously. But still, it felt a little like I was abandoning her by leaving. You're going to think I was drunk, but I whispered to her that I'd be back."

Lawrence held his head to one side, thinking this over. "I do see why you wanted children," he murmured, low enough that Nico wouldn't hear. "Your instinct for...what would you call it? Anything I think of seems macabre under the circumstances. Anyway, what I'm trying to say is that I admire the depth and sensitivity of your feeling."

Molly nearly made a joking remark but instead she thanked him. "And so, the cops came and I showed them where she was and they were doing all their forensic stuff and I just walked home. I thought maybe I was intruding and they were too polite to tell me to get lost."

"I really don't think you have to worry about that. I'm sure they would issue whatever instructions they needed to," said Lawrence. "So that's it? You've been holed up ever since, doing plumbing repairs and learning masonry, or whatever it is you do all day?"

"Pretty much. I saw the Bennetts leave to go to the station, or the morgue, I guess. I didn't offer to go with them. I figured that no one tagging along was going to make that trip any less awful."

"Unimaginably so," said Lawrence, and the two friends shared a look of pain, thinking of what the parents must be going through. "All right, well, I'll tell you what I've heard."

Molly sipped her kir and waited anxiously.

"I happen to know someone who knows someone...and the word is that Amy Bennett was not raped, but there was evidence of 'sexual activity.' Which means the police are looking for a sociopath of the murderer-rapist variety, and not, oh I don't know, a jealous ex-friend or something like that."

"Not a surprise, huh? I mean when a young woman goes missing, isn't that the conclusion everyone jumps to? Raped then murdered? Or in this case, apparently not-quite-raped? I'm not sure it makes much difference."

"I rather thought you would say there was relief in knowing she hadn't been."

Molly shrugged. "If she were alive, sure. Dead? What difference does it make?"

They drank extra-big sips of their drinks. Molly had been looking forward to dinner, but found she had lost her appetite entirely.

"I also hear there's been a date with Rémy."

"Good Lord, who *are* your sources?"

"You ride through the village in his truck, people are going to see you. And then, you know, tell everybody they know. Gossip in Castillac is everyone's favorite sport. It's one of the reasons you fit right in." Lawrence grinned at her and waved Nico over. "Get this woman a plate of frites, stat. Extra-crispy," he added, just to annoy the cook.

"I know it's selfish, but that's a whole lot worse," said Molly, putting her elbows on the bar and slumping.

"What's worse than what?"

"If Amy had been killed by, say, a crazy classmate who was jealous of her success, then the rest of us would be perfectly safe. The violence would be contained, you see?"

Lawrence shrugged. "Maybe as far as that one crazy classmate goes. But if envy is the trigger, then what keeps your neighbor from doing you in because your roses look so much better than hers?"

Molly laughed at the image of Madame Sabourin sneaking over to La Baraque in her housecoat, with a garrote in her pocket.

"I'm afraid none of us are ever all the way safe, the way we might wish," said Lawrence. "And I will admit that I moved to Castillac for reasons similar to yours. No, no divorce," he said, waving her question away before she could ask it. "Just a lot of family unpleasantness that was better walked away from. When I came here on a vacation, I was totally smitten with the beauty of the village but also the warmth of the people living here. I thought I could leave the dysfunction and judgment of my family behind, and make real friends here. I canceled my return ticket and settled in to embrace the tranquility of Castillac."

He and Molly laughed. "Oh, the irony!" said Molly. And they cracked up again, arms around each other, so happy to be exactly where they were, murders and abductions notwithstanding. Sometimes the hum of fear can make people giddy, especially with Nico throwing in the odd free refill.

36

It was cold and it was late, but Molly decided to walk home instead of getting the taxi. She smiled at Vincent on her way out, waved at Lawrence who had decided to have one last Negroni, and set off for rue des Chênes and home. The village was quiet. All the shops locked up tight, only a few lights on in houses and apartments along the way. On the edge of the village she could hear the faint sound of pop music coming from somewhere, so faint she could hardly make it out.

The moon was nearly full and she needed no light to see.

Her mind was filled with a jumble of thoughts: how she hoped Dufort would come through with an arrest, because having a sociopath on the loose was less than comforting; how much she loved Castillac and had no regrets about moving there; how the walk to La Baraque seemed farther when the weather was cold.

She turned up her collar and walked faster to warm up. She was on the final bit, a straight stretch of road about fifty yards from her driveway, when the lights of a car appeared behind her.

Her brain paused, but only for a second. And then she flashed on what she had seen but not noticed she had seen. She knew who killed Amy Bennett.

She knew who killed Amy Bennett.

And if she was right, he was on the road behind her. Coming for her.

He knows I know.

She began to run but of course the car was gaining on her. She left the road and pushed her way through Madame Sabourin's hedge, running without thinking for La Baraque. As she ran she frantically pawed in her bag, searching for her phone, but it was not there. She grasped the mace on her keyring and made sure it pointed in the right direction.

When she got to the wall between her house and Madame Sabourin's, she bent down and ran hunched over until she reached a large tree covered by an out-of-control climbing hydrangea, and she buried herself among the thick vines, pushing her back up against the trunk of the tree. She was breathing so heavily she thought for certain he would be able to hear her heaving from far away.

Molly watched the car drive slowly down rue des Chênes. He was not rushing. The headlights swung into her driveway as she knew they would, the car creeping along, the slow speed scarier and more disturbing than if he had been speeding. Her breath was not returning to normal and she wondered if she was going to hyperventilate. And why had she not simply rung Madame Sabourin's doorbell, and called the police from there?

Well, there was no helping that now. She watched him get out of his car and walk up to her door. She had known who it was but still it gave her a shock to see him. She watched him knock, then jiggle the knob.

He saw me run through the hedge, does he think I would be inside now? Waiting for him?

Molly felt a flush of fear run through her body and for a moment she thought she might lose control entirely. Her legs were going to give way and she would crumple to the ground, useless to defend herself against this evil man. For a moment she saw Amy's hand sticking up out of the dirt and she started to lose it.

Calm down, she told herself desperately. You can't think if you don't calm down! If he has a flashlight, he'll spot me in a second, she thought, adrenaline flooding her body again.

I need a plan.

But her brain resisted. Her thoughts were flashing, jagged lights—incoherent and undecipherable. She had never in her life been this frightened.

He began to walk slowly around the side of the house, toward Molly. She sucked in a long breath.

Okay, if he gets any closer, I'll have to make a break for it.

It had been a long time since Molly had sprinted. Years, probably. But she waited in the shadows of the climbing hydrangea, watching the killer as he tried the front windows of her beloved house, and got mentally prepared to run for her life.

37

1991

Vincent hated school. He was only six, but his classmates mocked him mercilessly for his grubby clothing that did not fit. He could not read and did not seem to understand the concept of reading, as though he had never seen books before. His first teacher had recommended testing, but he was deemed intelligent enough not to need any special services. Everyone at school, teachers and fellow students, thought him dull, and before long the teasing moved on to someone else, and Vincent was left alone.

In some ways, the isolation was worse. At school, he was among other people much of the day, but they did not seem to see him, did not reach out to him or involve him in what they were doing, and the pain of this was torture for the young boy.

One day he walked home from school by himself as usual. His father was off doing farm chores he said, but Vincent knew that meant driving the tractor to a field out of sight of the house, and drinking himself into oblivion. His mother was home, however.

His mother was *always* home.

When she caught sight of him that day, her eyes glittered and he knew that was a bad sign. She ran to him shrieking and slapped him on his bare legs, yelling about how he had failed to make his bed that morning. He did not cry but stoically stood still and waited for the first burst of rage to pass.

He knew it was only one in a series. That was how it always went.

Vincent had an older brother, but he had run away as soon as he could and was never heard from again. No one ever came to the lonely farmhouse at the end of the road—no friends, no relatives, not even any salesmen passing through.

Vincent was trapped there with his mother who beat him and rained insults down on his small head, and there was nothing for him to do but endure it. On that particular day, at six years old, Vincent felt his hatred for his mother grow inside him like it was a separate being, taking over his body. He welcomed the hatred because it made the beating hurt less. It gave him strength.

He knew that he would make her pay someday. He would make someone pay.

All he had to do was wait.

38

2005

Molly was about to make a move when a cloud slid over the moon and the yard went dark. There was no streetlight, no light coming from the neighbor's, and Molly's heart stopped pounding quite so hard.

Please don't have a flashlight. Please.

She could just make out his shape as he came around the side of the house, a slow-moving, darker space in the blackness. Molly held her breath, eyes pinned to him, trying to stay completely motionless.

Vincent stopped. She thought she could see him cock his head, as though he were listening for something. He stood like that for what seemed an eternity. And then the black shape started up again, moving toward the house. He pushed on a window but the latch held fast.

And then the cloud slipped away, and the light of the moon fell on the yard, so bright she could read the license plate on the taxi and make out the plaid pattern of Vincent's shirt.

Molly tried to press herself against the tree so that the vines would hide her, but she knew if he looked in her direction, the pale skin of her face would probably glow. Somehow she needed to distract him, to send him away long enough that she could make a break for it. Slowly and carefully she felt around on the ground with the toe of her shoe. He went out of sight around the back of the house and quickly Molly stooped down and grasped a stone from between the root of the tree.

She could hear him trying the French doors.

The door banged as he closed it. She knew he had gone into her house. Frantically she disentangled herself from the vines and ran toward Madame Sabourin's house, praying she was still awake. Not wanting to make noise, she tapped on the door, peering into a sidelight hoping to see her elderly neighbor. A light was on in the back.

And in a moment, Madame Sabourin appeared, smiling when she saw Molly, and opened her front door.

"Call Ben!" said Molly, trying not to get hysterical. "Lock all the doors and call Ben right away!"

Madame Sabourin acted without asking any questions until the house was secure and Ben on his way, and as she put on a kettle for tea, Molly put the stone she had been clutching on the kitchen table, and told her everything she knew.

39

Alphonse came out from the kitchen, gave Molly a kiss on both cheeks and a big hug. "Lunch is on me," he said, wiping a tear from his eye. "I hear you solved the murder and I can't tell you how grateful I am."

Molly's eyes widened. "How did you hear that already? I just left the police station five minutes ago!"

Alphonse's eyes twinkled. "We have our ways, Molly. Now come, sit at the bar and tell us your story. Nico, pour her a kir."

Molly smiled half-heartedly. "I don't know that it's time to celebrate," she said. "As I'm sure you know, since you people always seem to know everything—Vincent has fled. No one knows where he is."

"The innocent do not run," said Alphonse, shaking his big head.

"Not usually. Dufort wasn't telling me the details, but I got the impression he may have solid DNA evidence, so if they can just catch him, they'll get a sample and undoubtedly it will match. But in the meantime...there's a sociopathic murderer on the loose. Which is why I decided to have lunch here instead of in my own kitchen."

"A good plan, Molly."

"And when Lawrence gets here, I'm going to ask if I can sleep at his place until Vincent is behind bars."

"Did Dufort say you are a target?"

"He didn't have to. I already have been, Alphonse!"

"Just so," the old man said, shaking his head. "No one is safe until that man is in prison. And to think I served him at least a meal a day for years now! Right over there!" Alphonse pointed to the small table in the corner by the door, where Vincent was always found if not behind the wheel of his taxi.

"I know! I rode in his taxi a bajillion times! I put the *Bennetts* into his taxi!" Molly and Alphonse looked at each other, their eyes wide, still barely able to comprehend that this man who was part of the daily fabric of their lives had turned out to be a killer.

"Oh, Molly!" said Lawrence, peeling off his coat as he came in the door. "I just heard. Are you all right?" They kissed on both cheeks and then hugged.

"Yes, I'm totally fine. My thighs are a little sore from running. Maybe we could start working out together?"

"Never in this life," said Lawrence. "Now tell me—how in the world did you know it was Vincent?" Alphonse nodded and leaned forward. Nico put down the bottle of Campari and gave her his full attention.

"Well," Molly said. "First let me say that I was completely clueless all along, until the final moment. I guess all of us had wondered, at some point, was this evil person, this murderer, someone I know? But I'd never gotten any farther than that. I had no list in my head of all the creepy people I'd met in Castillac that I thought might be capable of murder. People here—they're wonderful."

"Molly! Get to it!" Lawrence almost shouted in frustration.

"Yes, well. You know the Bennetts were staying in my cottage. So I brought them food from time to time, and had various reasons to be inside the cottage just in the normal course of things. And what I noticed—that broke my heart—was that they had brought bags of things for their daughter, just like you would if you were visiting from your child's home country. You know—you'd bring things the child was fond of, but thought perhaps couldn't get, living in another country."

The three men listened intently but were still mystified. "Go on," urged Alphonse.

"And also, I took a lot of trips in Vincent's taxi. My house is close enough that I should just walk home, but I don't know, sometimes I'm lazy, and Vincent seemed pleasant, and it was so easy just to get a ride home that way. And I didn't even realize I saw it when I saw it, if you know what I mean...but on the floor of the backseat of Vincent's car was always a bunch of trash. It was annoying to me, and I would push it under the seat with my foot.

"It didn't occur to me at the time to wonder why the backseat of Vincent's taxi was littered with wrappers of English food—McVitie's biscuits, Cadbury Flake bars, that sort of thing. Things you could find in a French city, sure, if you knew where to look. But not so much at the *épicerie* in Castillac, right? And—I noticed this because it was unfamiliar and weird—a bag of something called salty licorice. It's German, apparently. Makes me gag just thinking about it."

"Amy got in Vincent's taxi that night, after the celebration right here at Chez Papa. She was drunk. She had her stash of English goodies in her bag, got the munchies, and dug in during the ride, leaving her wrappers on the floor. Who knows how long Vincent drove around with her before hurting her? Could have been fifteen minutes. Could have been hours. Even the next day. But somewhere along the line, Amy had her last meal of junk food that reminded her of home."

Nico was shaking his head. "But Molly, couldn't any tourist have left those wrappers behind?"

"You think people in Castillac are feasting on McVitie's and salty licorice? Not likely," she added, "but of course it's possible. And if they had, and Vincent wasn't guilty, he wouldn't have gotten worried that I would put it together. He wouldn't have had any reason to come after me last night." She shivered slightly and Lawrence put an arm around her shoulders.

"Why didn't he just clean out his car?" wondered Alphonse.

"I think in cases like this, there's an element of keepsakes," said Lawrence, and everyone understood and recoiled at the idea. "Maybe those wrappers were something he kept to remember Amy by—to remember the night he had with her."

"A memento of hurt," said Nico quietly, and they all bowed their heads and couldn't think of anything else to say.

MOLLY SPENT that night at Lawrence's. She called Dufort to let him know, and he said he would send Maron out to cruise by a few times just to keep an eye on things. In the meantime, he and the force were doing all they could to find Vincent and bring him in.

"So are you going to tell me, or do I have to drag it out of you?" said Lawrence, once they were ensconced in his deep armchairs with down cushions, directly in front of a blazing fire.

"Tell you what?" asked Molly, honestly having no idea what he was talking about.

"Well, you were nearly attacked last night. Had to run for it, and the murderer is worried you can identify him."

"Um, yeah?"

"So where did you *sleep* last night, Miss Sutton? I don't think you went home alone, did you?"

Molly blushed. A deep blush that started around her collarbone and moved up to her face, making her so warm she had to fan herself. "I'm surprised your sources have let you down," she said mysteriously, and then would discuss it no further.

They toasted thick slices of bread on the fire, and ate it with immense hunks of the most delicious sheep's milk cheese made by a woman who lived just outside Castillac. Lawrence poured them tall glasses of mineral water, and they finished up with some squares of Côte d'Or chocolate with hazelnuts.

The two friends talked long into the night, and Molly fell into a deep sleep in Lawrence's bed. He insisted on taking the sofa in the sitting room, and she agreed for just this one night, grateful for a safe place to rest. When she was ready for bed and turned off the light and sank into his luxurious bedding, she realized just how stressed and frightened she had been for these last weeks, and conked out immediately.

Molly and Lawrence slept late. They were just drinking their first cups of coffee, not quite awake enough to form sentences, when Lawrence got a call.

"Âllo?" he said, sounding nearly French instead of the Californian he was. "Really? No kidding...that's very good news....all right...see you later, thank you my dear."

"Let's finish up these cups and then trot over to Chez Papa," said Lawrence. "I know it's not quite lunchtime, but it sounds like the celebrating is already seriously underway and we don't want to miss it.

"Dufort caught him, Molly. Apparently he was hiding in a cave up by the Sallière vineyard. No weapon or anything, gave himself right up."

"How did you get all that in that ten second phone call?"

Lawrence just laughed.

"It's fantastic news. I'll just change out of my nightgown before we go."

"Only if you feel like it, Molls," said Lawrence, gulping his coffee and reaching for a heavy sweater.

40

Everyone cheered when Molly and Lawrence came through the door at Chez Papa. The fireplace was going for the first time that fall, a new waitress was passing around plates of free hors d'oeuvres, and the restaurant was filling up with villagers in a festive mood now that the nightmare was over. Dufort was talking to someone just inside the door, and Molly edged up next to him.

"Molly!" he exclaimed when he saw her. He grabbed her by the shoulders and kissed her hard on each cheek. "We never could have done it without you! In fact you did so much, I think I should put you on the payroll!" He was beaming at her and she felt a blush creep up that she sternly ordered to go away. She was impressed that Dufort showed no irritation at having a civilian—and an American at that—take all the glory.

"I'm just sorry I didn't realize it sooner," she said. "Not that it would have made any difference to Amy."

Dufort pressed his lips together and nodded. "Well, Vincent is locked up now, in our small jail for the moment. He'll be transported to a larger facility in a day or two." Dufort got serious, and then he leaned close to Molly's ear and said, "You know, he's sort of pathetic. He has admitted to the crime and he's offering no defense. He's just sitting there, stoic but beaten down, like he's ready to take whatever punishment is coming his way."

The noise of the party was getting loud and Molly just shrugged. She found it interesting that the chief gendarme was able to find any empathy at all for the man he had wanted so fervently to capture. She couldn't say she felt the same way. The fewer murderous sociopaths around, the better, was her line of thinking. And of course, Dufort would agree, even if he was unable to see the man as a monster.

Molly wanted to ask if Vincent was responsible for the other abductions—Valérie Boutillier and Elizabeth Martin. But the middle of an increasingly raucous party didn't seem like the right place.

Marie-Claire Levy appeared from the back room and came up to Dufort with a rather shy expression. He smiled at her and slipped his arm around her waist. Molly tried to keep her surprise out of her expression; she'd thought he was single, but now...?

Thérèse Perrault came over to kiss Molly on both cheeks and thank her. The young woman's eyes sparkled, and she laughed and lifted her glass to toast Molly, which Molly thought was very generous of her. The other officer hadn't come to Chez Papa—he had always seemed a little chilly, that one.

Just then they were hit with a draft of cold air and Lapin appeared in the doorway. He had not been seen since his night in jail, and he looked hesitant and unsure of himself.

"Lapin!" cried Alphonse, "come in and have a glass!"

Molly crossed her arms over her chest and sighed.

"La bombe!" said Lapin, spying her. But then he looked away, uncomfortable.

Perhaps something good came out of being a semi-suspect, thought Molly, daring to drop her arms.

Nico was passing a tray of drinks. He turned to go back to the bar and then changed his mind and spoke up. "You left with

Amy," he said to Lapin, his voice low and unusually serious for Nico. "So what happened? How did Vincent get hold of her?"

Lapin hung his head. Molly noticed tufts of hair growing out of his ears and for some reason that made her feel pity for him.

"I put her in his taxi," he said softly.

"And why did you not tell me that, when I asked you?" said Dufort.

"Why did you lie?" Perrault added, accusingly.

"Because..." Lapin started, but then bit his lip. He looked up at the ceiling, and then passed his hand over his face. "Look, he's my age. We were in the village school together, though not friends. Vincent didn't have any friends." Lapin paused and mopped his forehead with a handkerchief. "And then, you know, after school I started my antiquities business."

"Junk dealer," said Nico in a low voice.

"One of my first jobs," continued Lapin, "was at the Cloutier farm. Vincent's family. His father had passed earlier, but they called me when his mother died. I was very pleased, my business was just starting, you understand, so I was grateful..."

All of them—Molly, Dufort, Perrault, and Nico—leaned in to hear what Lapin was saying over the din of the party. "I didn't have an easy time of it after my mother died. Far from it. But when I saw the Cloutier farm...." Lapin wiped his brow and looked up at the ceiling. "He was living in filth. No running water, no heat. I'm telling you, the smell of garbage and excrement inside the house made my eyes water. I guess his mother had lost her mind at some point. Vincent told me he was not allowed to throw anything away. This was of course years ago and I have had many jobs since, and have witnessed the insides of houses that strangers had never seen—in short, I have seen plenty of ugliness, I will tell you. But nothing has approached the squalor and degradation of the Cloutier farm. Not even close.

"I did what I could to help him, got the place cleaned up and sold so he could make a fresh start in his own place. But you know, you don't outgrow damage like that."

"So..." said Perrault. "You felt sorry for him? But what about Amy? You're not sorry for her?"

"I will never get over that I was the one who put her in his taxi," said Lapin. "And yes, I am also not ashamed to say I felt sorry for him. Sadly, it was too late to save the girl anyway, by the time I heard she was missing." And then Lapin moved through the crowd, shouting out to a friend, leaving the others looking at each other with wonder.

"I see," said Dufort to Molly. "I had been wondering why Vincent had gone after you but not Lapin. I thought perhaps it was simply because you are female. But possibly the fact that Lapin had been kind to him when his mother died—that may have saved Lapin's life."

"Wow," said Molly, for once speechless.

Dufort said, his voice like steel, "Vincent denies any wrongdoing with Valérie or Elizabeth. But I will tell you right now, if I find any evidence that he is lying? He will not see the light of day outside prison ever again."

MOLLY DIDN'T LEAVE La Baraque for a week after the party at Chez Papa. She needed to cook for herself, keep getting to know the nooks and crannies of her house, root around in the garden, and figure out how to get the fire in the woodstove to stay lit. Lawrence came over for lunch one day, and she talked to Madame Sabourin over the wall as they were doing the last bit of garden cleanup for the season. But other than that, she wallowed happily in solitude, listening to the blues as loud as ever.

The high emotion of the previous weeks left her feeling depleted at first, even though she was secretly a bit giddy at having not only found Amy but solved her murder. But the events had another effect, an unexpected one: She wasn't sure she was ready after all to shut the door on romance quite so firmly.

That's not saying she had anyone in mind, at least, not anyone she would admit to. But the Bennetts had made a serious impression on her. In the midst of the worst grief imaginable, they had had each other to hang onto. And Molly was sure that if they were asked whether making their family had been a good idea, even knowing about the terrible thing that happened—that they would without reservation say that they were glad. That they were happy and grateful to have had Amy, to have known Amy, even though the loss of her was unbearable.

Molly was washing dishes and turning all this over in her mind when she heard a banging on her front door. She went to answer it and the orange cat sidled under her feet, causing her to trip and fall on her knees. "*Va t'en* you horrid creature!" she shouted. She had fallen on a rug so was unhurt, and scrambled up to answer the door.

"Hello, Molls! I bet you could use me for a little cleanup around the place, while you attend to more important matters!" Constance came bouncing in the house, wearing her trademark high-top sneakers. Molly noticed her hair was matted in the back. The two women waved to Thomas as he turned his motorcycle around and took off.

"All right then," said Molly, halfway amused. "Come on in, I'm afraid there's plenty to do."

THE END

NOT READY TO LEAVE CASTILLAC?

Here's the first chapter from The Luckiest Woman Ever, Molly Sutton Mysteries 2.

❧

Chapter 1

In the grand old mansion on rue Simenon in the center of Castillac, sitting in a deep armchair covered in a fabric so expensive it could have paid for a small car, Josephine Desrosiers was watching a game show. She was wearing a nightgown her husband, long dead, had bought for her in Paris thirty years earlier. She blinked as the host talked rapidly in his forced jolly tone, lights on the set flashing as a contestant managed to mumble out the correct answer.

Madame Desrosiers was seventy-one, and her hearing was as sharp as ever. She heard the door to the kitchen close three floors down even though Sabrina, the housekeeper who came each morning, was a quiet girl and not remotely a door-slammer. Josephine got to her feet and snapped off the television set, then smoothed the cushion of the armchair so it looked fresh and unsat-in. And then she nimbly climbed into her vast bed with its ornate posts and carved headboard, and squeezed her eyes closed.

Sabrina could not clean the entire four-story house in one day, even as young and hardworking as she was. That day she did all of the first floor and most of the second, but never came up to Madame Desrosiers's bedroom. Madame Desrosiers had told her that she was very ill and did not have the wherewithal to see visitors, including Sabrina, so she was left alone. She had a box of crackers under her bed and a bit of Brie that was past its prime—quite enough sustenance thank you—so she never rang the servant's bell.

When Madame Desrosiers heard the door softly shut at the end of the day, she slid out of bed and turned the television back on. Then she did her exercises in front of an enormous gilt-framed mirror, counting her movements, bending to the right and then the left, breathing heavily from the work of reaching for her toes. She was preparing for the best part of the day, when she sat at her desk and wrote letters. Each one was a harassing and maligning and instructing sort of letter, every single one of which, when opened, was greeted with the same feeling of deflation and even shame in its recipient, just as Josephine intended.

Josephine Desrosiers had been a lucky woman, in material respects. Her family had not been wealthy, but her husband had invented something that made him millions. (She couldn't say what exactly—something electrical, she believed?) And now she was able to play the significant role of Rich Widow, complete with younger members of the family gathered at her feet, hoping for the odd crumb to fall their way.

Well, there was one family member who did that, anyway: Michel, her nephew. He would likely come around tonight as he usually did late in the week, trying to butter her up. Very occasionally she wrote him a small check. She liked sometimes to think of herself as bountiful, and with impressive self-control, she denied any connection in her mind between Michel's attentiveness and the money she gave him. As she thought of Michel, the doorbell sounded and she heard him let himself in. She was not quite dressed and she enjoyed making him wait. Josephine liked the idea of the young man sitting in her salon, twiddling his thumbs, with nothing to do but look forward to the moment when she appeared at the top of the wide, curving staircase.

A vanity table stood in a corner of the expansive bathroom off her bedroom, covered with crystal bottles of perfume and old tins of eyeliner and foundation. She sat gazing at herself in the mirror, brushing her wisps of white hair straight up. She dabbed her fingertips into a pot of rouge and reddened up her wrinkled cheeks. She applied lipstick and blotted it with special blotting papers. It occurred to her, not for the first time, that some music might be pleasant to listen to while she made her preparations, but the record player had broken decades ago and she had no wish for anything ugly and modern in the house.

Finally, with a spritz of perfume, Josephine Desrosiers was ready to greet her nephew. She was spry for her age and she had no trouble with the stairs. She nearly hummed to herself as she descended, but stopped herself because she thought humming was a low-class pursuit. Her nephew, chewing on a fingernail, was sitting on the very edge of the sofa cushion, his brown hair falling down over one eye.

"Ah, Michel, *comment vas-tu?*"

Michel jumped up from the sofa and kissed his aunt on both cheeks, murmuring the most polite murmurs he could come up with.

He loathed his aunt.

He thought her mean and narcissistic, which did not take an abundance of perception.

"What would you like to do this evening, my dear?" he asked her, so solicitous he almost believed himself. "How about a bit of television? I hear there's a new—"

"Television is vulgar," said Madame Desrosiers.

"Ah. Well, shall I take you out to dinner then? Are you hungry?"

She considered. She did like to enter a restaurant and see the people she knew jump up to come say hello. But on the other hand, the tiresome service! The expense! She had lost her appetite for food years ago, and she didn't see the point in spending that much time and money on something she wasn't especially interested in. "If you would make me my usual," she said.

Michel sighed inwardly and went to a sideboard. He took a dangerously fragile cordial glass from inside the cabinet and placed it on a silver tray. Then he poured some Dubonnet from a crystal decanter and took the glass to his aunt. The stuff smelled musty like the rest of the house and he did not breathe until she took it from him.

He would have welcomed a drink himself, but had learned that helping himself, or even asking politely if he might join her, was a mistake. And with Aunt Josephine Desrosiers, you did not want to make mistakes. Not if you wanted to escape without a cruel dressing-down.

And definitely not if you wanted to inherit her money.

ALSO BY NELL GODDIN

The Luckiest Woman Ever (Molly Sutton Mysteries 2)

The Prisoner of Castillac (Molly Sutton Mysteries 3)

Murder for Love (Molly Sutton Mysteries 4)

The Château Murder (Molly Sutton Mysteries 5)

Murder on Vacation (Molly Sutton Mysteries 6)

An Official Killing (Molly Sutton Mysteries 7)

Death in Darkness (Molly Sutton Mysteries 8)

No Honor Among Thieves (Molly Sutton Mysteries 9)

GLOSSARY

1:

véritable..............real
pâtisserie.............pastry shop
très cher............very expensive
bonjour..............hello
parterre...............formal garden enclosure
mille-feuille..........type of pastry, also called a Napoleon

2:

La Baraque...........shed, house
notaire.................government official
gîte......................rental, usually by the week
enchantée..............enchanted
banlieue................suburb
bon......................good. All right then.

3:

potager.................kitchen garden
café crème.............coffee with whipped milk

4:

à tout à l'heure.......see you later

5:

pain au chocolat.........chocolate croissant
flic...........................cop
gendarmerie...............building where gendarmes live
politesse.................politeness

6:

comme ça.................like that
bonsoir....................good night
la bombe.................. stunner, sexy woman
bonne nuit, mon petit chou.......goodnight, my little cabbage

8:

bienvenue...............welcome
mon Dieu...............my God
bien sûr..................of course

9:

Maman..................mother

10:

pardonnez-moi.........excuse me

11:

ma chérie..................my dear
Á la tienne!...............cheers
fliquette....................female cop

12:

comment allez-vous............how are you?
merci bien.......................thanks very much

17:

mes amis........................my friends
à tous............................to everyone
bonne nuit......................good night
pigeonnier......................pigeon house

19:

la métairie......................farm

20:

mec...............................good guy
aux amandes....................with almonds

21:

bordel............................mess (also bordello)
pas de problème...............no problem

22:

absolument......................absolutely
légume............................vegetable

23:

apéro.............................apéritif, cocktail
deux chevaux..................classic Citroen economy car
pineau............................an apéritif made in the Charente

24:

je ne sais quoi.................hard to describe quality

33:

s'il te plaît......................please

34:

C'est un bordel ici!............it's a mess in here!

ACKNOWLEDGMENTS

Tommy Glass and Mariflo Stephens—you are the best editors in the world. Flowery, effusive thanks to you both.

Special thanks to the crack team of Christiane Rimbault and Geneviève Debussche-Rimbault, who helped me avoid insults to the beautiful French language and get the details of the gendarmerie straight. Je vous remercie de tout coeur.

ABOUT THE AUTHOR

Nell Goddin has worked as a radio reporter, SAT tutor, short-order omelet chef, and baker. She tried waitressing but was fired twice.

Nell grew up in Richmond, Virginia and has lived in New England, New York City, and France. Currently she's back in Virginia with teenagers and far too many pets. She has degrees from Dartmouth College and Columbia University.

www.nellgoddin.com
nell@nellgoddin.com

Made in the USA
Monee, IL
19 January 2023